Gary Barker is four⸺⸺⸺⸺⸺⸺⸺⸺⸺⸺⸺⸺⸺⸺⸺⸺ l
organization that wor̶k̶s̶ ̶.̶.̶.̶ ̶⸻⸻⸻⸻⸻⸻⸻⸻ ı
America and in the Middle East to prevent violence. His
first novel, *Luisa's Last Words*, about civil war in Guate-
mala, was published to critical acclaim in the Netherlands. He has been awarded an Ashoka Fellowship and
an Open Society Fellowship for his research and activ-
ism. Barker lives in Washington, D.C.

Michael Kaufman is the author or editor of seven books
of fiction and non-fiction. His first novel was the prize-
winning *The Possibility of Dreaming on a Night Without
Stars*. For thirty years he has worked internationally to
promote gender equality and end men's violence. His articles and books have been translated into a dozen languages. He lives in Toronto, Canada.

The Afghan Vampires Book Club

Gary Barker & Michael Kaufman

The Afghan
Vampires
Book Club

World Editions

Published in Great Britain in 2015 by World Editions Ltd., London

www.worldeditions.org

Copyright © Gary Barker & Michael Kaufman, 2015
Cover design Multitude
Image credit © Ed Drew, courtesy Robert Koch Gallery, San Francisco

The moral rights of the authors have been asserted in accordance
with the Copyright, Designs and Patents Act 1988

British Library Cataloguing-in-Publication Data
A catalogue record for this book is available on request from
the British Library

ISBN 978 94 6238 049 3

Typeset in Minion Pro and Calibri

Distribution Europe (except the Netherlands and Belgium):
Turnaround Publishers Services, London
Distribution the Netherlands and Belgium: Centraal Boekhuis,
Culemborg, the Netherlands

'The first casualty when war comes is truth.'
US SENATOR HIRAM JOHNSON, 1916

'The deepest sacrifice of those that we ask to go to war is not the possibility that they may die or their colleagues may die, but the sacrifice of their normal unwillingness to kill.'
STANLEY HAUERWAS

The Captain

February 27, 2025

The captain's room is at the end of the wing, dark but for light seeping from the bathroom. The room, larger than most, has six beds, all empty except the one by the window where he lies. Cold midnight air pushes through the slightly opened window, briefly lifting the thin green curtain and then releasing it.

The squeaking of a nurse's shoes recedes down the hallway and then is gone. All is quiet again. For nearly two months, his ears have been his only link to the outside world. From other rooms he has heard ragged breathing, and midnight crying kept at bay during the day, and shouts as a roadside bomb explodes in a fellow soldier's sleep. He knows this terror. Terror burrowed into the folds of the men's brains so deeply they no longer remember what life was like before. Before the Second Afghan War.

He takes his mind away from all that to the vision of a woman he has loved and lost and swears he will find again.

Medics found him in the mountains, half-buried in snow. At first speechless, unresponsive, almost depleted of life.

He heard shouts. Orders. Jostling him onto the stretcher. Deep thumping of helicopter blades. He shouted and thrashed and begged them to forget about him and save *her*. 'Save *her*!' he had yelled over and over until they drugged him back to sleep.

9

He ended up here in Germany at the Landsfuhl Hospital near the Ramstein base, where he has remained since, alone in this large, empty room.

But before they will send him home, they want to know what he remembers—what happened that day in that remote corner of Afghanistan. And what happened to all the others who were killed.

He opens his eyes and stares at the ceiling, imagining patterns and shapes in the faint light. They will return in the morning with more questions. Again, he will pretend to be disoriented. And the next day, and the next one, until they are convinced.

Each day, there is a man who stands in the corner. Short, in a civilian suit, always listening, never asking questions. A few days earlier, as he was feigning sleep, the captain heard the man in the suit speak. *If he remembers a single thing, make sure he'll never say a word.*

He closes his eyes, thinks he hears a sound, a rustling of silk, opens his eyes and, as much as the restraints allow, turns back and forth to stare into the darkened room.

He forces his breathing to slow down. He forces his eyes to close.

He knows he is close to convincing them he remembers nothing. That he's just another vet whose memories have been charred by war and scrambled by the meds he was fed to keep him in battle. He believes, he hopes, he prays, they will leave him alone, that they'll think he'll be one more soldier huddling on a street corner or hiding in his bed. One more who will not ask questions and who knows that if there were truth to be found, it was long ago buried in some forgotten place.

He cannot sleep, has barely slept for nights on end. He knows he won't truly sleep until he is far from this hospital and can finally tell what happened that day.

The Journal of
John Murakami Fox

April 9, London

It had been Alistair's idea to start the club—almost two years ago. We were already well into the Second Afghan War, the one that came after the Obama withdrawal and the short-lived Russian occupation that followed. I thought the club was folly, really, a desperate act of frustration over this recycled war. But I humoured him.

Alistair Thomason-Thorpe, seventy-one years old, two decades older than I, but determined to live the life of an English gentleman from before he was born, fragrant pipe tobacco, 'old boys', and all.

Our conversation that night had drifted pleasantly to the theatre season, updates on various acquaintances, and then back again to the latest reports from our current wars.

After discussing one particularly heart-wrenching item from the States, Alistair said, 'I can no longer tell which stories are true and which are pure fiction, my dear John.'

Alistair subscribed to more than twenty papers and magazines, from *The Times* to *Tatler*, *The Times Literary Supplement* to *The Independent* and *The Guardian*, as if he were on a one-man crusade to keep print journalism alive. Even one of the tabloids landed on his doorstep each day.

He had read me a story about a group of vets who formed an armed gang, invaded a casino on a reservation in Wisconsin, threatened to spill a 'swimming pool of blood', refused to surrender and were gunned down by a SWAT team, along with many other poor souls gambling their wages away. Thirty-three dead.

'According to this in-depth journalism'—with two fingers he held up one of the local tabloids as if he were holding someone's used underwear—'the veterans said they hoped to cleanse themselves of all the barbarism they saw, or committed, in Afghanistan.' He had taken a thoughtful puff on his pipe and then said, 'I never did understand this notion of self-cleansing violence, do you, old boy?' Alastair didn't wait for an answer. 'I do love this headline, though: *Vampire Vets Meet Bloody End.*' He looked up at me and then said, 'Do any of you actually report anymore or do you simply re-post what you find online?'

'Why bother searching online?' I said. 'We simply run the press releases.'

'I'm serious,' he said. 'We should start a society. A club perhaps.'

'Of...?'

He took a moment before he said, 'To collect all these terrible, barbaric, and unbelievable stories.'

As he said this, I glanced at the picture of his son, mounted in an art deco frame and sitting alone in the middle of a dark oak bookshelf.

'No thanks,' I said.

'But why not?'

'I already do that for my day job. Collect all those stories.'

Two days later I received a handwritten letter. Alistair was perfectly capable of turning on his tablet and sending an email but he relished old-school style.

The letter was headed: 'The Afghan Vampires Book Club: An Invitation.'

He had sent the same letter to five others: a fellow amateur historian, two journalists, a short story writer of some renown, and his favourite antiquarian book dealer.

We were to gather the most improbable, disturbing, unbelievable, and absurd stories—fiction and non-fiction—that were coming out of the two-and-a-half decades of the start-and-stop Afghan War, as well as the ongoing Syrian-Lebanese-Turkish war, the Venezuelan campaign, and the new counter-insurgency efforts in Indonesia and Argentina, and post them on a website. It was, he conceded, more of a storytellers' club, but he preferred the sound of 'book club', just as he preferred books, especially leather-bound, to any other medium. I think he tossed 'vampire' into the name as a nod to the bloodletting threats of those casino-invading veterans, although perhaps it was merely acknowledging the absurdity of the whole exercise.

He wrote that once a year we would meet at his country home near Oxford, where he would announce the winner. The prize would be a case from his wine cellar, a coveted prize ever since most of the Northern Hemisphere's grape production had gone awry.

'The goal, my dear friends, is to figure out if the story is true or pure invention.

'Only then,' his message continued, 'will the winner take home the wine.'

I had phoned Alistair. I'm certain he would have preferred a letter but I wouldn't have known where to buy a stamp. Again I said no.

The next evening I was having an almost peaceful dinner with Sandra, who, at the time, hadn't yet started her A levels. I shouldn't have been surprised to learn that she already knew about Alistair's idea since he was her godfather and one of her sources of after-school employment. 'He asked me to register a domain and set up a website for him.' There have been years when she sees more of him than of me. I believe that would be every year since she was born.

My wonderful daughter—she would not use the same adjective for me, I know—heading, she hopes, for medical school after her gap year, that is if I can somehow save enough money working as a serious journalist to help her. This mutual desire is perhaps the one thing Sandra and I have agreed on in many years.

A few days later I had flown off again, to Delhi. But it wasn't long before I received Sandra's note: 'Hi John. www.Afghan-VampiresBookClub.com Check it out!'

I could not say *no* to my oldest friend. And I would do just about anything to reduce my daughter's animosity toward me. Who knows, she might even start calling me 'Father'.

In the first year of the competition, the winning story was about a French aid worker who fell in love with an Afghan woman from a Taliban family and convinced her to flee the country with him. Anyone who knew anything about Afghanistan knew that couldn't end well. On the way to the airport, they disappeared. Their car was found more than 200 kilometres away with the suitcases still in the boot but no blood and no sign of gunshots or struggle. Months went by before anyone heard anything else of the story. The French government sent investigators, US inspectors poked around, but nothing turned up. Nearly six months later, a package arrived at the French Embassy, addressed to the French ambassador from 'the people of Afghanistan'. Inside was a small box with a note that read: 'After your men look at our beautiful women, they'll never have eyes for another.'

You can imagine what was in the small box.

It was easy to figure out the truth versus fiction question on that one. Not even a crazy Frenchman would try to date an Afghan woman in Afghanistan.

By the second year, as the challenges of making a living as a journalist increased, even for one who has books, prizes, and more than a few scars from his war reporting, I started using the site to find story ideas. It had become an open (if anonymous) website with postings from one and all. The challenge was sifting through the imaginative conspiracy theories, the pedestrian conspiracy theories, the absurd rumours, paranoid fantasies, and stoned jokes concocted late at night in a barracks, in hopes of finding the hint of a real story.

In its first two years, I hadn't even posted a story on the site let alone won the competition, though of course this didn't bother me. It was merely a pastime for an old friend and a small source of income for my daughter.

Both Alistair and Sandra were as persistent as biting insects, intent as they were that I take this year's competition more seriously. The hook for me came from a posting by a US veteran who claimed to have the real story behind the Vod Am massacre, which had been a scoop for me just a few months before.

Cody was his name. I wrote to him. He ignored me. I wrote again and asked if I could meet him. He said 'Maybe', and three days later wrote to me again to say, yes, if I could come to Baltimore.

If an idea is hot, I can get expenses paid by Judith in Brooklyn. Though Judith's business is thriving as one of the more successful agent-editor-management-epub houses, the enthusiasm and support of Judith and her staff is conditional on how high I happen to sit on the charts.

My social media lines were static. My world journalist rank had fallen to 482. My credibility index was still high, but my name recognition was spiralling down.

'Judith. Me.'

'Jesus, it's only seven here.' I heard the rustle of cellophane as she unwrapped a fresh pack of her Marlboro Easy Trippers. I heard her light one and take a short toke. I waited.

'Ah,' she finally said, 'nothing like the first hit of the day. So glad I live in a civilized state.'

'Listen, I think I've found a big story.'

'Your stories are always gonna be big. I must be time travelling.'

'Judith, pay attention. Something happened at Vod Am. Something they covered up.'

'The army always covers its mistakes.'

'This is different.'

'How?'

'I don't know yet. There's someone I need to interview.'

'Where?' I heard her take her second toke.

'Baltimore.'

No sound until there was a gush of air as she exhaled. 'What?'

'Baltimore.'

'Why?'

'I want to eat crabs. And talk to a vet who knows things.'

'Call me only when you've got a book.'

April 12, Baltimore

Cody had a face so scarred it looked as if he'd fought in all the wars Afghanistan had ever been through as well as those yet to come. Remainder of a boot-camp build, now rapidly in decline. Greasy hair, starved look. Blood-shot eyes. He couldn't have been more than twenty-three.

We met at a bar outside of Baltimore; he'd brought along four of his fellow veterans.

Cody tapped a shaky index finger against the soggy tabletop. He leaned forward and said, 'You need to know this', as if he were about to tell me the greatest secrets of the last quarter century. And then he wrapped a twitchy hand around the bottle of Budweiser. His face was stretched taut, making his eyes bulge, all puffy and alarmed.

The other four were veterans like him, only where Cody's eyes were wild, theirs had that vacant look I'd seen too many times before. Two were watching me, one was watching his own hand clutching a bottle of beer, the last was staring into the distance as if watching a movie replaying in his head.

Finally, Cody spoke. 'No one, I mean no fuckin' body, is saying what happened in the Vod Am Massacre. They don't want you to know...'

I knew all there was to know. Not a single American soldier had survived. Two hundred and eight killed. Thirteen never found. I had been the first journalist to arrive at the scene and the first to file, just lucky that I'd been visiting Bagram at the time. It was my story.

Cody said, 'You tell me this: did they ever announce that shit about their bodies? I mean, how they got killed?'

I said, 'Your standard Taliban ambush, only far bigger. Nastier. They've had years to get quite good at it. Their home-made bombs have gotten better.'

Cody smiled grimly. His mates nodded, robot-like, but ready for him to deliver the final blow.

'Well, they don't know shit.'

'I'm afraid I was there. I saw what happened.' This wasn't exactly true. By the time I arrived, almost all the bodies had been zipped up and carefully lined up for the helicopters.

He shook his head.

'I was there, too,' Cody said.

'You all were there?' I asked the rest of the men, but none of them answered.

'No,' said Cody. 'Just me. Cleaning it up. Finding the bodies in the snow. Taggin' 'em.'

'So you know that no one survived.'

'One man did,' he assured me. 'A captain. They dug him out of the snow or found him in a cave nearly a week later.'

'What was his name?'

Cody shrugged. 'Don't know.'

Momentarily, I was distracted by the screen on the wall above the bar. A CNN-Huff reporter was doing a stand-up outside a police station, her best urgent journalist expression plastered on her face. The graphic said, 8 VETS INVADE TULSA POLICE STATION. I turned back. Cody was staring at the screen.

'Friends of yours?' I said.

'Fuck you.'

This was clearly going nowhere. I opened my wallet to settle the tab.

One of the others, a large man with tattoos riding up his arms like a map of rage, laid a massive hand on my forearm.

I closed my wallet and cupped it between my hands.

Cody spoke. I listened. Occasionally, one of his friends spoke. Two hours later, my mouth was still shut and my wallet had opened three times when I bought one more round and then another.

Later

Alone, I ate steamed crabs at the harbour. I piled the shells on the brown paper that covered the table. I drank more beer. I wiped my hands carefully and took out my phone.

I typed a text to Judith: 'Got it!' But before hitting send, I erased it. The army, as she was keen to remind me, was always trying to cover up its mistakes. And every war produces rumours on top of lies to cover the truth, which is part of the reason Alastair started the Book Club. The problem was, when I asked Cody if anyone could corroborate his story, an expression of great weariness came into his eyes.

'Where's this captain? Is he still alive?'

Cody said, 'Yeah. But he doesn't want no one to find him.'

'Hard to get an interview with a man who doesn't want to be found.'

'He probably doesn't fuckin' trust nobody with what he's been through.'

I nodded.

'Did you see him yourself?'

'No. They found him a week later.'

'Anyone know his name?'

Cody turned to one of his mates, a short, narrow-shouldered man, African-American, who until then hadn't looked me in the eyes.

'I know how to find him,' the second man said. 'He hangin' low.'

'And?'

'Cody gonna write him. Maybe he check you out. Maybe he trust you.'

I nodded again.

'And then?'

The second man said nothing. I turned to Cody.

'And then?'

'Not up to me. Not up to you.'

April 15, Baltimore

Three days later, I was still waiting to hear from Cody's mystery man.

My stroll around Fell's Point trying to find a decent morning cappuccino was disturbed by a sharp bang. Before I realized it, I was down on the sidewalk, my arms flung over my head. It turned out to be a minor traffic accident. I stood up a moment later, brushing off my trousers, embarrassed as hell, kicking my foot against a crack to pretend that was the cause of my mishap and not the imaginary suicide bomb that had just gone off in my head.

Some reptilian part of the brain was reminding me that my home is Islamabad.

But I'm always there, aren't I? Margaret had left me because, she said, even when I wasn't over there I was over there.

April 16, Baltimore

I woke after my fourth night in Baltimore and considered hopping on the train to DC, but couldn't think what I would cover in Washington that wasn't already in the direct feeds from the government. I checked the Web. The US is talking about yet another round of peace talks with the Afghan Taliban. The India Grand Corruption Trial continues to astound even my jaded eyes. Indonesia's seething. The bite-sized Egyptian Coptic Republic is facing a new drought. One-third of Portugal and Spain is now made up of autonomous subsistence agricultural collectives that the EU can't figure out how to tax. Maldives is half underwater.

I searched bars for my vets, enduring several hours of watery beer to no avail. One bartender told me to try again after the benefit cheques arrive.

June 12, London

I'd long since given up on hearing from the mystery man.

I had been home in London for two months, although I suppose 'home' should be in quotations.

When I came back from Baltimore, Alistair had listened patiently to my story about Cody and his friends, interrupting only to ask questions about how I could stand the anaemic beer in the States, how I could eat such large portions of food, how I could stomach having religion constantly shoved into my face, etc., etc. I knew it was a screen for all his anger about the US so I ignored his tiresome barbs.

He was intrigued by my first-hand account of the type of veterans we'd been reading about.

'A sorry lot they are,' he finally had said.

We both knew his cavalier answer was but a flimsy shield against his own demons.

Later

I received an email from a name I didn't recognize. The subject line: *Cody sent me.*

I immediately tried to reach Cody to see if this was the person he'd told me about. But Cody was nowhere to be found. Veterans Affairs was, as usual, no help. Eventually I found him. Or, rather, found out about him. A short note in *The Baltimore Sun*. Nasty way to go.

June 19, Charleston, South Carolina

Only 8 a.m. but already Charleston is steaming. I walk along the sea wall as instructed by the mystery man. The once-gorgeous houses facing the harbour had withstood the Civil War and a couple of centuries of hurricanes, but The Storms have made them look like a row of crack houses. I reflexively check the sky: The Storms had come even earlier last year, months before the normal hurricanes.

A solitary woman walks in my direction, a soldier's posture. I slow down, meet her eyes, but she simply says hello and sweeps past.

Two runners overtake me, one moving effortlessly, the older one panting so hard I rehearse CPR manoeuvres in my head.

A battered Kawasaki 750cc motorcycle pulls up, both bike and driver dusty as if it's been an all-night drive.

The driver doesn't even flip up the visor as he tosses me a helmet. I scrape out some cobwebs, slip it on, and awkwardly climb up behind him.

Off we go. It's taken all of ten seconds.

Like the rest of the planet feeding steadily on revelations, leaks, arrests, and extraditions, my driver seemed to have acquired a paranoid need for security.

We don't drive far before he parks on one of the colonial residential streets edging downtown Charleston. We get off. We pull off our helmets and he says, 'I'm Tanner. The captain.'

'Is that your first or last name?'

'Take your pick,' he says.

Only then does he reach for my outstretched hand. Doesn't try to crush me, which I like.

He is taller than I by a head, but then again, I'm only 5'8". His neck and face look tense and for a moment his eyes dance around as if watching for spies. Then he chuckles, as if recognizing he's cast himself into a thriller. I like that too.

He can't be much more than thirty. His hair has an old-fashioned Brad Pitt shagginess which flops over his ears and forehead, so he must have been out of the army for at least a few months. His cheekbones are prominent and his muddy brown eyes reveal a sense of certainty. Not brashness, just certainty.

'Hey,' he says, 'it's been a bit of a drive. I need a piss, a coffee, and a good long walk.'

I feel comfortable with him. I'm eager to hear what he has to tell.

After he grabs a take-away coffee and we head back outside, I ask if I can record him. He stops walking. He stares around as if noticing for the first time where he is.

He juts his chin out in a gesture of agreement.

We walk together in tight patterns criss-crossing the historic quarter. He has a slight limp. He talks, I listen, not fully believing all that he tells me. But his voice is calm and sincere. He doesn't sound crazy.

At lunchtime we find a restaurant where we eat pulled pork and drink some decent local brew which, I expect, even Alistair would approve of.

'You up for more?' I ask. Tanner continues to quietly recite his story in the now-empty restaurant and then back out on the streets.

The sun is low on the horizon when his story finally reaches the massacre in Vod Am.

It's dark when he says he has to go.

'There are still lots of details I need to ask you,' I say.

He shrugs. That's all I get for now.

'If I'm going to pitch an article, I need to be able to reach you.'

He says, 'I don't want an article... This is a book. You're a writer. You take my story and write a book. This will sell. Heads will roll.'

'Ghost it?'

'I don't want my name on it. Reasons should be obvious.'

'I don't even know your real name.'

He smiled. 'Tanner Jackson will do fine. You can be the author. I just want half the proceeds. I'll make certain you know how to get them to me.'

'I'm not sure,' I say.

He gives me a look that tells me he knows I'm in.

CHAPTER 1

It was another patrol. That's what we do in this war—patrol. We study to engage the enemy, to strategize and plan, but it seems like all we fucking do is patrol. And then just like that they're in your face.

You never know where they're coming from. The crack of guns and snap of bullets sailing past you, missing you but hitting your buddy. That dry, alkaline smell of concrete pulverized by RPGs, the sound of incoming mortars. The ground is shaking, you're shaking, your ears are ringing, you have that metallic taste in your mouth, and everything tenses, and then, just as suddenly, it stops. You breathe. You breathe again and think maybe it's really stopped. And then it fucking starts again.

Blindness. That's what it feels like. Like you're in the dark and they can see you but you can't see a fucking thing. Which rocks are they behind? Which house? Which wall?

Worse yet, when you look up, you see the walking and running robes and burqas, the turbans and scarves, the kids and the women, the goats. It's anyone's guess whose side anyone is on. You don't even trust the goats.

And then there's your own guy next to you. Williams, tucked inside all his gear, his helmet with the built-in electronics, his don't-fuck-with-me sunglasses, his pounds of armor, and you'd like to believe he's a war machine who can read hostile terrain and knows what's coming. But then you remember he's a fucking nineteen-year-old who misses White Castle hamburgers and never ventured farther than the shopping mall in the next town. He's a kid who desperately needs the other guys to think he's tough but he's still laughing at fart jokes for fuck's sake and he's supposed to be covering my back and making the smart decisions about which of those running man-pajamas he's supposed to shoot at.

I'm lying in my cot, trying to read, and I look over at Williams reading the *Hustler* that's been doing the rounds. I say, 'Williams, try not to grab your crotch every thirty seconds while you're reading.'

And, like always, he says, 'Sure, Captain. But it's been an awful long time.'

'For all of us. That doesn't mean we like watching you play with yourself.'

Sometimes they'll ask what I'm reading, gawking at my books as if they were extraterrestrial objects.

And then it's lights out. You're always tired enough to sleep, but sleep isn't always kind. Then up and back out for patrol. Our handbook calls every patrol a mission, though we know better.

It's the missions we live for. Missions, when we've got someone to go after. Intel tells us where they are and out we go. Williams' teenage brain says that patrols are dry humping. Missions, he says, are real sex. Williams doesn't read *Penthouse* or *Hustler* at night after we've had a mission.

That's when I saw Katherine. On a mission. Makes sense now that I think of it. Katherine is definitely a mission and not a patrol.

We're in our FOB, me and my eighty-nine men in Bravo Company. This small base was called Victory's Camp, but most of my guys called it Victoria's Cunt—or simply 'The Cunt.'

That morning starts like it usually does: roosters crowing in the distance, freezing cold in the mobile units we call home. My mom would have said we looked like trailer trash, which was her biggest fear of what my brother and me would become. We're about a klick from a village and, when the wind's blowing east like it was that day, we hear the morning call to prayer. This was late October, the night's cold but warming up during the day. Back in the summer we caught the smell of lavender, now it's only cold dry dirt and stone.

Last few days the Taliban had been stepping up attacks over the region. We took that kind of personally because this was one of the few areas where our guys and our NATO allies had been doing the hearts and minds stuff, building clinics, schools, and roads. Off and on, that's our new strategy, new for about the twentieth time. Then we just go back to bombing the shit out of everyone. I'm a lot happier when I think we're doing some good.

My men gear up. Kevlar, ceramic pads, full body armor, extra ammo, first aid kit, water. You're suddenly a walking three-hundred-pounder.

I deliver my morning sermon to the whole company, reminding them of our rules of engagement. Protect the population. Engage the enemy. Stay alert. No needless radio chatter. No panicking. PID all targets. And most importantly, look out for each other. 'All of us are coming back alive. Even you, Williams (or Ross or whoever I chose to pick on that day). I want all of us proud of what we've done this day. You with me?'

Taliban's gotten better at the IEDs all these years, better at hiding them. Better at the remote switching and the sensors. Better at turning our soldiers into small bits, which is better at turning those of us who survive into walking basket cases. And I keep giving these speeches to my guys every morning.

I wait for them to respond. They're all still trying to wake up. A few are stamping to fend off the morning chill, a few are hopping from leg to leg as if they've just decided they should have taken a crap before leaving, a few are sleeping on their feet.

Then I yell, 'I can't hear you!'

They're young men and expect the football coach treatment. Anyway, I kind of like it when I know that they know their lives depend on me. And they know my life depends on them. A few guys nod at me. Even Williams doesn't seem like such a dumbfuck as he looks at me with those little-boy eyes of his.

I'm Bravo's company commander and we're at Victory's Camp along with one other company from our battalion. I have four small platoons, each led by a lieutenant responsible for his eighteen men, plus my headquarters team. Whenever possible, my headquarters team is out on patrol with one of the platoons.

Today, we're with 1st Platoon, driving slowly along craggy roads, passing goat-herders in man-jammies and their families going about their business. I'm thankful for every mile traversed without hitting an IED.

After an hour of worrying about everything—that cart, that little kid with the playful eyes, that pile of bricks on the side of the road, that stand selling rice or peas—I start tuning out because you just can't keep your mind set on high volume like that: even if there is enough adrenalin, the stuff eats you up if you stay on it too long.

They've gotten good at this shit. Think about it, right? A few hundred bucks takes out a million-dollar vehicle. I imagine the bad guys crouched in their caves or compounds, dreaming all this shit up. I mean, the IED is the fucking best way to drive us crazy. Has been for decades now. Your brain is moving in too many directions at once and after a while, you can almost smell the wires frying. You get too jittery, too paranoid, and bang, you've just wiped out another family and any goodwill you thought you had built. Figure that every civilian we kill recruits them another ten, twenty soldiers. Not to mention that my nineteen-year-olds, the ones who still have souls, get a little fucked in the head when they realize they've just killed someone's grandmother or child.

We're in three vehicles. The platoon's two Cougar 6x6s that hold ten each, and our smaller version that has six of us: me, Williams, Garcia, our radio man Rodriguez, Deezer behind the wheel, and Mikey strapped in up on the gun. The vehicles are beat up and patched together like the Cubans used to do with those old American cars. This ain't like the first Afghan War, that's for sure.

We get radioed that a clinic ten kilometers west is being hit with indirect. I radio over to Lieutenant O'Keefe, 1st Platoon leader. Someone has put on some old-as-shit Metallica and I can barely hear what he tells me. Rodriguez radios our Afghan National Army counterparts to meet us at the village. We radio our other platoons, but the closest is now thirty minutes away.

The dirt road leads past dead poppy fields and into the village. Typical stuff: a central square, brick and mud houses, small compounds, a scrawny little market that you know sells eggplants and onions and dried-out meat encrusted with dust and flies. An old mosque, long ago blasted away on one side and rebuilt a couple of times, with bricks and plaster that don't match. Men are coming and going from it like they always do. Williams says, 'Don't look like no fighting here.'

The men have flowers in their hair and dark eyeliner under their eyes. Some walk holding hands. Garcia loves this. He says, 'Tough guys. Hajji lock up their women and then put on their makeup and walk around holding hands.'

I tell him to shut the fuck up.

The health clinic is on the far side of the village. At first it's quiet, but then we hear shots coming from up ahead. Rodriguez radios to find out where the fuck the ANA is. A minute later we get word they've been ambushed coming in from the north.

This just got worse. We've got no interpreter with us. I can barely ask the time of day in Pashto and I'm the linguist in the group. It suddenly becomes obvious this whole thing is a trap.

When the clinic's in sight, I hear O'Keefe order his two vehicles to stop. I listen in as he talks quickly to his men: Watch for booby traps. No chatter. PID your targets. Let's get home in one piece.

I watch his 1st Squad pile out of one Cougar and immediately split into their two fire teams, one flanking left, the other right, both heading north in the direction of the reported attack.

Deezer drives us straight ahead behind the health clinic. Beyond it is a large open expanse and beyond that, nearly due north, some hills and rock outcroppings. The enemy might be in those hills ready to start firing, they might still be in the village although I doubt it.

This clinic, like most, is a simple, whitewashed stone building. There would be one or two examining rooms and a room for surgery. One room crammed with four beds for men, another for women. Out front a corrugated roof hangs over a spot where the men wait when they bring women. This one is run by one of the international charities.

I take Williams, Garcia, and Rodriguez with me, and we drop behind a wall. Not even six months ago, Garcia, our drone man, would have already launched two of his birds that would be skimming over the countryside. But since the Chinese figured out how to scramble our signals, any jihadi with twenty-five dollars and two AA batteries puts our drones out of business.

We watch O'Keefe's 2nd Squad working up a narrow dirt road, mud buildings on both sides.

For a split second, my brain works to register the high-pitched, whirring sounds.

Fuck.

It always takes too long to figure out when direct fire is coming. By the time you hear it, you're already fucked.

The guys from 2nd Squad are yelling at each other, firing, scrambling.

'Get the fuck down!'

'Up there! Those rocks!'

'Moving right… Cover… Cover.'

'Three hundred meters!… They're three hundred meters out!'

'Come on, I need you!'

'Get down!'

'Craig, I need the two forty. Come on, let's go!'

There's rapid fire from the gun and then, 'I'm jammed! God dammit. I'm jammed!'

Williams yells that he can crawl along the low wall below

their line of sight and make it to the front of the clinic compound to see what's going on. I give him the nod and he's off.

I listen as 1st Squad calls in: they've got a partial visual on the enemy up in the rocks above the village. I tell Rodriguez to call for air.

'Incoming!' someone yells from a block away.

'Incoming!' other voices repeat.

And the big shit comes in.

Dust flies, rubble in our face, the ground shakes.

Our ears are ringing. I wipe the dust away from my mouth and taste the rubble and the dirt. Some blood smears the back of my hand.

'Anybody hit?' I call out.

'No, sir,' they all yell back.

Williams gets me on the comm. 'Captain, this woman just got shot. Running to the clinic. She's just lying there.' Williams sounds scared. 'Oh, Jesus, she's pregnant. Maybe she's having her baby.' Then he says, 'She's screaming,' but now we can all hear her screaming, too.

'How close are you?'

'Twenty, thirty feet. But she's exposed.'

I order him back. He comes crawling along the wall.

'She's gonna get hit lying there.'

Jeffreys suddenly tumbles to my side. He's 1st Platoon's medic and he heard Williams.

Jeffreys says, 'Want me to get to her?' My first responsibility, and his first responsibility, is to our men.

I hear shelling up where 1st Squad is supposed to be.

'How long for air support?!' I yell at Rodriguez.

'Twenty minutes.'

'Fuck, Rodriguez, tell them we'll be goat feed by then.'

'On it,' he says, although I know they'll get here as soon as they can. This is what they live for. At least they used to be fast when we had enough birds in the air and had enough fuel to keep them going all the time. These days they rubber-band their planes together like we do our Cougars and we all have to ration fuel.

More mortar fire, this time closer.

The woman's screams are louder. I radio O'Keefe and tell him he's going to open fire to draw attention away from us when I give him the word. I point at my men, one by one. 'Rodriguez, stay here. Williams, head back along the wall. Jeffreys, you and me follow. Garcia, take up the rear. When we get in place, we make the call to O'Keefe, and Jeffreys and I go for her.'

The woman is still screaming. Fucking dogs are barking like mad.

I'm behind Williams as we make our way along the ground. His boots are a few feet in front of my eyes. More indirect hits nearby.

No noise on the radio, but my men are yelling instructions and warnings and commands at each other.

Williams stops almost at the clinic. I slither to his side and inch my head around the corner. The woman is twenty-five feet from us. Moaning now. Worse than the screams. She's facing us, clutching her abdomen. There's blood in the dirt.

She sees me. Her desperate eyes search mine. Her bright, powder-blue burqa is covered in rubble and dirt. She's pulled it away from her face and it's ridden halfway up her legs. Her head is exposed. She's a goddamn teenager.

Before I have time to move, direct fire slams around us.

'Williams, Garcia, hold your positions. Fire only if we're

getting shot at. Jeffreys, you're on the left, I've got right.' I radio O'Keefe and a moment later their firing starts.

'Let's go. Now!'

We both jump up and run like madmen, half doubled over, stiff and working to keep our balance with all the body armor. Bullets snap as they whiz over our heads. Another shell not far away.

I slide to the ground at her side. 'It'll be okay,' I say, making my voice soothing, knowing she wouldn't understand English.

I pull her arm over my shoulder, push the billowing fabric out of the way and wait for Jeffreys to lift her other side.

'Jeffreys, on two... one, two,' I start to lift her but it's dead-weight on the other side. I look over and Jeffreys is face down on the ground.

'Jeffreys!' I yell.

He doesn't move.

Jeffreys is my first responsibility. I know my orders but still I hesitate, not sure who to carry first.

I pick him up and run like crazy toward the clinic compound, almost dropping him as I round the open gate and dive to the ground. I turn and glimpse the staff and patients huddling inside the clinic. There are burqas and men with beards and children, maybe ten or fifteen people crowded into the waiting room, their faces wide-eyed in fear. Even if we built the place, they don't like us here. We attract the Taliban.

'Rodriguez! Man down. Call it in!'

No answer.

'Rodriguez!'

'Copy! Captain. Air support ETA five minutes. Calling Medevac. Over.'

I put Jeffreys on his back and tear open his Kevlar vest. He's taken a shot in his chest but the vest stopped it. He's had the shit knocked out of him and might have broken ribs and internal bleeding from the impact. 'Jeffreys!' I yell, but he's unconscious.

I call to Williams and Garcia on the other side of the low wall. 'Williams, over here, stay with Jeffreys. Garcia, cover me. I'm going back for the woman.'

I'm about to tell O'Keefe to open up with everything we got, but right then there's a fresh salvo of incoming fire and mortars directed at 1st and 2nd Squads. Without waiting, I'm running like hell, zigzagging across the dirt, tumbling down next to the woman, snatching her as she screams and then running like hell with her in my arms back near the clinic door where I drop behind a short wall.

I motion with my arms toward a man inside the clinic who looks at me from just inside the clinic doors. He hesitates. I wave at him frantically. I point for him to stay low and come along the wall. In a moment, he and another man are at the woman's side, carrying her in. The back of her burqa is dark with blood. She's stopped moaning. I don't know if this is good or bad.

And then I hear the music. The sound of two A10 Warthogs over us and a second later rockets firing into the hills. That's a beautiful sound, our bombs going off and their guns going silent. That's the fucked up thing that war does to you: I rejoice at the sound of men being killed.

Still careful, I duck back to Garcia and Williams.

Everything is quiet. No shots. Nothing.

O'Keefe yells to his men to keep down. 'Keep your eyes open. Watch your flanks.'

It stays quiet.

'Rodriguez, what's the ETA on Medevac?'

A moment later he calls me back. 'Twenty-five minutes.'

'Shit… Williams, I'm taking Jeffreys in.'

Williams knows the clinic staff won't be happy and I see his expression.

'Fuck that,' I say. 'Cover me.'

I throw Jeffreys over my shoulder and, crouching, move fast. When I reach the open clinic door, I see the patients and a few doctors and nurses, two of them ex-pats, foreign medical types. The place is a dank room and even from outside I can smell anxious sweat and disinfectant mingling with the smell of the goats tied up in the small yard outside the clinic.

I lay Jeffreys down at the doorway.

To the first doctor I see, I call out, 'You speak English?'

He comes quickly to the door. 'Yes, certainly,' he says in accented English.

'I've got a hurt man, Medevac's more than twenty minutes away. I need you to bring him in.'

He hesitates. We both know what can happen if they're seen as helping us. I stab my hand toward Jeffreys and yell, 'He was hit saving—'I point inside—'that woman's life.' I draw myself up and bark in his face. 'Bring him in now.'

He yells something in Pashto and two men rush out to get Jeffreys.

'Thank you,' I say.

I follow them inside as they put Jeffreys on the floor. The Afghani doctor, short, thick black hair and baby-face chubbiness, feels for Jeffreys' pulse and I hold open the vest so he can get to Jeffreys' chest.

'A little slow but steady.'

Jeffreys starts to stir and I hold his hand.

Rodriguez calls on my comm.

The doctor says, 'I don't know if there's internal bleeding.' His eyes dart to the door. 'Please.' His eyes hold mine, and in a strange way they make me feel safe. He has that Afghani softness that I always find incredible. In the midst of all this shit, these guys recite love poems at the drop of a hat, and have a hospitality you find nowhere else. I feel ashamed for intimidating him. I feel ashamed for risking lives by coming inside.

Rodriguez reports that one other man has a minor wound, little more than a scrape. I slump against a wall outside the clinic and feel immensely tired. 'Stay alert!' I snap into my comm when I hear chattering.

A nurse, greeting me in Pashto, comes out to offer me water. I place a hand to my heart. She lowers her face and says *salaam.*

I look past her into the clinic and see the back of a woman, wearing scrubs and with hair tucked into a surgical cap.

She turns and looks at me. She wears a surgical mask and protective goggles so I can't see her face, but I know she's a westerner by the way she holds my gaze.

She comes to the clinic door and stops right in front of me. Then I recognize her. Her eyes. The way she holds herself.

'How is she?' I ask. I know I'm talking too loudly because my ears are still ringing from the explosions.

'Stay out of our way,' she says, 'and she might have a chance.' Her voice is muffled by the mask, and fogged by my fatigue.

I watch as she returns to the tiny operating room. I can see the backs of the legs of a nurse and doctor leaning over the operating table.

I'm studying her when she seems to fly out of there, returns to face me, and strips off her mask.

I had worked years to get over those eyes and that voice. She would say that I hurt her. She stares with the same angry look I used to know so well.

'I heard you were over here,' I say.

She doesn't respond.

'Tanner, I...' She looks to one side and then at me. 'I have to get back to work.'

'I thought it was a big enough country that we could stay out of each other's way,' I say.

As I walk away I can feel her eyes like a laser-targeting system on my back.

The Journal of
John Murakami Fox

July 28, Islamabad

The voice of the first *muezzin* drifts through my open window. I am already awake. It is that in-between time, hovering between darkness and light, when the world still holds promise. Even here. The sky is light, the sun not yet up; I see Venus over the top of the neighbouring apartment. I am almost a happy man for I have not yet remembered where I am and why I am here.

The *muezzin* calls men to *fajr*, the dawn prayers. Of course I don't go. Church of England types, lapsed or otherwise, aren't given the warmest of welcomes. Still, Imam Ali, the leader at the small mosque from which the call to prayer comes, is my friend, as much as I have friends in Islamabad. We talk about religion, my utter lack of belief in all of them. We talk about politics. We talk about our children. Samir doesn't approve that I am separated from my wife and daughter although he says he understands.

He once told me he would miss me when I return home someday. 'Where's that?' I asked.

He stared at me when I said this with a look that was part blank and part tolerant of an insolent remark about something one does not joke about. Perhaps my humour doesn't translate across cultures. Or perhaps he thought me pathetic.

Within seconds, the beautiful, haunting notes are interrupted by a blast from one loudspeaker and then another and another, each vying to make the biggest impression on Islamabad. The sound is squawking, distorted. Poor Samir Ali: his *muezzin* is drowned out once again.

'What would The Prophet make of all this racket?' Samir once asked me. I didn't answer because I've learned, even with Samir, not to speculate on such things.

Later

Back when I met him in Charleston in mid-June, Tanner and I had struck a deal. Better to say, we struck an idea. I'd take the recording from our walk, write a chapter, then send it to him for corrections and answers to my many questions.

He had given me a list with email addresses and passwords, each to be used for the back and forth on only a single chapter. When we finalized that chapter, we would drop that address and move on to the next one. He had produced a second list of numbers of what he said were throw-away SIM cards to call once and only once. He told me to phone them only from a disposable SIM card. He was expecting trouble.

First I'd gone to DC and then back to London where I had fact-checked every detail I could. Everything checked out, at least the background and the characters. Of course what made the story sizzle was precisely what nobody else knew, or at least didn't *yet* know.

As I had told the story to him, Alistair listened with his eyes shut, his hands folded in front of his face, his lips resting on his fingertips. Sometimes, he'd nod, open his eyes, ask a thoughtful question and, once I'd answered, close his eyes to signal me to continue.

In the end, he said, 'We've got them. Finally, we've got them.' There was no triumph in his voice; it was quiet, sombre. But his eyes weren't on me. They seemed transfixed by the photograph of his son.

As I was leaving, most uncharacteristically, he said, quite solemnly, 'Be very careful, John.'

The next day, I had phoned Judith to pitch the idea.

'You said you'd be here last week.'

'I needed to get back to London. Listen, I want to change the deal.'

'Oh, God.'

'You were right.'

'I'm always right.'

'Do this as one of your serialized e-books.' A new chapter at regular intervals on her serial site.

'I'm listening.'

'We can promote it through our Book Club as well.' I told her about the Afghan Vampires Book Club.

'How many unique visitors?' she asked.

I told her.

'Per week?'

'Per year.'

'Nothing to give anyone a hard-on,' she said.

'If it does well, you can sell it to a regular e-book and print publisher.'

I heard her take a draw on her cigarette, or maybe it was a joint.

I waited.

She said, 'I like it. That is, if I like it.'

August 6, Islamabad
In the week since Chapter One was published in late July, more people have visited the Book Club each day than in all

of the past year. The site is still anonymous, but interest in the topic is hot, Judith's site is linked to the Book Club, and, lucky for those of us who live by hit count, word gets around.

Most of the online comments to the Book Club are the usual drivel, although there are a few worth keeping my eyes on. One I could swear is from one of Cody's buddies. 'Finally, the truth begins,' is all it says.

I sent Tanner the next chapter almost two weeks ago, but there's still no sign of the corrected chapter in my inbox.

August 8, Islamabad
Judith sent me the numbers on Chapter One downloads. 'Not a bad start,' she says.

Sandra wrote me to say that one of her male friends thought the book was brilliant. Given that she has seldom mumbled even a word about my writing, I perked up. Trying to maintain my journalistic *sangfroid*, I wrote back to ensure she hadn't told anyone of my (or her) connection to the Book Club and she immediately wrote a teasing note saying of course she had not.

When I last passed through London, Margaret said I still had a chance with Sandra. That it might still be possible for us to have something resembling a father-daughter relationship. She said that as far as she was concerned, I didn't deserve the chance. But there it was. I suppose even my ex-wife can't always be wrong. After all, there was a time when I still saw something in her.

Ah, sweet lies! There was a time when she still saw something in me.

August 11, Islamabad

Tanner's corrections and additions to Chapter Two arrived. I worked on it solidly for a few days then sent it off to Judith and Analia, her copyeditor. It will be back to me in two days and then should go live by end of the week.

August 18, Islamabad

Off to Kabul to earn my living for a few days, to do stories for the main UK daily I write for and, under a pseudonym, for one of the tabs. Maybe Margaret is right. Maybe I'm a hack British journalist after all; I do love the thought of a splashy 72-point headline.

As usual, at night I skim the news feeds. Another story that's perfect for the Book Club, this one about six Canadian vets killing themselves. Sitting together in a circle in a basement, all of them in their uniforms.

Alistair writes to ask if I've seen it.

'John,' he wrote. 'More stories of the living dead. The poor bastards.'

Sweet dreams to you too, old boy.

CHAPTER 2

After the attack on the clinic, we try to pry information out of the locals. Get nowhere. By the time Medevac comes, Jeffreys is talking and as they take him away he calls, 'See you soon.' We continue on patrol. Lieutenant Vance and the 3rd Platoon join us.

Back on the road, I try not to think about Katherine, but half the time it's a losing battle.

In the next village, I have a run-in with Hernandez, one of Vance's men who he's always complaining about. I come upon Hernandez and Pfizer questioning a young Afghani, probably mid-twenties. The guy is on his knees, hands behind his head. Hernandez, with a smirk, points his weapon down into his face.

'This one got something, Captain.'

'How do you know that, Hernandez?' I say.

'Guy his age, nice sandals like that, clean man-jammies, you tell me he don't get around.' He turns to the guy, 'Fuckin' *hajji*. I'm gonna string you up with your bitch mother.' The ANA guy translates and the guy starts babbling and you don't have to know a word of Pashto to understand what he's saying.

'Chill, Hernandez. Use your brains for once.'

'Prefer to use my boots to kick his balls to a pulp. Sir.'

I come up to within a foot of him. I lock my eyes on his and don't like what I see or what I feel. He's getting pleasure in this and he wants me to know it. Pfizer is standing there, waiting to see who's going to win.

'You're in Bravo Company, Hernandez,' I say, slowly without raising my voice. I move closer. 'Am I clear? We don't do that shit.'

I can't stop thinking about Katherine. And that gets me wondering if we saved the woman and her baby—but I know that's only an excuse to seek out Katherine again. I replay the scene over and over. I imagine it might be possible to be in the same room with her and not feel an ache that threatens to drown me. Then again, I wonder if the pain does me some good. At least it's something—something that's mine, something not from here, something that reminds me I once had a life outside of all this.

When we're heading back to Victory's Camp, we pass by the village and I order the vehicles to stop at the clinic.

'Captain, shouldn't we get back to The Cunt before dark?' O'Keefe radios back.

I reassure him we will. 'Give me two minutes to do some diplomacy.'

I turn to Williams. 'Hey, Williams,' I say, 'you still got those cookies?'

'My Girl Scout cookies?'

'Yes.'

'I was just going to open—'

'Williams, you didn't know this, but you were saving them for the nice people who took care of Jeffreys when they weren't supposed to.'

'But I…' He pouts like a little boy.

This time we pull our vehicles in front of the clinic.

I hear the evening call to prayers, and I hear the bells on goats as boys herd them home for the night.

I love Afghanistan in the late afternoon.

The thin, wispy clouds that look like a loosely woven carpet overhead. The dry, cold winds and big skies that make you feel lonely even if you're surrounded by a hundred people. In those moments, I get why the Afghanis love their classical poetry. You look at that sky, you smell the lavender in the wind, and you want to recite poetry.

At the clinic door the same Afghani doctor appears quickly, as if to stop me before I go inside.

'Good evening, Captain.'

'Everything okay here?' I ask him.

'Yes, no more problems.'

Behind him, I see Katherine holding a baby and trying to feed it from a small bottle. No longer in her surgical uniform, she wears a headscarf.

'My men wanted to leave these for you and your staff. To say thanks. A treat from our home.'

The doctor takes them and places his hand to his heart. He is even younger than I had thought the first time, his hair cut short, modern, a polo shirt under his white jacket, bags under his eyes that I now see are from fatigue and not from age.

'And the mother, is she...?' I ask.

The doctor looks in the direction of Katherine.

Katherine looks up at me. Gently, she sets the baby down in a rough crib on the floor and walks toward me.

He says, 'She didn't make it.'

'Is there family? I mean...'

The young doctor says, 'The father was killed in the fighting this morning.'

'The father... was he—Taliban?'

Now Katherine is in front of me. She says, 'And if he was, are you going to take the baby prisoner?'

'One of my men took a bullet in the chest trying to save his mother. Two of my men are wounded. You didn't worry if *they* have wives or kids at home.'

I can feel the young doctor looking at us, wondering, I imagine, where all this venom came from. Or maybe not. Maybe he's just polite. Maybe he feels the same way about me being here, minus the ex-lover bullshit.

'I didn't come back here for *you*, Katherine.' I speak slowly, awkwardly. 'I came back to thank the doctor here. And to find out what happened to the woman and her baby.'

Again, I am walking away from her. Again, her eyes brand my back with anger.

Who the hell knows anything about love when you're twenty-one? I didn't, that's for sure. Maybe smart people choose lust and leave it at that. That would be enough, wouldn't it, when you're twenty-one?

We met at university. I went to high school in Asheville, North Carolina, and then got an ROTC scholarship to the University of North Carolina in Chapel Hill. I didn't know for sure I wanted to be in the military but I knew it was a way out.

My father, my biological father, was in Bush's Iraq war. Enlisted. He came back in one piece and then got himself killed riding his motorcycle. Drinking, no helmet. I was six when it happened.

My mother was truly sad for a time, but then the sadness turned to resentment that she went on to perfect. Maybe it was his fault, I don't know. I've seen war. I can't know what he was thinking when he went out on his bike after drinking that day, but I can imagine. I think my mother tried to keep from throwing her spite my way after he died but she wasn't always very good at hiding it from me. She was mad that he left her with nothing except me and a shitty military pension.

A couple of years later she got remarried to Lou, my stepfather and the resident asshole when I was growing up. He ran the body shop at a Toyota dealership. At least he treated my mother well, even if around me he acted like he had an Allen wrench up his ass.

Neither one of them cared for the military and neither one of them had gone to university, so I did all the applications myself, both for ROTC and school. Plus my mom and Lou had their hands full with Joaquin, my half-brother, who was a walking case study of adolescent delinquency.

Both Mom and Lou passed away while I was on my second tour of duty here. Both in the same year. She was barely 60. So now my family is just Joaquin and me, but he isn't talking to me anymore, so I don't really have a family, I suppose.

My grandmother, my mother's mother, didn't die until last year. She's my Hispanic family, the reason I learned Spanish, and probably the reason I didn't become a criminal like my brother.

And then there was Katherine.

I was studying international relations at UNC, trying to learn something about the world, thinking that if I was going to be an officer, I should know about the places I was going. She was in nursing school, in the combined undergrad and master's nurse-practitioner program. Pretty unlikely with our respective majors that we'd even meet, but the gods had plans for us.

It was a South Asian contemporary history course. No shortage of wars to talk about there—Sri Lanka, Pakistan and

India, Bangladesh, the Nepalese civil war, and part one of the Afghan war.

How to describe her? Nutmeg skin, green eyes, long, black, shiny, wavy hair that she usually tied up but that always seemed to want to break free. A face as distinctive as those of the empresses and princesses and women warriors carved on the ancient temples of Angkor Wat.

I think it was in the second class that she announced to us all that she was the daughter of a Sri Lankan mother, a Tamil, whose family had mostly been killed in the course of the civil war, and an American father, an aid worker, who married her mother and got her out of Sri Lanka. She was so full of rage when she announced this, like she needed to make it clear to all of us who she was and why the class mattered more to her than it possibly could to the rest of us.

I remember that first time I wore my ROTC uniform to that class. I always felt a little out of place when I wore it on campus. UNC is a liberal school and all that, but then again, after my mom and Lou and the crap they gave me about going into the military, I was pretty much ready for any shit or looks I might get.

But Katherine's look was in another league, another universe altogether. Her eyes cut into me.

From that day on, Katherine and I had a routine in class. Every time I spoke or asked a question, a few seconds later her hand shot up and she argued the exact opposite of what I said.

I relished going to the class. I would raise my hand, make an argument, and count the seconds until she responded. If she didn't, I felt cheated, like my day was missing something. It was like that ancient Warner Brothers cartoon with Wiley

Coyote and the sheep dog who guarded the herd. Arch-enemies, sure, but it's what they looked forward to.

So one day, I was walking out of class, and my mother called my mobile. It was when Lou was starting to have heart problems.

My mother always spoke Spanish when she was nervous or angry. She had taught me a fair amount of it and I spoke it with my grandmother, too, so I can get by.

Katherine heard me speaking Spanish. I could feel her lingering close to me, acting like she wasn't listening when she really was.

'You speak Spanish?' she said, after I got off the phone. It was the first time she was looking at me in a way that was more curious than hostile.

'Yeah,' I said, and then paused, giving her a look like I couldn't give a shit. 'My mother is Hispanic and she taught me a fair amount.' For once Katherine didn't say anything critical or sarcastic and seemed to be waiting for more. 'My grandmother was originally from Mexico and she lived with us a few years when I was growing up.'

'I wish I knew more Tamil,' Katherine said, her voice almost wistful. 'I think my mother wanted to forget it.'

I almost said I was sorry to hear that, but I just listened. Later Katherine told me that I had passed the test. She explained that she was fed up with guys who felt sorry for her or made that pained face when she talked about what happened to her family in the Sri Lankan war.

I was getting ready to walk away, imagining this was the end of the conversation.

'I wouldn't have imagined you were half Hispanic and spoke Spanish.'

'I wouldn't have imagined you would even talk to me if you didn't have to.'

She smiled. It was the first time I had seen her smile. I could imagine that the pantheon of Hindi gods and goddesses had worked in a rare show of unison to craft her smile. I was awed.

I mumbled something about getting a coffee and she said sure. Three hours later we were still talking.

By the time we walked out of the student center I was pretty sure I would soon be in her bed or she in mine. This I knew for certain: I was stupidly and madly in love with her.

'Captain,' Williams says to me from the back after we've driven forty-five minutes and are getting close to camp. 'Earlier, I started telling you…'

I have neither the energy nor the heart to tell him I'm just not interested, so on he drones.

'It's this crazy shit I heard from this ANA guy. Like this village, way up north somewhere. These other ANA guys found every villager dead, but they didn't see no bullet wounds. No blood or nothin'. Couldn't figure out why Taliban would attack them and couldn't figure out how they got themselves killed.'

Garcia hates when Williams goes on about things and interrupts. 'So brainiac, you got the name of the village so we can pass it on to intel.'

'No, but Jennings from Alpha said—'

'Alpha Company are a bunch of…'

I tune them all out for the rest of the drive back to Victory's Camp. My body's stiff from sitting and it hurts to climb out of the Cougar, but the cool night air feels good and I gaze up at the billion stars sprawled across the high-altitude air. Most of my men head straight to the canteen. I stop Rodriguez and ask him to radio to see how Jeffreys is doing.

I'm walking to my quarters to dump my gear and grab a shower when I see a cigarette glowing by the trailers where Alpha Company bunks. I can't make out the face but I know who it is. The cigarette smell is acrid, and I know only one man who smokes Afghan cigarettes.

'Tanner Jackson.' He isn't calling, as much as affirming his spite for me in that smooth and taunting voice of his.

He steps out and blocks my path. 'Heard you guys took hits for a pregnant chick. I'm guessing she must have been real strategic.'

'Captain Ditka,' I say.

'We found two labs where they were making IEDs. Also a weapons stash. Drone jammers. RPGs, mortars, the whole shit.'

'And let me guess, no one captured alive?'

I start to pass around him, but he continues. 'You and I have different clientele, Jackson. You bring flowers for the moms, we go after the bad guys.'

I hear the muffled pop of his fingers as he flicks his cigarette to the ground. His voice softens. 'You're not a bad officer, Jackson, but you gotta find your center. Remember why we're here.'

As I walk away, he calls to my back. 'There's no such thing as being in a war halfway.'

The Journal of
John Murakami Fox

August 25, Kabul

Alistair once told me about an American woman he met at Oxford in the 1970s. She had taken a year off to backpack across Europe and Asia, and Alistair claimed he'd never forget her description of her first morning in Kabul.

'She was the adventurous type, on her way from Iran to Pakistan,' he said.

'When there still was one country called Pakistan,' I replied.

'No war was going on at the time. Nor were there any journalists or soldiers or mercenaries or disaster vultures trying to make a million bucks or two.'

'And not many crazy fundamentalists, I suppose.'

'So, that first morning, the sun was rising as she and a friend climbed up to the roof of their guest house. She said she was haunted by the sounds: the creaking wooden wheels of carts, the tinkling bells on the necks of goats, and the call of a *muezzin*. Later, she wandered through the dusty city. People were friendly, she never felt threatened. There were alleys with cafés and bakeries. The first hippie she met told her where to get the best Hungarian goulash in town.'

Now, it's a long-term war zone. Now, you have trouble finding people who remember when it was something else. It's a city of concrete blocks, concrete walls, concrete barricades. Razor wire and bullet-scarred monuments, HESCO barriers, checkpoints and guards. Private generators pump noise and exhaust into the dusty air. A city where UN staff are, under their latest directive, allowed to go to only six restaurants other than in the main hotels. Where they aren't allowed to stray more than 150 metres from their vehicle or come within 100 metres of military personnel.

Three-and-a-half million people crammed into neighborhoods without running water, with sewage dribbling through open ditches, and with electricity for only a couple of hours every day or two. All this not far from the palaces of the narco-warlords who run the government of Afghanistan for us.

Later

Only when I pressed him did Alistair admit that this was Joanne, his American wife, the mother of Ryan. The woman who tore his heart out when she decided to return to the States without him. The woman he blamed for letting their son join the US Army.

August 28, Kabul

Judith reports a 90 per cent return rate for Chapter One readers coming back to buy Chapter Two. Plus tens of thousands of new readers. Dutiful daughter (seeming to forget her years of resentment towards me for my years of virtual absence from her life), reports that visits to the Book Club continue to climb. So far, our book is still not front page news, but both Judith's serial book site and the Book Club are starting to get some social media buzz.

I catch a news item. This time it's a bunch of veterans who went berserk in the Atlanta airport. Complained about the newest body-search technology. Came back a couple of hours later with semi-automatic weapons. Not pretty.

For a moment I ponder the fascinating American ability

to stare at the obvious and not see it. Then I think I shouldn't cast the first stone. After all, I carry the passport of a country that still has a monarchy, however symbolic it is, and still fights in this war too. Seems to be our accepted role: dutiful lapdogs.

I scan the images from the Atlanta airport massacre, everything captured on video.

And everyone back home thinks it's dangerous over here.

CHAPTER 3

A few weeks later, along with Alpha Company, we were sent back to Bagram. Normally we'd have stayed longer on a rotation, maybe doing most of our tour out there. But something was up. Things were not going well, even though they would never say it. For every IED we found, there were fifteen more planted. Not only did they get better at making them and hiding them but they also got faster in laying them. We could go back to a place a day after we'd cleared it, and there would already be new ones. And for every clinic we protected, they blew up two in the district next door. Anybody who talked to us in the daytime might turn up dead that night. And then there was that weird shit Williams was going on about, about the Taliban up north who only attacked at night, about dead bodies but no gunshot wounds. Guys were getting spooked. Any of the old-timers who had been in the First Afghan War said they hadn't seen anything like this.

I noticed Williams shooting baskets and I headed over. 'Captain,' he said, grinning. 'A bit different from down at The Cunt, ain't it?'

Victory's Camp was small, squalid. No decent shower. A short row of reeking latrines. Nothing for the men to do but watch the same old DVDs on their computers, reread old magazines, play cards, and complain. Nothing close to real food. Half the time you were tense out of your mind on patrol, the other half so bored you wanted to be out on patrol.

Bagram is like a small city. Planes come and go around the clock, stores sell DVDs and junk food, jewelry and carpets, motorcycles and cars, to be delivered when you get back home. (The salesmen always say 'when,' never 'if.') Internet works except when they don't want us communicating out, like when we hear about a KIA but they haven't yet reached the next of kin. Graffiti in the toilets reminds me of junior high, only the scrawl is about NCOs and chaplains instead of principals and teachers; the taunting scribbles are between the ones who brag about how many people they've killed and the ones who just want to go home.

Streets are named California and 1st Avenue. A few buildings are 1970s Russian vintage, but there are rows of prefabs and tents and those big portables with toilets and showers.

Anyway, it was good to be in a place where I wasn't tense all the time. We still walked around with our weapons, ate with weapons slung across our backs, crapped with our weapons propped against the cubicle wall, but we pretty much knew we wouldn't be using them.

I would find myself staring across the plains at the mountains. Back in the summer, the base of these mountains was carpeted with green, but now, in the last days of fall, their craggy peaks were thick with snow. Maybe I had a premonition I'd end up in those mountains far too soon.

I was talking to Williams. He stopped dribbling, got quiet, and couldn't look me in the eye.

'Captain,' he said. 'Those stories about the roving Taliban. They say they're using some kind of weird chemical or biological or...' and on he went.

It was more of the rumors that were swirling around the base but as far as I was concerned, all they really meant was that we just couldn't make ourselves admit we'll never really understand this place.

Our Cougars were back in the shop. All their fancy digital communications useless. Screens were going blank, freezing up. Rodriguez said the only things he trusted were a clear old-fashioned shortwave radio signal and a voice he could recognize. The rest, he said, were toys. Toys that some company back in Detroit or Atlanta or San Jose was getting rich on. And toys the terrorists could jam.

I was usually busy with meetings and admin crap, but once in a while I'd play a game of basketball with my men or ping pong with O'Keefe. I read. We worked out and did training exercises. Some of the guys went in for the devotionals and Bible readings. At least they were calmer for a few hours afterward. Then again, Hernandez seemed to always come back acting like he had a license to kill straight from God. And we talked about the Taliban.

After a few days of this, I was ordered to Kabul for some training and took O'Keefe and Williams along. We caught a drive to Camp Julien, the old NATO base in Kabul, turned over to the Afghan government a decade or so ago, but now theirs in name only.

As much as Kabul stinks, it was good to be somewhere with a few trees again—the entrance to the base is on a tree-lined street except along the tall concrete wall where the trees have been amputated for security. You could see their stumps standing like sentinels all down the road.

I'd done anti-insurgency training in officer training school back home, but since nothing seems to work, they keep coming up with new theories. Hence a new four-day, anti-insurgency course. Some smart guys from Princeton and Stanford, and some other smart guys from the Pentagon. When we finally admit we lost this war for the second time, it won't be for lack of smart people.

On day two, over lunch, I was sitting in the coffee shop along with dozens of NATO soldiers, a few Afghanis, and a bunch of civilians. People had their laptops open, writing home, checking email or the news.

'I guess this means we're supposed to talk,' I heard a woman's voice say.

I looked up and saw Katherine. She wore cargo pants and a purple sweater, marking herself as not being military but also not a corporate or UN type. A light parka was tucked under one arm.

I stood up.

She said, 'We're all stuck in Kabul. No one's telling us why, but you guys forced us to leave our clinics. They claim it's for our safety. As if it could get more dangerous, between the Taliban attacks and your brilliant intelligence getting in our way.'

'You mean protecting you.'

'We're better off when you don't come around.'

'I doubt that.'

She studied me, her angry look parked in neutral. 'Remember the doctor in the clinic? The one who took care of one of your men?'

I slowly nodded, knowing what was coming.

'A day after you… *defended* us, we found him dead outside the clinic. They left his head in the doorway for us. Dogs were eating it.'

'Shit, I'm—'

'You guys don't know the first thing that's going on out there.'

Finally, I said, 'What was his name?'

She hesitated, as if first deciding if I deserved to know.

Eventually she said, 'Behnam. It means "good". "Honorable".'

There was silence between us, then I spoke. 'When you told me you wanted to come here, I should have figured we'd eventually cross paths in some nameless village.'

'Barikju. It has a name.'

'Whatever.'

'It's not *whatever*. It's a place with people who have lives and homes.'

'You know what I mean.'

'Yeah,' she said, 'but you don't know what *I* mean, do you?'

Her words hung in the air like a dare. Would I take the bait? Go back along that old path?

We had crashed into each other's lives those first months together in university. It was the fall semester of my fourth and final year; she was finishing her undergraduate degree in nursing but had two more years to become a nurse-practitioner.

She was at my apartment or I was at hers almost every night. We both had roommates but it was as if they ceased to exist. They probably despised us: if you're not in love, it's hard to watch. It looks fucking crazy.

There were days she'd swear she needed to study for an exam, or that she was behind on an assignment, or that she had study group. I'd say it was okay, of course, that I'd miss her but I'd see her the next day or the one after that, and that I had to study too. But every time, late at night, I'd hear her lean her bicycle against my window and snap her lock and tap gently on my window.

'Tanner. Tanner? You awake?'

And seconds later she'd be in my room, the street lamp casting shadows on us, her clothes on the floor, my boxer shorts lost under the covers, her hands and her mouth on me and mine on her. She'd show me how she wanted it, usually with her on top, her hair loose and falling in my face, rocking back and forth until we were both spent and exhausted and mumbling *I love you's*. Then we'd fall asleep in that wonderful stupor that only great sex can bring.

In the morning she'd wake me up far before I wanted to. She'd say it was the only time we had to talk. Some days, she'd try to talk me out of the army, others she'd ask about my family, and when I told her about my real dad dying after the Iraq war, she listened gravely, maybe finally understanding what I was doing.

'Promise me you'll be one of the good ones,' she'd say.

She said her mother told her stories of a few Sri Lankan soldiers who were not cruel. She said she wanted to believe that I could be honorable, that it was possible to be an honorable soldier.

But other days she'd start at me again.

'Tanner, don't do it, please. You're too smart for the military. You have too much to offer. You can teach, or get your master's, or PhD, study military history if you want. Or teach Spanish. You said you'd like that.'

I'd smile at her and kiss her neck and whisper to her in Spanish and try to change the subject.

And so the months went by, ticking down to the bittersweet week we each graduated.

She cried while I packed up my car. Driving away that day was the hardest thing I'd ever done, like I needed gargantuan muscles just to start the car and point it down Franklin Street. After I had been on the road for about an hour she called me and told me that it wouldn't work, that she couldn't wait for me, that our lives were going in directions that were too different, that it made no sense. And then I became silent and she could hear me controlling my voice, trying to keep from showing how sad I was, and she hung up. She called back an hour later and said she didn't mean it, that she wanted to try and asked how often could I come back to visit.

It went on like that for more than half a year.

Fortunately for us, officer candidate school was at Fort Benning, Georgia. Every month I'd drive up for a weekend. Sometimes her roommate would be away and the campus would be empty and we'd make love in the living room or in the kitchen.

At some point I realized we were having sex more often than we talked and when we were done we slept or pretended to sleep or turned on the TV.

I had become part of the army. And she was getting closer to a humanitarian career.

On one of those visits, we didn't immediately go to her bedroom and pull each other's clothes off. She just stared at the floor and out the window. Soon I was gone.

I cried part of the drive back. I felt empty inside, half dead. Then, for a moment, I was relieved that I didn't have to pretend to be someone I wasn't. But a minute later I felt like I'd been kicked in the gut.

I tried to write her an email. I tried dozens of times to tell her I missed her and that I understood, that I loved her and wanted to find a way to be together, or tell her that I would wait for her if she needed time to think things over. But I never did. The hurt was too deep.

It was a Friday night, about a month later, when I received her text.

'I'm in town. Where can I find you? I need you. I miss you.'

Fuck, I thought. Here we were as if we were back at university with her knocking on my window late at night. I was excited, and yet terrified of opening old wounds. I wanted to turn off my phone, pretend I didn't receive her message, but instead I tapped a response.

The guard on duty at the entrance to the base was smiling as he watched us kissing and embracing like movie lovers.

But that feeling didn't last. Sunday was February 10. *That* February tenth. 2/10. Like everyone around the world, we were transfixed by the horror at the winter Olympic stadium. We watched in stunned silence, in agony, both sensing where it would lead.

Right back to Afghanistan.

And now, six years later at a NATO military base in the Second Afghan War, soldiers walked by us with their weapons, and Katherine was here, dressed as if she'd just come from class. We stood like sentries, facing off.

'We can't simply march in and make them into who we want them to be,' she said.

'But maybe we've kept another 2/10 from happening.'

'Tanner, this isn't a contest about who's right. These are people's lives. This is our government's pathetic attempt to try to make them into something else and kill them when they disagree. Hardly a recipe for preventing terrorism once and for all.'

We were right back in our South Asia political science class, but this time I wanted nothing to do with it.

Without a word, I sat down; she followed.

'How long have you been here?' My tone was lifeless. I

could have been interviewing her for a job.

'Almost two years,' she said.

'It's what you wanted.'

'They need us. I believe we're doing some good.'

'We believe that too.'

'But do *you*? Do you believe all that?'

I didn't answer at first.

'You know, Katherine, I only know what I saw that day when that Olympic stadium exploded.' My voice felt wearier than a thirty-year-old's had the right to be.

She seemed to be studying me. She cupped her hands under her jaw and rested her elbows on the table and, like that, I was back in Chapel Hill—at the library, in a bar, or my apartment kitchen table. Back then she'd uncup her hands and reach across the table for mine.

'Kat... Katherine, look, I won't get into this. We're both trying to do a job we believe in and—'

'Don't even try to compare us.'

'Yeah, but here you are, working in a clinic we protect. Hanging out on our base.'

'My conscience is clean.'

'Mine too.'

We stopped and took deep breaths at almost the same time.

When she spoke again, she almost whispered. 'Tanner, God, I mean... I hoped to avoid seeing you in Afghanistan... I spent so long just trying to forget you.'

I stood up. 'Then consider me forgotten.'

The next week back at Bagram was a blur. Our course ended, our briefings and new training sessions began. The new plan—Full-Court Press, they called it—was a hodge-podge of all the previous strategies. They described it as 'man-to-man defense' with a platoon assigned to each hot village—to get to know it, to be part of it, to breathe with it—along with a 'full-court press' with all our firepower focused on the trouble spots. They said we were going from reactive to proactive. Or something like that. The more they explained it and the more they tossed in various sports metaphors, the more it made no sense, the more it showed how desperate we were getting. I was thinking we were as clueless as the British back in the 1800s and the Russians in their first venture here in the 1980s and their second, which went just as badly.

And we were to give an ultimatum to the humanitarian organizations, like Katherine's. You want to stay in the country, you act as our eyes and ears. You become part of our network. You help us target our enemy. Don't like it and we suggest to the Afghan government that they cancel your work visa and put you on the next plane home.

The biggest thing the intelligence guys kept talking about was a group in the northern provinces they were calling the 'Nomadic Northerners.' It was even worse than Williams' most far-fetched story. It might be one mobile Taliban group, although the way the reports were coming in, it could be a dozen. They were showing up in remote corners of remote provinces and used the dirtiest tactics: murdering medical staff, placing IEDs in dead animals and on children, hiding bombs under burqas, and quietly killing without bullets, slitting throats or using one of the new Russian poisons supposedly banned by the UN. They didn't seem to have local friends—they didn't seem to care about winning hearts and minds. Turns out dumbshit Williams knew something before I did. Maybe I should have listened more to his crazy stories.

Going after them was the assignment we all wanted: the worst assignment, but the prize assignment. I caught Ditka from the corner of my eye. For a second it felt like we were all back in elementary school, hoping to get picked by the teacher.

The next day, we waited as each company was called out along with the district it was assigned to. We in Bravo Company were to secure a district in Balkh. Alpha Company would be in the next district over. Once again, we'd share the same combat outpost set smack dab in between. We were going north but not nearly as far as we had hoped.

Our superiors pretended they actually knew where the hot spots were, that we had enough intel to find the bases of operation for the Nomadic Northerners. And they'd rewritten the rules again—'engagement with the safeties off.'

'Colonel Lovejoy,' I said, raising my hand to our battalion commander during one of the briefings. 'Is it good for these aid workers to be our eyes and ears? Pretty risky stuff.'

'Captain Jackson, they speak the language, they draw the enemy in, they tell us what they see. This is a tracking war. The NGO types will be our bait.'

'Sir, there's no way they'll go along—'

'Jackson, we're not idiots. We don't announce this to them. We simply restrict their movements and insist they report any security breaches to us.'

'But Colonel, doesn't that violate...'

Lovejoy wasn't even looking at me anymore. 'Yes, Captain Ditka?'

'Jackson likes the Boy Scout approach. Light a campfire, sing "Kumbaya," and they'll put down their weapons and hug us.'

'Make your point, Ditka,' the Colonel said, but he was barely suppressing a smile.

'Colonel, the full press works if you let us do our job. Get the aid people out of the way and let us treat everyone as a potential hostile until proven otherwise.'

'You've got your orders.'

It turned out I had mine. I was supposed to stay in Kabul for two more weeks to assist the battalion intelligence officer talking to the aid agencies in our region and working out a communication process. I was thinking what a pain this would be, especially because one of those groups was Katherine's and after our last encounter I didn't want to see her again.

The Journal of
John Murakami Fox

September 15, Islamabad
An SB blew up another market, this one in the south end of
Islamabad. I spent the day stepping through the horror. Trying not to breathe through my nose. Trying not to smell the
shit. Interviewed whom I could but everyone was either too
stunned, or too angry, or too sick of answering the same in-
ane questions. Wrote it up, sent it off to my main UK paper,
knowing it will be cut down and buried, knowing that few
people will even bother to read it.

September 16, Islamabad
Tried to make it through the wall into Rawalpindi to get reactions from my Taliban contacts about the bombing. I was told
the bombing has shut down the border crossing.

Too bad. In spite of all the Taliban prohibitions on the other side, it's a relief to get out of Islamabad and into a real city.

Judith sends me a message: 'Sales tracking upward. Keep it
coming!'

I write to Tanner, pressing him to move faster on the corrections.

CHAPTER 4

When I went for the first liaison meeting two days later, Katherine was there. The day before the meeting, our battalion intelligence officer got dysentery. I guess they figured the humanitarian organizations were secondhand news so they figured a captain like me could handle some simple liaison. I brought O'Keefe with me, with Williams as our escort and guard.

We were in a nondescript meeting room in a nondescript one-story building in a nondescript walled compound. All the aid agencies were behind high gates, behind walls and razor wire, and, at the entrances, steel-reinforced security cages and cameras, the same old shit from more than twenty years ago. I heard that in the early years of the first Afghan war back after the post-9/11 invasion, Kabul was party central: NGO types, advisers, corporate vultures, and UN staff worked hard all day and played hard all night. Soldiers grumbled about having to leave their weapons in their cars to get into the parties but, at least in Kabul, fear was not yet the air everyone breathed.

Fifteen aid agencies sat around the table. None of the corporate partners were there; they were all run through the embassy. These agency reps clearly didn't want to be within a mile of me. They grilled me with questions about our new strategy. I pretended it made sense. I jotted down their questions that I didn't have an answer for and told them I'd raise them with my superiors. The whole first meeting was tense, especially when I told them they'd need our OK to leave Kabul. We hated each other even before we began talking. We didn't even start to create our communications plans.

Katherine asked one question. Her voice was reserved but she didn't set into me like some of her colleagues did. When the meeting was mercifully over and I was gathering my things, I caught her gaze as she left the room.

'That was friendly,' O'Keefe muttered. 'They're a bunch of—' O'Keefe stopped. Katherine stood beside us.

'Captain Jackson, do you have a moment?' Her voice was professional. 'I'd like to discuss the next meeting's agenda.'

'Williams, O'Keefe, wait for me at reception.'

O'Keefe raised his eyebrows to ask the obvious question. I ignored him and waited for them to leave.

She opened her mouth to speak. Paused. Then she asked if I wanted another coffee, as if she needed to buy time. I said I was fine.

She still didn't look at me when she said, 'The other day, we didn't finish talking. I want to ask you how you are… I want us to stop feeling angry at each other every time we walk in the room.'

I didn't tell her I'd been thinking about her every hour since the day at the clinic, that I was thinking that anger could only be this intense if you really cared. I didn't tell her the war was going from bad to worse and I felt I was being dragged down with it. I didn't tell her my commander was an idiot and one of my fellow captains was a psychopath. I didn't tell her that my ideals were getting tested. And I didn't say that I'd spent more than six years wondering if there was something I could have done differently.

Katherine had left that day, 2/10. Few words came to either of us. She said she needed some time to think. She said she still loved me. She said she didn't know. I said she was repeating herself. She scowled at me.

Both of us were in a hurry. She had more than a year before her graduation, but she desperately wanted to go to South Asia. I wanted to go anywhere.

For three weeks we didn't speak. The mushroom cloud of 2/10 hung over us, as if any contact between us would be too toxic to bear.

She was always on my mind. I desperately wanted to see her. To be with her again.

I had a long weekend and I drove to Chapel Hill to surprise her.

I was about to knock on the door, when I heard voices inside: Katherine's and a man's. I could make out only some words, but it sounded affectionate, intimate. I knocked. I should have just driven away, or at least gone back to my car and phoned her. Instead, I knocked again.

It took a moment before Katherine spoke from behind the closed door. 'Who is it?'

'Hey, it's me. I wanted to see you… I didn't want to leave it that way.'

The silence that followed said it all. I heard her speaking to the man inside.

'Tanner… I… just a minute,' she said, the door still closed.

When she finally opened it, she didn't step out to kiss me. I recognized the post-coital languor in her eyes.

'You didn't waste any time.'

'We knew this wouldn't work, Tanner. We're too different. You won't change. You want to go to war.'

'The only thing I want is you.'

She looked away.

72

'Tanner... I can't do this any longer...'

'I never pretended to be anyone I'm not. I never lied to you. I never tried to make *you* into someone else.' I went on and on, but she was silent, which only goaded me on.

'Fuck you,' I half muttered and half shouted as I walked away.

And now here we were, in an antiseptic meeting room in Kabul.

'Tanner, I want to talk. I mean I want to be able to talk to you.'

I opened my hands with a skeptical 'I'm listening' gesture.

'We're both here, so far from home and... I'd at least like to be able to talk to you. Can we do that?'

Absently, as if we were still sitting at my tiny kitchen table in Chapel Hill, she touched the shirtsleeve on my left arm, above the scar. Then, as if realizing what she had done, she quickly drew her hand away.

'Your family?' she asked still looking where her hand had just touched my arm. 'Are they okay?'

I told her Mom and Lou had died. She asked questions. She said how sorry she was. It was a long time before she spoke again.

'And Joaquin? How is he?'

'What can I say? Totally fucked up.'

Not just cutting his older brother on the arm with a flick knife. Not just desperate to prove to his older brother and his father, my miserable stepdad, that he wasn't a pussy.

I watched her eyes as I said, 'He's in prison. Accessory to murder.'

'Oh Jesus.'

'He was bragging about it, what his friends had done. I told him he needed to go to the police, tell them what happened, especially if he was innocent. He wouldn't go. I was the one who turned him in.' I paused before continuing. 'Anyway, last year he wrote me an email from prison. Said he never wanted to see me again.'

'What—'

'Mom said that's what killed Lou... Maybe it's what killed her, too.'

I didn't see Katherine again for almost a week, though I thought about her every day, and even when I tried not to, I went to bed thinking about her each night. In spite of the hurt and the anger, she was right that we were both here, and that we were so far from home and from anything that made sense. And for me, she was about all I had left from home.

My company was still at Bagram preparing to head north. The reports on the Nomadic Northerners were getting more gruesome. Villages where five or ten people would be found dead, no gunshot wounds, bled to death it looked like, some decapitated, others poisoned. Real eighteenth century kind of shit. I was relieved to be busy—calming my men, gathering information, doing the usual admin bullshit—and to be focused: my favorite state of being. But even with all this on my mind, I kept thinking about Katherine. Maybe we could just talk. That would be enough.

The second meeting with the NGOs was on a mild, sunny November day. As I got things started, Katherine hadn't yet arrived and I felt a jolt of disappointment. I explained that Major Chan from the battalion was recovering and would be taking over for the next meetings. And, I joked, 'He'll actually have some answers to your questions.'

Just then, Katherine came bustling in. 'Sorry,' she said, handing me a file folder. 'Just finishing the information you requested about our clinics and locations.'

I glanced in the folder. Lists. Maps. Descriptions. And an envelope. In small letters she had written on it, *Open before meeting ends.*

I waited until O'Keefe was explaining our communication plan before I did so.

There was a card key inside. The note read: *There is more to say. More I want to say. Sheraton. Room 515. I'll be waiting. K.*

It took us longer than it should have to reach the Sheraton, recently rebuilt after the last iteration got blown to bits for the third time. There were new barricades, new checkpoints every time we drove through town. Security outside waved us through and inside brushed us past the civilians putting their belongings and bodies through the metal detector, the X-ray machine, and pat-down.

Williams and O'Keefe eyed a big-screen TV in the sports bar. 'See you shortly,' I said. They both told me to take as long as possible. They thought I was meeting with the UN liaison staff.

At the elevators, two more private security toughs waved me forward. They asked what floor I was going to. I told them and showed them the room card. They scanned it and then pressed an outside console; inside the elevator there were no buttons except for the lobby. The fifth-floor hallway was deserted, surveillance cameras watched me. I stopped at 515, took a deep breath, inserted the key, saw the light go green, and opened the door.

Katherine was sitting in a chair near the window reading a book. The sky was pink from the plastic blast film covering the glass. She was wearing a long Indian cotton skirt, a swirl of purple, green, and blue; her loose hair touched her shoulders.

She closed the book. I stood at the doorway, the door still open, my heart racing. I made myself breathe deeply.

'You don't have to say anything, Tanner.' Her voice was serious. Then she looked at me in a way I hadn't been looked at in years: desire, familiarity, and affection blended together.

I did not want to move; I did not want this moment to disappear. At the same time, I had the overwhelming feeling that it could only get worse from here.

She said, 'Tanner, I still want you. I know I hurt you. I know I was unfair.'

Still I didn't move.

'I was an idiot. I was so young. We were both so young. I didn't know what I wanted or what was important. I was a fool—'

'Kat, you've never been a fool.'

'You haven't closed the door.'

I didn't move.

'Tanner... Tanner, I'm sorry.'

I closed the door and stepped into the room. She moved to the foot of the bed, her eyes still locked on mine. I stood, silent.

She said, 'If you don't want this, don't say anything. Just go. Now.'

Still at a distance, I studied her face. I looked at her hands the color of nutmeg, at her hair and her sea-green eyes. The waist of the skirt softly hugged her hips and I imagined slowly undoing the buttons, one by one, and letting it fall to the floor.

I thought: *Walk back out the door.* I thought: *We've been through this before.*

I dropped my backpack to the floor and went to her.

The Journal of
John Murakami Fox

September 20, Kabul

Even for someone who has received his share of threatening phone calls, this one spooked me. They're never fun, but after the first several dozen, you learn not to take them too seriously. You write things, you annoy people, you feel proud to have annoyed them. They try to scare you. All in a day's work.

I had bought an extra throw-away mobile phone this afternoon in case I needed a safe number that couldn't be traced to my name.

I was charging it when it rang.

I picked it up.

A man says, 'I've been reading your book.' American accent.

'Which book?' I say.

'One about the captain and his girlfriend.'

'And?'

'And I've been reading your website.'

No one is supposed to know it's my website, but then again it wouldn't be all that difficult to find out. 'I don't have a website.'

'There are people even less enthusiastic than I am about this story of yours.'

'I don't know what you're talking about.'

'Cut the bullshit, Fox. You should know the type of trouble you're stepping into.'

'Who are you?'

'All that matters is that you should be worried about your daughter. And yourself. And what could happen if you continue.'

I hung up.

The spectre of Snowden and all the exiled, jailed, and disappeared whistleblowers and journalists hangs heavily over my profession. You do the job, and you try not to get spooked by the threats when you write things about powerful people and powerful institutions. And when they mention your family, you have to assume it's a sign of desperation.

I know this one is bigger than anything I've ever done. The threats are no surprise, really.

The call itself isn't what spooked me.

What spooked me was how the bloody hell anyone knew the phone number.

September 21, Kabul

One good thing happened today: a beautiful email from Sandra. That's not something I've often received from her. Perhaps never. Sandra says some kids at school who don't even know I'm her father are talking about the e-book. (Perhaps it's more surprising that they even pay attention to this war.) I called her on Skype and asked if that's because she's bribing them to read it. She said she was proud I was her father. I definitely hadn't heard her say that before.

Well, there you have it. Margaret once said that Sandra was growing up without a father. I dare say that was true. She said Sandra wouldn't even know me. Probably true as well. But she does have a father, and behind the anger at me that Sandra has nurtured over the years, I still want to believe that deep down she cares about me. Which makes my absence even worse.

Later

I saw the feed as I was checking email for the final time to-night. The US was waking up to the news that Homeland Security and Los Angeles police uncovered a cell plotting to put a hallucinogen in the city's water supply. I turn on the TV. CNN-Huff has a graphic up: 'LA + LSD = Terror!' A commentator on Fox News rants about how we must redouble our efforts to extinguish the jihadist elements. Minutes later, out comes the news that the masterminds are five fresh-scrubbed, beard-free, white-as-snow, born-again Christian army veterans. Not missing a beat, the pundits shout about the need to increase the military budget.

Afghanistan is feeling like a country club.

Later

Before going to bed, I phone Alistair. I tell him about the threatening phone call yesterday. I tell him they had my throw-away mobile number as soon as I turned it on. I tell him I threw that phone away, but I'm not sure why I even bothered. I tell him I assume this call was being monitored.

He says, 'John, whatever happens, this is worth it. This is important.'

Yes, I think, as I lie in bed. But I don't know how much Alistair is hoping to better the future, and how much he hopes to assuage his own ghosts.

CHAPTER 5

'Tell me what you're thinking,' she said, her tone wistful.

I had gotten out of the hotel bed and was getting dressed. I gave her a look that said I did not want to talk even though I knew we needed to. Finally I spoke.

'I missed you. More than… I don't know. I mean, it was like you hurt me so much I needed to start hating you or something. That's what I spent years doing. Hating you. Fucking wasted years.'

She was silent.

'He turned out to be an asshole,' she finally said.

'The other guys are always assholes,' I said, smiling.

She smiled back.

'I want to believe this is happening, Kat. But… That's all I can say. I want to be together. I want you. But I can't go back to *that*… to you loving me one day and rejecting me the next.'

'I'm sorry,' she said. 'For everything.'

I nodded, relieved and uncertain.

'Tanner, I want to see you again.'

'Me too.'

But I didn't call her before we left for Balkh, nor did she phone me.

We'd been in Balkh province less than a week and we'd already lost two guys from our company, one lightly wounded and expected back in a week and one killed in an RPG attack. He'd only joined us a day before deploying and I barely knew his name. It was Melvyn Banks. The men are pissed off and ready to fire, ready to do what they've been trained to do. Alpha Company is with us—even Ditka is managing not to be a total jerk. He must know I'm already too strung out to take any of his shit.

The wounded one is Lieutenant Vance and, since his recovery is going to be quick, Lovejoy tells me to take over Vance's platoon until he returns.

That morning, I've got Williams and Rodriguez with me. We're all quiet inside the Cougar. It's cramped and smells like a football locker room after a losing game. Damn thing probably hasn't been cleaned since the first Afghan War. We're not out for an hour when we get word of an attack in a nearby village.

We arrive in a village. Completely empty. No goats, sheep, or dogs wandering. No people. Never a good sign.

We've got my platoon and O'Keefe's, so we're almost forty men in total. I radio instructions to the other three Cougars, one behind, the other two heading in from different angles.

It's really quiet now.

O'Keefe radios me. 'Bodies, Captain. I got… five, no, six, Afghani men. Can't see any weapons.'

I turn and yell to my men, 'Get ready to roll,' and yell instructions on the radio to the other vehicles to fan left and right through the village and one to go right through to the other side to provide cover.

I look back at my men. They nod and I nod back.

We're out of the Cougar and running to the edge of a wall of rubble where we can see the bodies.

'Fuck,' Williams says as we fall behind the wall. 'What's that smell?'

I turn back slightly toward him and say in a low voice,

inches from his ear, 'Williams, keep it shut.'

The smell is enough to make us all gag.

I glance over and see 1st Squad on one side of the road. I send 2nd Squad down a parallel alleyway.

'Shit, they killed the sheep and goats,' Williams says.

I'm trying to look in all directions at the same time, spotting snatches of O'Keefe and his men as they go between the houses and small shops, little more than huts really, on my left, 2nd Squad along the alley or path between them, and Garcia in front. I'm thinking of my other two platoons out on patrol. If the enemy is still around, they heard us coming from miles away and I'm thinking of calling in the rest of my guys.

Garcia is well ahead of me down the alley heading toward a disemboweled goat and I know somewhere in my head that I should yell for him to stop even though he's still a long way from it but I'm keeping my eyes on everyone and I'm concentrating on the gaping windows of all the buildings around us and I'm listening to my comm for what's happening with the other squads. And then Garcia takes another step, and I say, 'Garcia, watch...'

He's still twenty paces from the goat when the fucking thing goes off.

I'm blown backward, the air is thick with dust and it takes me a few seconds to realize that these globs of stuff on me are either pieces of Garcia or the rotting goat.

I stagger to my feet, my ears ringing. I make my way to where Garcia was. I've got this crap all over me and I'm gagging and turn down a side street so I can vomit out of sight of my men. Behind me, I see Williams down on his knees and I can see through the dust that he's holding his hands to his head and not because his ears are ringing but because his best friend over here has just been killed. The night before, Garcia was showing Williams a picture. I was reading but watching them at the same time. They understand each other. Garcia said this was his girlfriend. She looked barely old enough to be legal. He said they met in an Internet chat room. She loves Grand Theft Auto Next Gen3, which, he said to Williams, is so cool. 'Hey Captain,' he'd said, calling over to me. 'How lucky is that?' Williams answered back for me, 'Fucking lucky.'

I go back and drag Williams to his feet and I can see he's doing all he can to hold himself together. I allow him to lean into me as I pull him up.

'Captain...' he says, in the slightest whimper.

'Williams, stay alert.' I grab his shoulders and give him a light shake until he looks at me. 'Williams. We need to find the assholes who did this.'

I lightly pound a fist on his chest.

I call for the medic to get a body bag from the Cougar. I tell my platoon sergeant to get a fire team to recover what they can of Garcia.

I lead Williams and the rest of the squad up one street, down another, no sound, no bodies, everybody gone. There is nothing and no one in this village.

We drive to the next village. We have no ANA with us.

It's just like the village before. There's nobody on the road. Fucking strange. Goats but no herders.

O'Keefe is calling from up ahead.

'Talk to me, O'Keefe.'

'Something's up there. Hang on... Women, a bunch of women.'

'O'Keefe, stay in your vehicle.' I call my 2nd Squad sergeant in the other Cougar. 'You guys flank me on the left and right. Eyes open. Weapons ready.'

My men look at me. Weapons ready with a bunch of women is not usual. Williams looks tense; Hernandez has this expression like this is what he was born for.

We're out of the Cougar and facing maybe twelve or fifteen women, all in bright blue burqas that cover them from head to toe. Even their eyes are behind that lacey lattice. Everything around us is gray and brown and covered in dust, and these women are wearing brilliant blue burqas. They're mesmerizing, surreal.

They watch as we approach, our guns aimed at their heads. 'Where are the men?' I yell. 'Men? *Mardâ?*'

Silence.

'Where are you going?'

I am pointing with my hands first to the ground and then in the direction of the other village.

Silence.

'Where are you going?'

This time I yell even more loudly and I move in closer, waving my gun so they can see it.

'Where are the men? *Mardâ?*'

Silence. They back away from me. My men are moving up closer to them. I turn to them and nod. *Watch out.*

I yell again at the women, 'Where are the men?'

One of the women starts blabbering but we can't make any of it out. I think I hear her say something about night and men, but those are the only words I can recognize.

'Captain,' Rodriguez says over the comm, '3rd Platoon's calling in. They're engaging the enemy. Ten clicks away.'

It's about 1530, just a couple of hours shy of sunset. I don't want to be out here when it gets dark.

'Captain,' Rodriguez says, '2nd Squad's found more bodies.'

I move a step closer to the women.

To my left Williams does the same but Hernandez walks up close to one of the women and uses the tip of his rifle to lift up her burqa as if he's looking for something. Any other day I would have busted him in the head for that, but I don't stop him this time.

I yell at the women again.

'Where are you going? Where are the men?'

'Captain,' Rodriguez says.

'What the fuck? We're in the middle of—'

'Captain, 3rd Platoon's under heavy fire. Want support. They need orders. Two platoons from Alpha are coming here. ETA less than one minute.'

I stare at the women thinking I should be able to read something, anger, fear, anything, but through their burqas I can't even look them in their eyes.

'Men? Men? Men?' I point to the men behind me, one at a time. 'Where are the men? Tell us! Do you want to fuckin' die?'

The woman is blabbering again.

I gesture for her to point.

'Point. Point. Fucking point!' I yell. 'Men? *Mardâ*?'

'Captain,' Hernandez says, 'I saw something move under that woman's burqa.'

Again, Rodriguez is shouting at me over the comm, 'Third Platoon calling again. Very heavy fire.'

I hear the Cougars from Alpha Company pull to a stop behind us.

My mind is flipping back and forth between Hernandez

and 3rd Platoon and Alpha Company.

'Captain,' Hernandez shouts, this time louder, more urgently. 'I'm telling you. Afghan bitch is hiding something. I know it—'

And just like, she steps toward Hernandez.

'Hernandez!' I yell.

Hernandez opens fire on the woman. Quick bursts, blood seeping onto her burqa and she's down and the other women are shrieking and moving down to help the woman.

We're momentarily silent, stunned. I swear I see Hernandez smiling at me with a smirk. My head's throbbing, the women are wailing, some reaching down to their friend, while others throw their arms in the air. I see Hernandez moving as if he's going to check the body to see if there might be weapons or a bomb.

'Stay back, Hernandez. That's a fucking order!'

All the other men are watching, their guns at the ready. Williams' eyes are still red and now they're also burning with anger and fear. I'm afraid he and the others may start shooting at any time.

Behind me, I hear the clomp of boots. I turn to see Ditka and his men running toward us, their weapons drawn. They can see what happened.

Before I can say anything, Ditka's men are pushing past us. He says nothing, only nods and makes a gesture with his hand, a mere flick of the wrist. Before I can understand what he means, I hear the series of pops and they're mowing down the women. I yell but the sound is barely out of my mouth when it is all over—short bursts, a few seconds and all of the women are down in front of us.

No movement, no wailing, no tears. Their blood purples

their bright blue burqas. Beneath their bodies, the dirt turns dark and wet.

'Ditka, for fuck's sake, what the...'

Ditka's voice is calm. 'You've got your orders, Captain. We've got ours. Get out of my way.'

He hasn't broken a sweat. In an instant I go from disbelief to rage and I want to rip the grin off his face and grind him in the dirt along with the blood. Without thinking I raise my arms and lunge at him. Ditka's men turn their guns on me. Two of my men grab me just as Rodriguez bellows again over the comm. 'Captain, 3rd Platoon's asking ETA.'

Ditka gives me his rattlesnake grin.

Not taking my eyes off him, I yell, 'Everyone, back to the vehicles. Rodriguez, pass the order to O'Keefe. Now!'

My men are still holding me, but I shake them off. We back away and move into the Cougar.

We've driven ten minutes toward 3rd Platoon. We're at the edge of the next village, my mind replaying every second of what happened. I feel like a thousand needles are poking into my brain. I'm replaying it for the millionth time, just at the part when I yelled 'Hernandez!'

I turn to look at Hernandez, only to see he isn't with us.

'Packer,' I yell back to the platoon sergeant, 'where the fuck is Hernandez?'

'I don't know, sir.'

'What's that supposed to mean?'

'When you were talking to Captain Ditka, Hernandez was talking to one of the Alpha guys and the two of them just took off. He said—'

My stare tells him to shut up. 'Packer, didn't it occur to you to fucking tell me?'

'Rodriguez, call Alpha. Tell them to report on Hernandez.'

Before he can do that, 3rd calls, still a couple of kilometers away. The enemy has fled. It's quiet.

I stop our Cougars in the village and we get out, weapons at the ready.

I look around. Another faceless, nameless, empty village.

No one on the streets, no animals, nothing.

The wind is picking up, whistling around the edges of the stone buildings and the leafless trees.

I make out a minaret 150 feet away. I point toward Packer and motion him to take his squad to our left. I tell O'Keefe to lead his men to the right. I take a squad straight down the road that should take us to the center of the village.

I look across and see O'Keefe sending his squads into each building, their guns pointed. They kick down doors. They push away flimsy curtains hanging in doorways. Each time, they come out shaking their heads. Then they disappear behind a wall that blocks their street from ours.

We inspect the buildings one by one. Nothing. No bodies. Just the wind.

I call the others. Same story on their sides of the village. Nothing but the wind.

We're near the village center.

'Second squad, enter from my nine o'clock.'

Packer calls in. 'They were here. We got a gun and some ammo lying on the ground at the edge of the square. Tire tracks, oil spots that are fresh. Looks like someone left in a hurry.'

We're hugging the walls. My head is pounding. But adrenalin is doing its job.

Packer is back on. 'Got a body.'

89

'Enemy?' I ask. 'Villager?'

'Negative, Captain,' he says slowly. 'It's one of ours.'

'Shit. Stay away. It could be rigged.'

O'Keefe and I are now converging across an open, rubble-filled space at the center of the village.

Packer's squad is moving into a compound. Low wall in front. A house or warehouse. Some empty wooden stalls and I realize it must be the market. Packer points. I can see the body, face down, the uniform, the helmet, the weapon on the ground next to it. Shoulder patches have been torn off, but he's clearly one of ours. No dust: he hasn't been here long.

Packer takes half his men into the market, sending the other team to the far side. I wait for the clear and take Boomer in with me.

We move toward the body, Packer now at our side.

I stop them. It could be rigged. But he could still be alive.

I tell everyone to back away.

Boomer goes first. This is his job. He walks slowly, on his own, toward the body. Looking for markings, wires, the hint of a detonator on the ground. I am standing well back, peeking around the edge of a building, trying to see the back of the fallen soldier rising and falling. Nothing.

Boomer calls back. 'Don't see nothing. Could be underneath.'

I join Boomer at the body. I take a deep breath through my nose, figuring if he'd been cut open to plant a device I'd smell it. Nothing. I look for blood around him. Nothing.

Boomer says, 'Looks clean, but let's feel underneath.'

I lay my gun on the ground. Slowly, I push both hands underneath, here, then there, as Boomer does the same from the other side. Nothing. No wetness from blood, nothing.

'Get out of here,' I say to Boomer.

He looks at me, questioning.

'Go. Stay back.'

I wait a moment and turn body over. The name tag torn away. Helmet and chin strap, cracked sunglasses covering most of the face. No pulse. I lay my ear against his mouth. No breath. I scan the uniform for signs of a wound or signs the body has been tampered with. Nothing. Not a single mark. But then I look at his face again. Something. I take off the cracked sunglasses, I unbuckle the helmet.

Before I can understand what I'm seeing, Packer and Boomer are at my side.

'Captain, that's… Shit, how in the hell, that's…'

I haven't taken my gaze from the blank stare of this dead man, his skin almost gray, as if he died in mortal terror and all his blood rushed away. I don't know if I have yet taken a breath. My mouth is so parched that it feels like my tongue is petrified. The wind, now colder as sunset approaches, is howling in my ears.

Packer says, 'Shit, that's Hernandez.'

We eventually made it back to the outpost.

Colonel Lovejoy had come up by chopper. I headed to the TOC to speak to him.

I was halfway there when a voice behind me called, 'Captain Jackson.' It was a sergeant from Alpha Company.

'What?' I said, impatient to move on.

'Captain Ditka would like to see you.'

'I'm busy.'

'Sir, Captain Ditka says you want to hear what he says before you talk to the colonel.'

I wasn't interested in matching the truth to whatever story he'd concocted for Lovejoy. But I figured I should know what he'd said.

I nodded toward Ditka's quarters.

He was there with two of his men. They were laughing, talking in low voices, as we approached.

Ditka dismissed his men.

'Captain Jackson. Back already? Wouldn't want to be out there in the dark now, would we? Real scary out there.'

'What do you want?' I said.

'Before you make a fool of yourself, Jackson, we found a bomb on one of those women. Seems your man, Hernandez, knew what he was doing. He saved all our lives.'

'The problem is, Ditka, you killed all those women before you knew that.'

Ditka raised an eyebrow and shrugged.

'The other problem, Ditka, is that you're lying.'

'Pretty serious accusation. You think I have a bomb ready to plant on her, Captain? You've been watching too many of those old police movies.'

'You fired into a group of women without sufficient cause.'

He smiled. 'Your man shot that woman. And who told him to? I saw her move at him. I heard you yell his name. He obeyed your orders and he saved our lives.'

'Bullshit.'

'There are two dozen men, mine and yours, who will corroborate the first point. And I've got a dozen who saw the device. Hernandez died in combat, killed for his bravery, and you're busy second guessing like a pussy.'

'Did you hear what happened to him?'

Ditka shrugged. 'Shit happens.'

'Not like that. He was miles away.'

'It's fucking combat.'

'How'd he get there?'

'How would I know?'

'You guys dump him?'

'Jackson, you're gettin' spooked. Taliban motherfuckers musta grabbed him. That's what they do. They try to kill us. If we don't do our job, they succeed.'

'He couldn't have gotten that far that fast with none of us knowing. It doesn't make any sense.'

'Who's not making sense, Jackson? Seems to me you're worried about protecting civilians and blaming someone else for your own mistakes when you should be worried about commanding your troops.'

'You killed those women.'

He had moved within a foot of my face. He was calm; I could smell his sour cigarette breath.

'I'll make my report. You make yours.'

He smiled his rattlesnake grin. I wanted to rip his face off.

Colonel Lovejoy was typing into his laptop.

'Permission to enter, sir,' I said, barging in.

He waved his hand at the space in front of the beat-up pieces of wood we call a desk. I stood stiff. Formal.

'Sir, I'd like to report an incident today in—'

'Captain, I know all I need to know. I spoke to Ditka, I spoke to three of his men. I just spoke to'—he glanced down at his notes—'O'Keefe.'

'Sir, those women—'

'Those women posed a tangible threat. Hernandez saved all of you. We don't like this sort of thing, but I don't believe

Ditka had much of a choice.'

'Of course he did. Sir.'

'Captain Ditka says he hopes you'll put in for a commendation for Corporal Hernandez.'

'But sir—'

'Captain,' Colonel Lovejoy said. 'The Taliban are using tactics out there that more than justify whatever force Ditka and his men used.'

'Colonel, we killed civilian women out there, possibly unnecessarily. We—' He cut me off. 'Unless you plan on taking this over my head, Captain, it's done. I'm contacting General Page with a recommendation to issue a statement before anyone else gets word of it first. Profound regret to see the Taliban involving women. Profound regret to see any loss of life. But particular sadness in losing one of our finest warriors who lost his life protecting his fellow soldiers. Any questions?'

I turned away from him for a moment and then looked him in the eye.

'Sir, I request you consider reposting Bravo Company.'

He eyed me. 'Captain Jackson... Tanner. Let me speak personally. I know this is difficult. You and Ditka have different—let's say styles. But you're two of my best and this is where I need you. This isn't about personalities. I don't give a fuck about whether you two get along. This is about sucking it up and getting the job done.'

I started to speak but he shook his head.

'I'm authorizing six days R and R for you and your men. The whole company. Rotate to Bagram. And, you, you have permission for a six-day leave. Hop on a plane. Get out of Afghanistan for a little while.'

I'd never heard of anything like this. Whenever a platoon

takes a KIA, everyone in that platoon gets three days to cool off. To prevent massacres. You could rotate to Bagram for that time. I'd never heard of an entire company getting six days downtime like this.

'You're giving me leave? In the middle of all this?'

'You and your men have earned it.'

'Starting?'

'As soon as you walk out that door.'

He pointed to the exit.

The Journal of
John Murakami Fox

September 26, Kabul

I phoned Alistair to ask what he thought of Tanner's latest chapter.

Alistair said, 'The murder of those women? I wasn't surprised.'

'It's getting huge coverage.' Most of it was focused on the difference between this account and the army's spin.

Alistair didn't respond right away, but when he did, his voice was grim. 'Yes, I'm not surprised that's how the army would spin it,' he said.

'And Hernandez?' I said. 'The soldier who was found dead miles from where they last saw him.'

'What about that?'

'Do you believe it?'

'Fog of war, old boy.'

'That much fog?' I ask.

With a cynical laugh, he said, 'Do you have any doubt, John? I can tell you from experience: none of them really has a clue what's going on.'

September 28, Islamabad

It's nice to wake up in my own apartment in Islamabad, even if it's as sterile as the rest of this city. The air conditioning blasts away in the still-blazing weather. I defy the heat and leave my window open at night just to hear the familiar voice of Samir's muezzin intoning the call to morning prayers. I do the unthinkable for an expat and walk to the baker two blocks away, where the yeasty smell of *naan* makes me salivate. Mrs. Bhatti arrives with one of the beautiful melons she gets from her brother—sweetly fragrant and perfectly ripe. You know you've made some strange career choices when Islamabad feels like a safe haven.

September 29, Islamabad

Safe haven mood is over. I was followed today. He didn't seem to be a state security type—they never mind being spotted, in fact they delight at making you nervous. I had parked the car and was walking over to buy a ticket for the Quaid-e-Azam Trophy First Class tournament, even if, without the Karachi teams, it's a shadow of its old self. As I stood in the short queue (but like all queues in former British colonies, painfully slow), a man with a light beard was watching me. Whenever I caught him staring, he quickly turned away. He was gone by the time I was told that the final match was absolutely, totally, completely sold out, I'm sorry sir, (head balancing side to side), but then, once I offered the ticket seller a little something for checking again, he was able to discover quite a nice seat.

I went to the supermarket and then the foreign currency store, where I bought a few things that Mrs. Bhatti never brings me, namely a good bottle of single malt and a fairly decent *sake*. When I came out to the parking lot, I saw the same man again, scurrying away from my car.

Turned the key, half prepared to be blown to pieces—even closed my eyes for a second—but apparently the lesser gods of foreign correspondents have other plans for me.

Phone conversations

JMF: Sandra, you are certain you haven't told anyone?

SANDRA: Father!

JMF: Any way someone could find out?

SANDRA: I helped Alistair register the domain name as a private listing. The average person couldn't find out.

JMF: But...?

SANDRA: It's the Internet, father. Pay attention.

Then

JMF: Alistair, have you told anyone that we're behind the website?

ALISTAIR: Are you daft?

JMF: I'm being followed... Alistair, are you still there?

ALISTAIR: But I have heard that from you before.

JMF: Yes, but...

ALISTAIR: But?

JMF: It's nothing. Listen, Sandra tells me there's been a huge jump in people visiting the site. We're in the tens of thousands of hits a week.

ALISTAIR: Perhaps I will finally be rescued from anonymity, old boy.

JMF: This isn't a joke.

[A long pause]

ALISTAIR: No. None of this is a joke. Do you know how worried I am that this will all get shut down before we get to the truth?

JMF: Me too, Alistair. But right now, I'm more worried about having a hood thrown over my head and getting dragged away in broad daylight.

CHAPTER 6

I walk out of Lovejoy's office and try to find out more. I ask my men. I ask Ditka's men. Nothing. No one saw Hernandez leave, or they won't say that they did, and no one will talk about what happened to the women. All I get are shrugged shoulders. Although he was an asshole at times, everyone liked Hernandez. I can feel my men looking at me like *what the fuck are you doing?* They want to mourn one of their fellow soldiers.

I take a long shower and I shave. I find my face again under the grime and dust. Then I call my men together and I say a few careful words about Hernandez. I praise the men for their bravery. I tell them we'll avenge Hernandez. I tell them they deserve the leave. I tell them that in six days we'll be back to find the guys who did this.

Within three hours, Lovejoy had arranged for helicopters to ferry us to Bagram. I pulled rank and jumped on the first one.

I looked down at the outpost as we were lifting up. I'll never get used to that feeling, like this noisy box you're sitting in is attached to a cable and there's a crane that's lifting you straight off the ground. I caught sight of Ditka watching and even at a distance I swear I registered his rattlesnake grin. Fuck him, I thought, and we were gone.

I was messed up in a way I'd never been since I'd signed up for the military when I was all of eighteen. This was not the normal bad shit. Out here, you always feel wired and jumpy. You never know who's gonna take a crack at you or from where. You're never really prepared to kill another human being; no matter how much training they give you, no sane human can kill without it sooner or later tearing you apart. Nor can I bear seeing one of my men die.

But this was different. I'd seen mistakes and civilian deaths, but I'd never seen cold-blooded murder like that. I've never been told to keep quiet. I relived the conversation with Lovejoy. No one could think I was telling Hernandez to shoot her. And even if I had, no one had told Ditka to mow down the rest.

This was my moment to question it all: the Father, Son, and the Holy Fucking Joint Chiefs of Staff. This was a massacre of civilian women. If those women had meant to blow us up, they would have done so, especially after Hernandez shot the first one. We were covering up a massacre.

By the early evening, we were back at Bagram.

I caught Katherine on her mobile. We had exchanged emails but I had spoken to her only once since the afternoon at the Sheraton. And now I was telling her I was on leave until Tuesday night with permission to get out of Afghanistan.

She asked if everything was okay. I lied. I said it was. She said she would phone me back in a few minutes.

I waited at the coffee shop, staring at the sea of soldiers without seeing a single face, gripping my mobile. On an impulse I had phoned her, but now I wasn't so sure I should see her again. Along that road, I thought, will come pain. Part of me wanted to jump on a flight all alone, shed my uniform and be an anonymous American tourist for a few days. And part of me wanted to be in Kat's arms, pretending she hadn't betrayed me and imagining we could be together.

I held my finger over the off button of my phone, I took a

deep breath, and then my phone rang.

'Tanner,' Katherine said, her voice like silk to my ears. 'Have you ever been to Angkor Wat?'

The next afternoon, Friday, we arrived in Siem Reap, Cambodia. A sense of vastness overtook me: green jungles, low mountains, thin haze that seemed to hang on the heat.

We stepped from the arrival area into a thick blanket of humidity that penetrated my clothing and woke up every part of my skin.

'Ah, finally.' Katherine sighed, as if she could read my mind. 'Humidity, as nature meant us to live.'

A motorcycle rickshaw was waiting for us. At the side of the road, Buddhist monks walked in procession, dressed in simple saffron-colored robes, their heads shaved, their feet bare or in sandals. In front of the small dwellings, miniature shrines perched on pedestals so spirits would stay outside and not try to mix with the living. I thought of the murdered women and wished them peace. And then I wished them to stay outside my head. I thought of Hernandez and found it in me to wish him peace. No matter what crime he had committed, I didn't think he deserved to end up that way.

Our hotel was a small lodge set around a courtyard: a fountain in a small pool, and a garden that was a tangle of deep green plants and large, waxy flowers. A quiet woman with watchful eyes and a child-like smile poured us glasses of fresh lychee juice.

Before the sun set, we caught a ride to a trail that climbed through the dense trees up the mountainside to a view of the temples. We walked quickly, glad to be outside after the day in airports and airplanes, thrilled to move without guards, without fear, outside of walled compounds. For the first time in months I was walking in the open air without a pack, rifle, armor, and ammunition. I felt as light as the silk blouse Katherine was wearing. And next to me, her fingers occasionally tangling in mine, was Katherine. I was no longer a soldier, no longer a jilted ex. I was just a man walking next to his lover.

Whenever the trail was wide enough, we walked side by side. Once, when she reached out and took my hand, I was instantly back in the Duke Gardens, way back when; then too it was just the two of us, a fading afternoon, the scent of gardenias, and she had turned and kissed me for the first time.

We reached the top of the temple just in time for the sunset. The Cambodian sky was pink, gray, and lilac. The humidity had dropped slightly and now rather than being overpowering, it felt like a soft, thin veil.

Below us, poking out through the canopy of the jungle, were the ancient temples of Angkor Wat.

Katherine pulled me to her. She kissed me and her breath was as hot and humid as the air around us, and she was sweating and I was sweating.

'When we're here like this,' she said, 'I can remember what it was like before, when life was normal. I can almost forget you're a soldier.' There was no irony or bitterness or criticism in her voice.

I wanted to say, *This week, Kat, for the first time I wished I was not,* but before I could find the courage to speak these words, Katherine said, her voice dreamy as if speaking to herself, 'But you are, aren't you?'

Words stuck in my throat. I looked out at the tops of the temples catching the last rays of the sun. I turned back to her.

'Right now, I'm just a guy who wants to be with you.'

She smiled, her lips pressed together, but whether it was a smile of joy or indescribable sadness, I could not tell.

We ate dinner in town. I was intoxicated with the smell of the jasmine flowers on the table, with the beauty of the jungle, and most of all with Kat. During our stopover in the Bangkok airport, I had bought her a sleeveless silk dress. In the candle-light, it shimmered, a rich, emerald green; it was made of the soft but rough-textured Thai silk.

She wanted to wander around the market after dinner, but when we got there she said, 'I didn't really want to see the market. I just wanted to stretch out the anticipation of what might come next.'

That night, I woke panting, unable to catch my breath. I couldn't form a clear picture of what I had been dreaming, but I was left with an intense feeling of dread. I was certain I had woken Katherine, but she lay curled on her side and fast asleep.

We stayed at Angkor Wat for four days and four nights. Saturday we went to the temples and marveled at the statues of the serpents and lions, and the goddesses and dancing girls carved into the walls. Some of the reddish carvings showed the whole Hindu pantheon of gods and goddesses turning from good to evil and back to good once again. Some sprang out of others' heads, some had animal heads on human bodies.

'My mother told me all these stories when I was little. I once knew the names of the gods.'

I smiled at her and she turned and moved close to me.

'I think my first erotic feelings were seeing some of these

images, of the Hindu gods and goddesses, their bodies entwined like that, the bare-chested men and the women with their perfect breasts.'

'Speaking of...' I said, and she laughed as I pulled her to me.

Saturday night the nightmare came again. This time it woke Katherine, but when she asked me what was the matter, I said it was nothing. A bad dream.

On Sunday, after more walking, more jungle, and more temples, we ate, and then read for hours in the courtyard. Katherine checked email on her tablet—'Not work!' she promised. Now and then, she reported news from her family. What her sisters were up to, and her parents. There was a time when I had started to think of them as my family too. I walked a thin line between wanting to dive headfirst into all of it again and worrying I'd be smashing my head in an empty pool.

'My friend Jan's in Bhutan. I think you met her. She says the mountains and the temples are stunning. No TV. Gentle people. Only place in the region not overrun by Chinese companies. Not a US face to be seen.'

I mumbled an acknowledgment although I didn't recall meeting her friend. Katherine continued with her report: another friend was getting married; one had just had a first child. This is what intimacy had once felt like with Katherine, and what it might feel like again.

We ate dinner, the flavors more delicate than the much heavier food of Afghanistan, then showered for the third time that day. We made love and lay in our bed under the mosquito netting, listening to the chirping and croaking of tree frogs and the hum of a billion insects and creatures of the night. I was drifting off to sleep.

Kat said, 'Ever been to Bhutan?'

I mumbled, 'Uh-huh.'

'That a yes or a no?'

'No.' I said, my eyes closed, dreams swimming not far away.

'One of the last corners of the world that hasn't been turned into a shopping center.'

'Mmm.'

'Let's go.'

'Mmm.'

'A cottage on a mountainside.'

I was drifting into sleep and didn't want to or couldn't respond.

Kat said, 'Tanner, listen for a second. I want you to know… we can be different this time.'

I muscled enough energy to groggily say, 'Okay, tell me when to pack.'

'I don't mean Bhutan. I'm telling you I want to be with you. When we're done over here. In Afghanistan, I mean. I want us to try. My contract ends in less than a year. Your tour of duty will be done.'

'Unless they extend us.' Now I was paying attention.

Kat ignored this. 'Let's meet in Bhutan. A year from now. I want to be with you. I want a life with you.'

'Sure,' I mumbled, as if what she was saying was of little consequence. But of course I had heard every word.

'Tanner. I mean it. I'm promising. I'm serious. Promise me. Bhutan a year from now. We start this. We start *us* again.'

Her words were like a lullaby.

She was talking about the Clock Tower Square in Thimphu, the capital of Bhutan. I soon fell asleep, but not before she made me promise that we would meet there.

The nightmare didn't come to me that night.

Monday was our fourth day, our last full day. We woke early and went to the main temple, Angkor Wat itself. Perched majestically in the middle of a lake, it made me feel the vastness of time, of wars fought, and of lives that went on. I wanted to feel this way all the time. I wanted to remember everything I saw and felt, everything Katherine and I said to one another.

We sat down on the steps on the side of the temple.

'Do you remember what you promised last night?'

'That I would go AWOL?' I said.

'No, that would be *me* dreaming.'

I said, 'Clock Tower Square, Thimphu, exactly one year from now. December tenth.'

In the afternoon, we took a *tuk-tuk* and walked to see some ruins carved underwater in a river. Compared to the temples we had seen, this area was nearly empty of tourists. I held Katherine's hand. We walked in silence. I was trying not to think about returning to Afghanistan the next day.

Suddenly, Katherine asked, 'Have you killed someone?'

'You really want to ask that?'

'Tanner, have you killed someone?'

'Probably.'

'What do you mean, probably?'

'Officers actually don't fire their weapons that often. Even on a mission, my focus is directing the company.'

She scoffed. 'You're saying you never shoot.'

'I do, but most of the fighting is done by my men.'

'You didn't answer my question.'

'Katherine, we're shooting across ravines, toward rocks on a mountainside, across large distances.'

'That makes it easier for you. You don't have to see their eyes.' Her voice was full of sorrow and anger.

'Don't, Katherine.'

'Why not?'

'We're fighting people who put bombs inside cars or in dead bodies. Who blew up a stadium full of people. They don't look us in the eye. They kill any local leader who opposes them, or worse yet, the guy's wife and children. There's no nice way to paint this war. Or any war.'

'Could you kill someone with your bare hands?'

'Kat, why does that matter? Why do you…'

'I want to understand what you think about what you do and what you have to do. We need to say these things. To talk about them.'

'Look, I can think of maybe one or two soldiers I know who seem to get into killing. The rest of us, we do it only when necessary. And we're torn up inside when we do.'

'Could you? Kill with your bare hands?'

'I suppose,' I said tentatively. 'I suppose if I had no other way to protect someone—one of my men, a civilian, you, myself… Yes, I suppose if there were no other way. Otherwise, it would be savage, wouldn't it?'

We continued down the quiet road through the jungle without saying anything, until I spoke again.

'When we were students, you told me about a Sri Lankan soldier who protected your mother against another soldier. Yes?'

She nodded.

'You said you believed it was possible to be a good soldier.'

She didn't respond.

'In spite of everything I see, I still want to believe it is possible to be a good soldier. To somehow be good in the midst of everything that isn't.'

I turned away from her and looked in the direction of the river.

'I'm not saying I always know what's right and what's wrong, but I do know I think about it every second I'm out with my men. You may not agree that we should be here, but at least I need you to trust that much about me. I would never kill someone out of spite or in cold blood.'

She reached her hand up to my shoulder and the edge of my neck.

She said, 'I come from a family destroyed by war, whose lives are devoted to ending it. This isn't easy for me.'

I turned to look her in the eyes.

'So consider it a capricious act of the gods that we're together and let's just get on with it,' I said, smiling.

'That's what I'm trying to do,' she said. 'That's what I want to do, Tanner.'

We climbed through the jungle and though we were only holding hands, it seemed our bodies were intertwined. We reached a small waterfall that plunged twenty-five feet onto a large stone slab and then into a shallow pool with more carvings.

We had worn bathing suits under our shorts, and we stripped down and stepped out onto the stone to stand under the water. It was a shock at first, far cooler than we expected. We were surrounded, protected, by green on all sides. We kissed under the waterfall and had to remind ourselves we might not be alone. She laughed and said, 'Only the gods can see us.' We sat in the shallow pool, ancient stone faces watching us.

'In that case, Tanner,' she said, picking up our conversation, 'I want it to be different this time. I hate how reasonably you talk about what you do.'

'You can say it, Kat,' I said gently with my mouth near her ear. 'I'm a soldier.'

'Okay, I can say it. You're a soldier. And apparently a wise one.'

She turned her body toward me and kissed me. Her skin was wet and electric and I wanted to wrap myself around her.

Katherine was again wearing the emerald-green silk dress. We were about to leave for dinner when she turned on the ceiling fan, pulled aside the mosquito net that draped the bed, and, with a swish of silk, pulled the dress over her head. She wore nothing underneath. I watched her, amazed, excited. She moved toward me and casually looped the silk dress around my neck and shoulders and let it slide over my chest and back. She let it fall to the ground and took my hands in hers. She was naked before me, her skin and hair smelling like the green of the waterfall. She pulled my hands up to her mouth and began kissing my fingertips.

'Whatever these hands have done,' she said.

She kissed them again and moved my left hand to cradle the back of her head. The other she kissed on the wrist.

'I trust you'll do right with these hands,' she said.

She pulled them both toward her mouth again, lightly kissing each fingertip.

'Do right with these hands,' she ordered me in a voice as silky as her dress, and then she moved one of my hands to her breasts and the other down between her legs.

We slept afterward, wrapped in each other's arms. But this time I had another nightmare and, this time, I remembered it vividly: I was standing alone in a large, open expanse, a runway maybe that went on and on, only there was a fence at the end and I realized it was a base, our base. From far off I saw horses coming, horses bearing soldiers, our soldiers, and I could see the dust they were kicking up and then I could see they were dragging something with their rifles or with a stick. I could recognize their voices—Williams and Hernandez and O'Keefe. They were playing *buzkashi*, the national game of Afghanistan, their version of polo in which a goat carcass substitutes for the ball. They were riding toward me and as they got closer I could see that each one was dragging a carcass. They were laughing. I could make out what they were saying.

'Gotta love this game. Men here have what it takes.'

They were approaching me.

'Hey, Captain, glad you're playing our game,' Hernandez says. 'Catch!'

Hernandez has thrown a carcass up in the air. It comes straight at me, hits me, and I feel flesh and slime. It is the body of an Afghan woman. And just as I'm staring at the body in front of me and wiping the guts off of me, I look up at Hernandez, whose grin is even more horrible in death. His whole abdomen has been cut open and his intestines are running out. But he never stops smirking at me.

'Tanner! Wake up, Tanner. You're having a nightmare. Wake up.'

I was fighting to catch my breath. I was still half in the dream. I tried to focus on what I saw in front of me. The early morning light came through the wooden venetian blinds and I let her hold me. But I kept my face away from hers, trying to hide my tears.

'Tanner, talk to me. What's going on?'

She hugged me tightly, and then coaxed me away from her and held me at arm's length.

She smiled. 'It's only a dream,' she said. But I knew it wasn't, and I did not speak. Then she said, 'I'm right here.'

In the security of that moment, in the warmth of her hand resting on my arm, in the knowledge we were together again, in my promise to do right, I told her what had happened in the village. I told her about the women in the burqas and all that happened after and that I knew they were covering it up.

As I spoke, she relaxed her touch and by the end of my story had pulled her hand away.

After I finished, she did not speak for a long while.

'Why didn't you tell me before?' she finally said, the calmness in her voice belied by her words.

'I…'

'Tanner? Why didn't you tell me?'

I shook my head, dumbfounded, knowing there wasn't a right answer.

'Kat, I tried to stop it.'

She said, 'You need to trust me. I'm—'

'Of course I trust you.'

'—trying so hard. I really want us to work. I…'

'You think I don't?'

'You have to mean what you said.'

'What?'

'Yesterday. You said you try to do right every day.'

'I just told you, I tried to stop it. I reported it. I—'

'And then you ran off with me for a romantic weekend. How could you? How could you see all that, be part of that, and then put it aside?'

'I have to put it *all* aside every day, Kat. We're at war.'

She wasn't listening. 'You went from that to *this*.'

She jumped out of bed and was shaking her arms, as if trying to dislodge something sticking to her. 'God, how could you just carry on? As if you hadn't just witnessed a massacre?'

'I had to leave. I had to be with you.'

'Tanner, I know you didn't do it, okay? I'm sure you tried to stop it. But your army did that. *Your* fellow soldiers.'

'And you know what the Taliban do.'

'Listen to yourself.'

'I didn't mean... I'm not trying to justify what we did... what *they* did.'

'You never stop thinking like a soldier,' she said.

I exploded, 'Because I am a soldier.'

We were quiet, paralyzed, as if the slightest physical movement would bring us closer together to a reconciliation that I knew she didn't feel at that moment and I wasn't certain I did either. Or move us farther apart, which carried its own symbolic weight. I wanted to ask her: *did this change what we said yesterday?* About being together, about going away together?

Maybe I was close to asking and maybe she sensed this, for she cut me off: 'Right now, I want to burn your uniform and shout all those things they shout at Americans, me included, when they want us to go home. But I guess I can't do that.'

She went for a walk, said she needed some air. I showered, dressed, and packed my bag. The taxi to the airport would arrive soon. I went into the courtyard and saw Kat coming from the road. She looked in my direction and slowed. She did not come toward me.

As I walked toward the restaurant, I sensed she was now behind me. I turned and looked into her eyes, which were red and tired.

'Do you want to talk?' I said.

'Did you pack?' she asked, the question stiff, formal, off-putting.

I nodded.

'I'll meet you in the lobby,' she said.

Two flights to reach Kabul. She spoke in monosyllables. During our layover at the Bangkok airport, she wandered off on her own.

She slept on the flight from Bangkok to Kabul. She pretended to watch a movie. She pulled a newspaper from her backpack, the *International Huff Times*, and read it. She handed me the paper, folded back to one article, without comment.

Not the usual burqa factory: Dresses fitted for suicide bomb vests, the headline said. Citing military sources, the reporter said that female suicide bombers were on the increase. The army had found some specially fitted burqas in rural areas and in a workshop in the heart of Kabul.

'Don't you see?' she said.

'What do you mean?'

'Your bosses, our government... I mean, I wouldn't put it past the Taliban, but is this part of our cover-up for what happened? Is this true? I can barely tell anymore what's true and what's trumped up, and I live in this place.'

I didn't think she wanted a response.

She said, 'How can any of us do right in the middle of all this shit when lies are packaged as truth? You tell me that, Tanner. When you figure that out, you tell me.'

For the rest of the flight she returned to her silence.

We descended into Kabul. The mountains were covered in snow. There was no snow on the plain and hills around the city, but the trees were bare. It seemed lifeless. It seemed like hell.

I felt Kat's hand on mine and I took it, gently, not talking, not looking at her. She was staring out the window. She said, 'I wish we could just forget all this.'

We waited for our bags. They came out together, side by side. She picked up hers and I grabbed mine. Just past customs there was a military liaison desk, where soldiers returning on commercial flights are met and escorted back to base.

I stopped. Katherine tried to smile.

'I'll call you,' I said.

She nodded, but didn't speak.

'We'll figure out a way,' I said.

She didn't speak.

'In a year,' I said. 'The Clock Square in Thimphu. December tenth.'

She nodded, but it was a lifeless nod.

I reached to embrace her, but she said, 'I've got to go.'

I went to the military liaison desk. I felt someone behind me and turned with a big smile on my face only to see a pimply-faced soldier with my regiment's insignia on his arm.

'Hey, Captain,' he said to me. 'That's some tan you got. Had fun?'

I caught one final glimpse of Katherine as she stepped out of the arrivals gate and into the dented SUV her organization had sent for her. It was all I could do not to run after her and go AWOL to leave all this right then and there. Perhaps if I had known what was about to happen, I would not have hesitated. Instead, I turned to the soldier and said, 'Let's go.'

I was back in my world.

The Journal of
John Murakami Fox

October 18, Islamabad

I wrote to Tanner: Please. I need to talk.

He sends the corrections to the next chapter. And the next and the next. Taking us right up to the final, short, concluding chapter that I'm still writing. But not a word from him about my obvious panic, as if he knew this was when the shit would start hitting the fan.

Later

I've had death threats before. Some on the phone like a few weeks before, and some to my face. Some I took very seriously. Some I laughed off.

Not this one.

I returned to my apartment from a press conference organized by the US embassy and USAID where they announced their next round of community development projects, this one supposedly better than the last one.

I unlocked my door—all three locks, the one on the knob, the one above the knob, and the German deadbolt I had carried back from Frankfurt two years earlier. I dropped my keys in the tray, glanced through the mail I'd picked up from my cubbyhole off the lobby, wandered into the kitchen, and poured a beer. A package the size of a shoebox sat on my dining room table. The wrapping paper was ablaze with lipstick-red hearts.

The superintendent didn't have my deadbolt key, but I went

down to talk to him anyway—didn't want to chance using my phone in case, somehow, that might be the trigger.

'No,' he said, indignantly, 'of course I didn't go into your apartment.'

I apologized. And then I said, 'There might be a bomb sitting on my dining room table.'

The building was evacuated. The bomb squad came. I was outside like everyone else and when they came out, one of the squad members held a blast box in his protected arms. They were talking casually as they put it into their armoured truck to take away to detonate. They approached the superintendent, who pointed to me. They were very polite: 'Who has access to your apartment?'

'No one,' I said.

'Who'd want to kill you?'

I asked how much time they had. And then they told me, 'Sir, the box seems to be empty. But still we must blow it up.'

'Empty?' I repeated.

'Light as a feather.'

They were returning to their vehicles when my cell beeped that a text had arrived. I clicked onto it: 'Shut down your website. No more chapters of your book. The next time the box won't be empty.'

Later

I bought yet another mobile, then checked into the Hyatt.

I rang Alistair.

'Alistair, I had a death threat today.'

'You've had those before.' I didn't respond. Then, with a more worried tone, he added, 'Haven't you?'

'This was different. Someone broke into my apartment.

Someone who knows my every move.'

'Do you believe it was the same person who rang you?'

'Likely. But who knows.'

'John, should we shut down the site? Forget about the book?'

I could hear that he didn't believe we needed to do this, but must have thought he owed it to me to at least ask.

'They're usually just trying to frighten you.'

'Except when they're not.'

I told him I'd call back tomorrow.

The next day I rang Alistair. I told him I wanted to stay the course.

I decided not to tell Judith about this. Not because she'd pull the plug on the book, but because she'd want to make a big deal out of it.

Late Night

Couldn't sleep. Wide-awake dreams of bombs in shoeboxes, bombs in my old laptop. Got up and checked email. One from Sandra, whom I haven't told about the threats. 'It's going great! Hits are blowing the roof off!'

Judith writes too: 'Sales are booming. You better start figuring out where to invest your earnings.'

October 19, Islamabad

'You're going to love the personal ads.' This was scrawled with a red pen above the masthead of the morning paper left outside my hotel door the next morning.

The Pakistanis still have some matchmaking ads in print, although nothing like what they have in India. I glanced through them, saw nothing, then read more carefully. There it was: 'British journalist with popular website, recently diagnosed with terminal disease, looking for wife for his final days. Visa to the UK guaranteed. Virginity not an issue.' It listed my new cell number.

I turn on the phone. Already, there are 148 messages.

In a near panic, I book a plane to London that leaves today. Tomorrow the new chapters will be posted.

CHAPTER 7

All the way from the airport to Bagram, I was silent in the transport. I was with three hyped-up sergeants just back from a week home and then a week in Bangkok. I tuned out their jokes and stories, but I couldn't get away from the smell that insisted I was back. I couldn't even call up the olfactory memory of jasmine and Kat. Here there was only the stink of exhaust fumes, canvas, machinery, and sweat.

'Hey Captain,' one of the men said. 'Tell me Bangkok isn't one wild place.'

I shook my head. 'Wasn't there.' They were waiting to hear more. 'Cambodia,' was all I gave them.

'Shoulda been there, Captain. You tell me it ain't an oasis of pussy after this desert.' Pulling out his phone, he said, 'You gotta see this one.'

I ignored him and stared down at my own phone.

Winter was descending. Snow covered the mountains in the distance. Dust swirled over a field of dead plants. I could almost see the cold reaching down to grab us. We passed a pile-up of cars from an accident.

I told myself again and again: *Only a year.*

But then I imagined her thinking: *How could this ever have worked?*

I imagined her thinking: *I love him.*

But none of this sounded convincing.

The ancient Humvee stopped and I jerked awake. It was the usual backup of vehicles lining up for the checkpoint. The three sergeants were silent. They were not thrilled to return and neither was I. But I only needed to believe this would be over in a year. I could do what I knew how to do, be a soldier just a little bit longer. I felt my heart pump a little faster. I was back in the war. However horrible it was, I knew how to do this.

In our common area, one of my lieutenants greeted me, dropping his *Playboy* and standing to attention.

'Captain Jackson.'

'Crenshaw.'

'Welcome back to the land that time forgot.'

I smiled weakly; at least he was trying.

'Forgot us, too,' he continued.

I raised my eyebrows.

'Alpha's heading far north in two days.'

'And us?'

'No word. Waiting for Strykers, they say, and fuel. But we figure there's more.'

'Shit,' I said.

'Colonel Lovejoy says he wants to see ya. You and Captain Ditka. Says I should tell ya and tell him when ya come in.'

Ditka was waiting in Lovejoy's reception area when I arrived, ahead of me as always. He went straight into his routine. 'Liberated some whores when you were in Bangkok?'

I didn't respond.

Colonel Lovejoy didn't greet us when we were led into his office. He was gazing at his laptop, obviously upset. He jerked his head toward the two chairs across the desk from him. 'I wish I could tell you exactly what we're sending you to face. Before Alpha Company leaves, your officers and NCOs will get the official stuff. But I want you to see what's waiting for you. It's not to leave this room and if it does you'll find yourselves on the wrong side of the stockade fence.'

He finally looked at us, staring until we each agreed.

'We got a photo from the ANA. Supposedly from Badakh-shan.'

Badakhshan was the northernmost province of Afghani-stan, pretty low on our radar. Taliban had never conquered the province even when they ran the whole country. Some years ago, some foreign doctors were killed up there. Taliban claimed responsibility, but most people didn't believe that. The Germans had a bit of an operation going until they pulled out. Russians didn't even bother with it when they were here the first or the second time. Other than a small presence to keep the airfield open in Feyzabad, I didn't think we were there at all.

'We've been hearing stories, so two weeks ago we sent in 10th Mountain. Late yesterday they had nine MIAs. Two hours ago, we received this photograph. You need to know that they were at least a hundred klicks from where this was taken. Rest of the company, minus these nine, are still no-where near. That squad lost radio contact and didn't show up end of the day. No sign of 'em. Like they vanished.'

I finally noticed his eyes—red, puffy, deeply circled with purple, like he hadn't slept in days.

'Take a look,' he said.

He swiveled his laptop to face us. Ditka and I leaned for-ward. The photo was dark and grainy, apparently taken in low light with a crappy camera or a mobile phone. Then I under-stood that it was foggy or misty. I began to make sense of the vague shapes. A dark wall. Stone, possibly plaster. Tall, with a door set into it. Ancient.

I heard Ditka suck in his breath and that's when I noticed.

What I first thought were stones or rubble along the top of the wall were severed heads. Eight of them completely within the frame and one halfway out. Nine.

'Could be fake,' I said.

'Zoom in,' the Colonel said.

I saw US ID tags hanging beneath each of the heads. My eyes met Ditka's and he said, 'Fuck me.'

I brought the photo back to normal size and looked at the faces, pale gray against the wall. Each was impaled on a spike, maybe going through the back of his neck but definitely coming out under the chin or through the face: poking out of a mouth, an eye, a cheek.

You think you can't see anything worse than you've already seen. You think seeing women massacred two feet in front of you is about as bad as it gets. But this place has a way of proving you wrong.

I said, 'That's like nineteenth century. They did that shit to scare the British.'

Ditka said, 'You scared, Jackson?'

Lovejoy interrupted. 'Well, it scares the shit out of me. How will our men react when they know they can be dragged off and impaled and that the almighty US Army can't do a fucking thing to save their asses?'

He paused, letting us take it in. 'That's why you're heading north.'

I said, 'What about 10th Mountain? Isn't it their territory?'

Lovejoy said, 'I have my orders, you're getting yours. I want you to find the bastards who did this and blast 'em under so much stone even their mothers won't go digging for them. There's no room out here for hearts and minds shit. Ditka, you're rolling first thing in the morning.' He looked at his watch. 'You've got ten hours to have your men ready. Jackson, you'll await my orders. You'll be heading up soon afterward. But when you go, let me tell you this. None of you are coming back in until you wipe out these motherfuckers.'

Outside I was walking away when Ditka snatched my arm, which I just as quickly yanked away. 'Let's get one thing straight,' he said. 'Up there, I make the rules. So tell your little girls to leave their dolls behind.'

'No, let *me* get one thing straight, Ditka.' I spat when I said his name. 'I couldn't give a shit what you call me. But you mess with my men, you question their abilities or you give them orders, I'll take it personally. If I so much as hear—'

Flashing his most arrogant grin, he cut me off. 'So you have balls after all.'

'Fuck you,' I said and turned away.

The days dragged on and then they dragged on some more. This was what we all hated the most. The waiting. The sitting around, feeling like we were doing nothing, knowing we were doing nothing. Nobody tells the civilians this, but this is what we spend most of our time doing. Lovejoy said he didn't have time to see me. His sergeant and chief lackey sometimes told me we were waiting for the Strykers they were sending us out in. That could mean that we'd be waiting until after Christmas. It could be that we were waiting to see what Ditka turned up.

My men started to tear at each other and anyone who got in their way. One day O'Keefe told me that two of his guys actually came to him to settle an argument over a DVD. Matrix said Dean borrowed it and wouldn't give it back; Dean was supposedly his best friend out here. O'Keefe told them to deal

124

with their own bullshit. The next day I noticed Matrix had a butterfly bandage on his forehead. Apparently from dealing with his own shit.

With my officers and NCOs, I studied maps. Some wondered why they weren't using helicopters and light infantry to make forays into the mountains, but I said the weather was deteriorating and, besides, they wanted us to be able to lay in for weeks or whatever it would take. Plus I didn't want to tell them that we were rationing fuel and that it took less fuel for the army to send men to Kabul to hang out for weeks at a time than to ferry them back and forth to the US.

We ran and worked out at the gym. We cleaned our weapons. I filled out forms and wrote reports that I knew no one would read. We spent money on junk food. Other than arguments, no one seemed to be talking much anymore. Even Williams, who normally prattled on for hours, had run out of words.

It was December and the nights were getting colder. We pulled out our winter gear. The only news we got from Lovejoy's office was that snow was piling up in Badakhshan like it hadn't in years.

Lovejoy was constantly in meetings. When I managed to speak to him, he kept saying, 'I know you're anxious to get out there' and 'Soon.'

By now it had been almost a week. It was driving me crazy just sitting around. But worst of all was the silence from Katherine. I'd convinced myself to give her some space, but it was all I could do to keep myself from texting her every ten minutes. A thousand times a day I pulled out my phone to see if I'd missed the chime when a plane was thundering to take off or land. She had written me one text, thirteen words: 'I'm trying. I know u r too. Will call soon as can. K.'

Another few useless days passed. I plodded through the dreary routine. We were a few days away from Christmas and a deep funk hung over the base—it didn't seem to matter what religion anyone was, the men and women all wanted to be home.

Still no word on when we were to leave. I tried to read intel reports. I tried to read a trashy novel. I tried to watch movies. But unless I was really engaged in something, I thought about Katherine, worried about Katherine, worried about *us*. Late one night, I broke down and texted her.

U ok?

Ages passed before I received her response:

Kat: Have to get back into field. They need us.

Me: Some v bad shit happening out there.

Kat: This is my job.

Me: Kat, I'm worried about u.

A second later my phone rang.

'Tanner, I'm not about to flip my life around because of your worries.'

'I'm not asking you to—'

'I'm on a mission here. This is what we do.'

'They're stepping things up. We're losing more men. This isn't the usual...'

'I read about it.'

Yeah, I thought, but you don't know the gruesome way they were killed.

'Please Kat, I—'

'I've been here as long as you. I know what's safe and not. We're sick of waiting for your approval to go where we need to go.'

126

'Just promise me—'

'I thought you phoned to see how I was.'

'I did.' I took a deep breath. 'I miss you, Kat.'

'Tanner, I miss you, too.'

'I can probably get leave to come into Kabul this weekend. Maybe we can...'

'Maybe we can. Call me, okay?'

I prayed for the weekend to come, I prayed that I'd see her. But I also prayed for this purgatory to pass so we too could get out of Bagram and back to what we were here to do.

I took my men, all eighty-eight of them, on a run in full gear. If I'm gonna suffer, they're gonna suffer, I figured. Even at midday the air was cool, but halfway through, two of them were puking out their guts and ten had fallen out. I felt stupid I'd pushed them so hard right before going into combat, so the next day I led them on a much shorter run without our gear. Even then, I'm sure just about everyone wanted me dead.

Only when I was sorting out another fight between a couple of my lieutenants, or pushing myself in exercise, or arguing with Lovejoy's lackey, did I get my mind off Katherine.

Two days later, still waiting to hear about weekend leave, I sent her an email in the middle of the night when I couldn't sleep. Short, maybe a bit too gushy, but fuck it, I was sick of not knowing what was happening between us.

Then, just as I was about to shut down my computer, an automated message came back: *Away From Office.* It read: 'I'll be out of mobile and email range for an undetermined time for field support work. In case of emergency, please contact Sally Gregg.' It gave Sally's email address and office number and mobile number for emergencies.

Something didn't feel right. It was the middle of the night, but I figured I wouldn't be the first person to wake up Sally Gregg.

A groggy voice answered.

'Ms. Gregg. This is Captain Jackson. Tanner.'

There was no response.

'We met briefly when—'

'Yeah… I remember,' she slurred. She fell silent again and I worried she had fallen back asleep.

'Sally?'

'Yeah… why're you calling?'

'I don't know if she told you, but, well, Katherine and I are friends. From university. And we—'

'She told me.'

'I just got an out-of-office email from her. I… can you tell me where she's gone?'

'Shit. Hang on.' I heard a light switch snap on. I heard the rustle of sheets. I heard a cigarette being lit and the sound of her taking a deep drag and blowing out the smoke. 'Yeah. I guess so.'

I waited.

A note of caution came into her voice. 'I'm not in charge of the approval process with you guys.'

'I'm sure it's fine. I just need to find out where she is.'

'She's gone to a clinic up in Badakhshan. They had to leave in a hurry. Forecast said lots of snow.'

It was as if all my blood drained right out of me. Any optimism I had felt five minutes earlier was flying away from me at the speed of light. *How much time*, I thought, *would it have taken her to phone or send me a text?*

After a moment, she said, 'You still there?'

'Yeah, I'm here.'

'What?'

Cautiously, I asked, 'Is everything okay up there?'

'Snow's coming down hard. No regular cell phone access. She's got a satellite phone, but it seems to be wonky. We don't have the stuff you guys have. We've gotten through maybe once or twice.'

'Email?'

'A couple times linked through the satphone.'

'I'm sure she's okay,' I said, trying to convince myself.

Sally laughed. 'She's tough.'

I wanted to say, *Yeah, but I've seen the heads on the spikes.*

That night, along with fitful sleep, the nightmares came, jolting me awake. When daylight finally arrived, my head felt drugged. I got up, showered, and headed straight to Lovejoy's office.

The lackey said Lovejoy was busy.

I said I'd wait.

He ignored me for the next thirty minutes.

The sergeant wandered into Lovejoy's office and when he returned said, 'It's your lucky day.'

Lovejoy seemed just as strung out as every other time I'd seen him. Without preliminaries, he said, 'Your men ready?'

'Colonel, I just heard that—'

'Been watching the weather?' he asked.

I had. I'd seen the reports. I'd seen the photos: clean white snow filling the mountain passes. Beautiful and treacherous.

He said, 'Winter's come early and it's a bitch. It won't be easy out there.'

'Colonel,' I said, 'have we authorized any NGOs to move into Badakhshan?'

He stood up and walked to the window, looking down onto the rows of brown tents. A plane came in, disappearing below my sight line.

'Were you told to continue liaising with them, Captain?'

'No, sir.'

'Anyway, no. No, we didn't. We didn't want them in our way.'

'I think one of them has gone up anyway.'

Lovejoy cursed and then said, 'Their fuckin' problem.'

I started to speak, but he interrupted me. 'Listen, Tanner. I've got some… let's say mixed feelings about the reports I'm getting out of Ditka. I gave him a long leash but he can go a little ape shit now and then.' Lovejoy walked back to his desk, picked up a piece of paper, read it, tossed it back down. 'I don't like him, but I need him and I trust him. Up to a point. But—I need to make sure we don't get any blowback from this. You following me? He's taking this to the edge. He needs to. I told him to. But I need to make sure he doesn't go over it.'

I nodded. Not because I agreed with him. I didn't, not with Ditka, not with Lovejoy, and increasingly not with most that was happening over here. I nodded because I wanted to protect Kat, and if I could get even a foot closer to where she was I would *yassuh* every inch of the journey.

As I stepped outside, I felt something I'd never felt before. For me soldiering was not about this. But at that moment, I'm ashamed to say I didn't just want to defeat our enemies. I wanted to kill them.

Less than twenty-four hours later, before the sun was even up, I gathered my men. They looked at me like Christmas Eve had arrived early, even though it was still twelve hours away.

I tried to motivate them for what was coming. I told them it was our job to give the country back to any Afghans who wanted peace. That we had lost time to make up. That we had our own men to avenge. That this was the most important mission they would ever be on. That we'd have to watch each other's backs. That I wanted all of us to make it back alive and to go home proud.

I didn't tell them about the photos I had seen. Lovejoy had repeated he didn't want it getting out at Bagram, although of course everyone knew the nine missing men had been found dead. A recovery team had been sent in and they'd probably been forced to swear on their mothers' lives they wouldn't breathe a word about what they saw until the brass decided it was to their advantage to leak it.

I did not tell them that the woman I loved was out there and I'd do anything I could to get her to safety.

They listened or pretended to. But I couldn't help think they looked at me as if I were speaking Greek. Or Dari. They didn't need motivation. All they wanted was to get out and kick some ass.

Our convoy was made up of nine aging Strykers carrying my eighty-eight men, plus nine vehicle commanders, nine gunners, and two interpreters, as well as a couple of trucks packed with food, ammunition, extra fuel, and tents that none of us had slept in since basic training: all the shit we would need, at least to get started.

The original plan had been to fly us in a Globemaster III packed with us and our vehicles over the mountains into Feyzabad, the speck of a capital of Badakhshan province. Alpha Company had done that a couple of weeks earlier. From there it would have been a day or two grinding along some dirt track to get up to the Darwaz district. But the northern part of the country had been blanketed with thick, low clouds for days and Feyzabad was now deep under snow. Rance, the commander of our Stryker fleet, said that in the summer we could probably make it to Feyzabad in a day or day and a half. With the snow it would be anyone's guess. It was a guess too if we would have enough fuel to get back.

In no time we were climbing into a range of the Hindu Kush that slices Afghanistan in half. We were taking turns riding on top behind the gunner. Whatever might be going on to the north, the morning sky was a deep blue and the sun rising behind us turned the mountaintops red, then yellow, and then a sparkling snowy-blue. Even when we had climbed and were right into the snow, the road was clear and we made great time to the Salang Tunnel.

We came out on the far side, onto the north of the mountain range, into a different world. The sky here had patchy clouds and even though it wasn't snowing, it had snowed heavily and the road was slow and treacherous. And so we traveled along Highway 76, 'highway' being maybe too fancy a word for what it was, and headed northwest toward the Pul-e Khumri junction.

Time frozen, we ground along. You try to stay inside your head. Sleep. Play cards. Write letters on your tablet or write in your journal. Trade stories. Sleep. Listen to music on your phone. Mainly you try not to think: about how uncomfortable you are, jammed shoulder to shoulder with no room to stretch your legs. About some guy farting and another whose team leader should be reminding him to brush his teeth in the morning. Most of all, you try not to think about spending hour after hour in a coffin on wheels, a Kevlar coffin some of my men called it, trapped inside if anything goes down.

We were well into the afternoon. We'd stopped every couple of hours so the men could take a leak and have a stretch. I was now back on top. We were down from the mountains traveling through a broad river valley, the water a chalky blue against the white snow on the banks. Up ahead was a near-ruined village—a collection of broken-down farms. I scanned them with my binoculars. A bright blue burqa was swaying on a clothesline. I saw no one. Just before we reached the buildings, we passed a rusty old tank turret on the side of the road, Soviet-era. I could make out a faded red star on one side. A woman, then a man, then three kids emerged from the turret like a family of raccoons crawling out from their burrow.

We were pushing to make it to the Pul-e Khumri junction before dark. There we could meet up with a convoy heading from Mazar-y-Sharif back to Bagram, and the town would be safer than stopping in the middle of nowhere.

Rodriguez was sitting with me on the back of the Stryker, perched atop a stack of tents and backpacks.

'Captain, did I tell you 'bout when I was out with our ANA guys on my first tour and we passed this minefield?'

I shook my head. I was watching the road ahead, the mud houses starting to build up as we neared the town. The sun was low off to the left. The air was suddenly much colder.

'So I was out on this supply mission in Herat, with the ANA guys, right? and we passed this minefield. There was those dinky signs put up by the EOD guys. Anyway, I look out across it and see a woman walking in front of a man. Behind the man were the goats. So I'm thinking that looks strange, right?'

'Rodriguez,' I interrupted, 'is this a story or a joke?'

'It's a story. This really happened to me.'

'I was just asking.'

'Jeez,' he said and didn't continue for the longest time.

'Anyways,' he finally said, 'so I say to our ANA lead guy, "That's not something you see every day, an Afghan man letting his wife walk in front of him. What's with that?" The ANA guys looks at me and smiles. Get this, Captain. He says: "Logical way to walk through a minefield. A man can get a new wife for nothing but goats are expensive."'

I shook my head.

'Gotta love this place, huh, Captain?' Rodriguez said.

We were traversing a valley. The land stretched endlessly to the north; all that broke up the expanse were scattered trees and mud-brown houses, perfectly square and symmetrical. In the distance, the setting sun painted the snowy mountaintops orange. The air was crisp and clean, cold, but not the bone-chilling cold I knew was on the way.

We both looked off to the left as the sun slipped behind a thick bank of clouds.

'Maybe more snow,' Rodriguez said.

I watched the clouds, then said, 'Maybe it'll miss us.'

The night was cold, just at the edge of freezing. At the Pul-e Khumri junction, we met the convoy in a field next to a big dirt parking lot filled with trucks, makeshift food stalls, tea shops, and vendors. Colored lights were strung across some of the stalls and shops. We formed the Strykers and convoy trucks into a circle, Wild West shit. We uncoiled barbed wire and created a perimeter, then pitched our tents against the vehicles. In the latrine tent we dug a couple of shallow shit holes. We bought bottled drinks and fruit from vendors. We bought wood and started a couple of fires. Most of my men were smiling.

We didn't have much to make us comfortable, but it was Christmas Eve. We'd brought along cooked turkey, stuffing, mashed potatoes, pies. A few men went out and chopped some branches off holly trees and decorated the Strykers. We sang carols and some of the guys opened small presents they'd received from home when we were at Bagram. I knew that all of them were thinking about family, parents, wives, girlfriends, kids.

We set up guard duty; the men would take turns through the night. The lucky ones got to go first or last. I was tired, but it was too early to sleep. I was sitting by myself on the back of my Stryker, twirling a sprig of holly; in front of me one man at the gun was talking to another beside him, both on watch. Music came from some of the parked trucks. I looked at the colored lights. Even out there in the middle of Afghanistan, they made me feel safe.

I felt my phone in one of my breast pockets and turned it on. A strong signal. I hopped down, told the guards at the opening to keep an eye on me, and wandered out about forty feet. I scrolled down to where I'd inputted Kat's satellite phone number, the wonky one Sally told me about. I had tried it a hundred times over the past forty-eight hours and never so much as heard it ring at the other end. This time it rang. My heart raced. It rang on and on, and then I heard a bunch of clicks and it went silent. My exposed fingers were stinging in the cold air. I tried once more, it rang, and there was a change of sound like it connected.

I turned my back on the camp so my men couldn't hear me.

'Katherine?' I yelled. 'Can you hear me? Katherine, it's me, Tanner.'

Music was coming from the parked trucks, but I could make out a voice.

'Tanner?' Her voice sounded like it was coming from the moon.

'Katherine, it's me… can you hear me?'

'Tanner?'

'Yes, I can hear you. Katherine—'

'Tanner, where are you?'

'We're heading north toward Badakhshan.'

'What?'

'Badakhshan. Darwaz District.'

'Darwaz?'

'Yes,' I yelled.

'That's where I am. Our clinic is snowed in. We're treating frostbite and pneumonia. They—'

For a moment I thought I'd lost her, but when she spoke again, her voice was suddenly next-door clear.

'It's supposed to warm up,' she said. 'Maybe melt.'

'You sound like I could reach out to you.'

'What? I can't hear you.'

'You're totally clear. Close.'

'What?'

'Can you hear me?'

'Sort of. This phone hasn't worked in days.'

'Kat, I'm coming there. Sally said you're way up in Madud.'

'What?'

'You need to get out of there.'

'Tanner, don't do this. I don't need you to protect me. Okay?'

'I mean it. It's—'

She laughed. That beautiful laugh.

'Tanner, Merry Christmas,' she said, and I could hear her smile.

'Kat,' I yelled. 'I'm losing you again. Can you—'

'Tanner, can you hear me?'

'Yes,' I said. 'Talk slowly. Yell.'

'I miss you...'

And then all I could hear was static on the line and the music coming from the trucks.

'Katherine...'

Only static.

'Katherine, it's not safe. You gotta get out of there. It's—'

More static. And the words 'Call ended' appeared.

I clutched the phone as if I could will the connection back. I looked back at the guards watching me, hoping they couldn't hear over the sound of the music, and the men talking behind them, and the winter wind whistling. I dialed again and again. Nothing.

No more blue skies in the morning. By nine we hit the snow. We stopped the Strykers in the middle of the two-lane highway and put chains on every other wheel. They'd get us through, but as the snow picked up, we were creeping along, trying not to slide off the road. The first sixty-five kilometers took us three hours. And this was an easy stretch: a reasonably good road, even worthy of being called a small highway. If we hadn't been worried about falling off the road, we might have thought it was a beautiful area to pass on Christmas Day, full of farmhouses, villages, and leafless groves of trees—pistachio, apple, and walnut, now hibernating for the winter.

The valley narrowed and the river wound, cutting through

mountains. We crawled along. The plunges off the side weren't huge, but a plunge of forty feet into a river is probably going to kill you as much as a plunge of a hundred. The men couldn't see out, but they could see the screen and not a single one opened his mouth for an hour.

The snow stopped and the sky cleared. The afternoon air started to warm and, just as Katherine predicted, although we were still three hundred kilometers away as the crow flies—and easily three times that along the winding roads—it was getting warmer, above freezing, and the road was turning mushy under melting snow. We stopped. It was great packing snow and some of the guys had a snowball fight.

The highway was decent all the way up to Talogan, where we made camp.

The next morning, the eastward road out of town was much worse. There were still trucks and mud-caked Toyota minivans—the *falang*, the 'flying coaches' of Afghanistan—but there were also donkey carts, horses, and a lot of people on foot. We drove until three, and before it got dark, made our camp.

With the sun down and the sky clear, the temperature plunged. My men ate standing by the fires. They headed early to their tents. Some threw their sleeping bags across the seats or along the floor of the Strykers even though it was a hell of a lot colder than sleeping in a tent. I wandered away from the fire. Like a puppy, Williams was at my side again.

'Captain, you know the stars?'

'The Big Dipper. That's about it.'

Williams was a farm boy.

'What sign are you, Captain?'

'US Army.'

'Come on.'

'Taurus.'

'Then it's one of your lucky months.' He turned south. Pointed up. Tried to describe the stars that formed the bull, but it was nothing I could make out.

So he said, 'Okay. See those three bright stars in a row. Angling up? No, not that high. Right there.' I saw his hand blotting out the stars in front of me. I tried to follow the line of his arm. 'That's Orion's belt. See that?'

And there they were.

'Okay. Follow them a bit to the right. They point to a curving band of lighter stars.'

I saw those too.

'That's his bow.'

'He's the hunter, right?'

'Dude, he's the greatest hunter. Nothing can stop him.'

'And what's he hunting?'

'That's the thing, sir.'

'What?'

'Well, it's you. His arrow is pointed right at the head of the bull.'

I looked at him.

He smiled, then said, 'Chill out, Captain. They're just stars.'

The next day, we started just as the sun was breaking and made it all the way to Feyzabad, the provincial capital that winds along another chalky-blue river. After all the villages we'd driven through, it was almost a surprise to see an actual town with some two-story buildings. At this time of year it was gray and brown and white.

We pulled into the airbase, once manned by the Germans

and now by a rump of our men who, apparently, had been joined by a company of 10th Mountain.

'You're fucking driving where?' was just about the first thing that Major Stankowski said. 'You won't get through, and if you do, you won't get back.'

'Alpha Company made it in.'

'Two weeks ago. Before the snow. Plus, your pal's a psycho.'

I looked out the window. The airstrip was built on a desolate plain in the river valley—and from here there wasn't a building, a tree, or a human being in sight. Even now, at the end of the day, the temperature was still above freezing.

'Looks like the snow's melting,' I said.

'Yeah?' he replied. 'Then maybe you'll get a run for a couple of days. Burns up your fuel, you know.'

He showed me the maps and satellite photos. Lots of mountains. Rivers cutting out valleys. Dirt roads that hadn't ever been graded. The very top of Afghanistan. Mountainous land bulging into Tajikistan. Almost no one lived there. We were going to the very end.

'Taliban's not up there,' he said.

'That's what they say.'

'That's what we know.'

'Maybe the Nomadic Northerners.'

'If they exist.'

'Major, I know about Mountain Brigade's men.'

He gave me a hard look.

I said, 'I saw the picture. We're here to get the bastards who did it.'

'They won't be that far north. No local support.'

'We'll get there. Our best intel says that's where they are.'

'Good luck. But remember, you still have to get out.'

Again at dawn, we'd fitted out the Strykers with extra fuel, food, and ammo—everything we could stack up and tie down onto the side cages and along the back. Major Stankowski convinced us there was no way our two supply trucks would get through. He said he'd try to reach us in a week with the Chinooks to bring in supplies if the weather stayed clear. He said good luck again and then said, 'You'll need it.'

The road was shit compared to the decent two-lane road we'd been on. But shit seemed like ice cream an hour and a half later when we turned north along the dirt track that would take us two hundred klicks to the end of the world. Stankowski had been right. If there had been any snow we wouldn't have made it: it would have been impossible to see where the track was and where it wasn't. But there'd been two days of melting and probably a few cars, pickups, and carts had come through, so even though it was slippery and deep with mud, we could see the track and didn't feel at every moment that we were about to drive off the road and down a mountainside.

I had tried again to reach Kat from town, but no luck. I had contacted Sally again but she hadn't heard a thing and was starting to worry. I didn't tell Sally where I was or why I was so worried too. Out here there was no cell phone reception. I tried our satellite phone but didn't get so much as a ring from her end.

One of the vehicles started having mechanical problems and we wasted half an hour trying to fix it. Another went off the road and got stuck in a gulley. We lost another forty-five minutes pulling it out, and by then the other one had totally died. Couldn't be fixed with what we had. We distributed all the gear and men among the remaining vehicles and got ready to head out, two hours wasted.

Two of our men blew up the Stryker. Five million bucks in a not so impressive explosion, but better than leaving it to the enemy to scavenge.

We hadn't driven more than five minutes when we got a call from the last vehicle. Looking back, they had seen movement around the burning Stryker.

Rance, the vehicle commander, asked if he wanted me to find a place to turn around so we could take a look.

Our gunners were ready. Our helmets were on, our rifles in hand. We knew someone was out there. As we drove toward them, I felt like those Russian sailors I once read about, trapped in a submarine and knowing that at any second this whole thing was gonna be their death trap. I heard a mumble and saw one of the men's lips moving, like he was deep in prayer. About what, I could only guess. Maybe, hoping he'd live to see his girlfriend back home. Probably, that the Stryker would hold together with whatever rubber bands kept it going, or that our fuel would hold out. There was no chatter until Williams said, 'Now I know what a deer feels like when hunting season begins.' We broke out laughing but suddenly went silent as we all thought about what he'd just said. We returned to our deadly quiet—quiet except for the pounding of the engine.

We stopped just as soon as the burning Stryker came into view—maybe two hundred meters away. I was asking for a status report when we got that *thud* and *schwack* and every way you try to imagine it, it was coming in. The gunners were firing back and we scrambled out the back hatches, staying behind the vehicles or throwing ourselves behind boulders.

We traded fire although it felt we were firing into nothing, and pretty soon it was only us shooting. We held fire and waited. And waited. I knew they had gone. I didn't think it was because they were as cold and tired as us.

There was no question of finding a place to make a camp that night. The moon was full, we had good headlights, and my vehicle commanders said we could keep going as long as no one minded poking along.

Men talked in quiet voices. Some nodded off. Williams snored. I drifted in and out of sleep, waking with a lurch whenever my head slumped down.

At sunrise we finally stopped driving so everyone could stretch and take a leak. Normally, that's a good time to get attacked, which is why when we were at Victoria's Camp we'd stand to about thirty minutes before sunrise so everyone would be awake. Here, I figured we were pretty safe, but we were still keeping careful watch.

The sky was getting lighter, although it would be another hour until the sun finally rose above the mountains. I walked away from the vehicles. We were in the midst of the most barren, spectacular landscape I'd yet seen. The mountains here were angular, sharp-edged, and heavy with snow. At their base, where the snow had melted over the past few days, the ground was flat, strewn with boulders, like the surface of Mars. Far to my left, across the narrow river, was a wild plateau—irregular, torn apart, as if a million-year cataclysm had forced rocks up into irregular mounds and then lava had spewed out, filling in parts of the landscape with twisted cords of iron. It looked biblical, Creation-like stuff. Snow had blown into long, high drifts that mimicked the mountains towering above. The wind whistled, pushing at me, and it seemed as if the rocks were moving.

These were the Pamirs, the mountains Marco Polo described as being so high that even the eagles had to walk to get across. If it hadn't been for the strip of half-defined road that wound along the side of a rushing river, tumid with the melt-off, I might have felt we were the only ones alive on the planet. I was surrounded by my men, but I had never felt so utterly alone.

We made it to Madud that day. Crawling along at five or ten kilometers per hour. Constantly stopping to make sure the road was passable. Some of the men started walking and every time the Strykers got a bit ahead, the men would soon catch up when we got stuck.

The sky was still cloudy, but patches of blue shone through. Behind us was a solid wall of gray clouds as forbidding as the mountains to our sides. Every mile we traveled north, the clouds seemed to be right behind and sometimes when the sun peeked out, it reflected off the fresh-falling snow that was covering our retreat.

Sometimes the men in my vehicle would trade stories about snowstorms and cold and who's been the coldest and what was the stupidest thing they'd done in the cold. I pasted a smile on my face, but I wasn't listening; I was, predictably, day-dreaming about Katherine. Imagining us together, less than a year from now, traveling to Bhutan, and then, what? What would it be?

The hours passed slowly and it was growing dark when we finally reached the village of Madud, a straggle of huts and small mud buildings. We drove around and looked for Ditka's camp. People stared at us, silent, unsure. Mothers and fathers swept up little children and pushed them behind their backs.

No one met our eyes, and that was the strangest thing of all. Usually when we drove around, people looked at us. Not necessarily with defiance or even curiosity, more as a statement that this was their land and they could look at whomever they wished. But here, everyone was doing their best to avoid our eyes. Some of our gunners up on top waved. No one waved back, not even the little kids.

Just past the village, we found an open area whose recent occupants had ditched a pile of empty MRE pouches, paper, and assorted junk.

Ditka and his men were gone.

CHAPTER 8

I walked through the village with four men and one of our interpreters—which, around here, meant he could translate Tajik. 'We're going to find out when and where Ditka's gone,' I told them, 'but first we're going to find one of the NGOs we met with last time.' Finding the small clinic was easy for it was the only building that looked like it had been built within the last century. There was a handwritten note on the door, in Tajik, Pashto, and English: 'We've gone north for two or three weeks in the countryside and villages.' At the bottom was Katherine's name and the name of an Afghani, presumably another nurse or perhaps a doctor. A shiver ran through me. I tried her again on the satphone. A few of my men were staring at me.

'If we're gonna let them come out to places like this,' I said, 'we should at least make sure they don't run into the enemy before we do.'

This time my men looked back at me as if I were rooting for the wrong team.

We knocked on several doors to ask about the other US soldiers who were just here. We had knocked on at least five houses before anyone would talk to us. An older man, his gums empty and raw as if he had just lost his teeth, gestured wildly and kept repeating two words. I turned to the interpreter. 'He said, "Bad foreigner. Glad he gone."'

The people here dressed differently. Few of the women were clad in burqas. Instead they wore long, intricately embroidered dresses in bright red, emerald green, and purple.

Most wore some sort of head scarf, either draped over their heads or tied under their chins. It felt like we were in another country, like we'd left the fundamentalist part of Afghanistan behind and entered the land of Genghis Khan.

Everybody's clothes—men, women, boys, girls—were brighter here, but worn and shabby. No one looked healthy or well fed. There was no electricity. I couldn't help but compare this area to the other places I had seen here. Afghanistan is a pitifully poor country when you leave out the businessmen, politicians, and narco-lords we've made rich. Up here in Madud, no one was rich; everyone was poorer than anything I'd seen. This was the Afghanistan of Afghanistan.

Between the one old man and two other younger men who talked to us, we finally got enough information to figure out that Ditka had left about four days earlier, right when the weather broke.

One young boy pointed up the dirt track leading north to Vod Am.

We had to find shallow spots over which to cross and re-cross the river, which wasn't yet frozen. In one area, the track disappeared completely under snow and we drove warily through the water. Once we had to drive way out across a plain to get around a landslide that had partially dammed the river and taken out the track. There were no villages, just isolated clumps of mud farmhouses. We didn't pass a single vehicle the whole day. A man walked in the distance, a huge bundle of sticks on his bent back. A family, riding yaks, crossed our path and we stared in amazement at the huge, shaggy beasts. Normally we would have been worried about IEDs but our intel said those were not likely a problem here. Still, I felt a relief every time we passed a long stretch of road and nothing had blown up under us.

By midday, the temperature had dropped well below freezing. The wind howled; the snow was closing in.

It was getting dark when we arrived at Vod Am, a village that looked even more destitute than the one we'd left that morning. We found Ditka's small camp outside town, pushed against a cliff face and protected on the other sides by concertina wire and sandbags. One bright light flooded the approach; two more shone off on the sides. As we approached we heard the throbbing of the generators.

Three guards dragged open the wire gate and we pulled inside. With our ninety-plus men, we would be doubling the size of the camp. But after the vastness of mountains and valleys we had been through, our nearly two hundred men felt like a pittance.

One of the guards said, 'Well, if it ain't the pussies from Bravo Company.' His words created a cloud of frost in front of his mouth.

I jumped down from the Stryker, stiff, freezing. The guard wasn't wearing a jacket or even a shirt, just his body armor vest.

I pointed to the two silver bars over my breastbone. 'Private, you know what these mean.'

He eyes locked on mine, his pupils huge, obviously stoked up on mind candy from the medics. I didn't turn away from him.

Lazily he said, 'Yes sir. Captain.'

As I stared at him, the snow started.

'Where's Captain Ditka?'

'Captain's busy.'

'Where?'

148

He shrugged. 'Captain says he don't want nobody interrupting him when he's questioning a suspect.'

'I'm not nobody, Private.'

I'm not sure if he would have told me and I'm not sure if I'd have ripped off his head, but I caught sight of Ditka marching my way.

'Jackson, what the fuck are you doing here?'

It seemed the strangest question, as if he thought we'd dropped in on a whim. But I'd be damned if I'd argue with another officer in front of our men.

I motioned with a wave of my head for him to step aside and, half to my surprise, he followed.

My voice low, I said, 'Lovejoy said you lost three men back near Madud.'

He didn't say a word.

'That makes twelve up here,' I said.

'We didn't just lose three men, like boom you're dead. We lost three bodies. Get me? We haven't found their bodies. Men who come over to serve their country and even their fucking bodies don't go home.'

'Think they're holding them as prisoners?'

'Listen, Jackson. Even if we're as stupid as you think, that might have occurred to us. They weren't captured. And if they had been, they wouldn't have survived after the blood we found near the gear they left. Everyone down here says these particular Taliban motherfuckers don't take hostages.'

'Tomorrow, we—'

'Tomorrow you stay out of my way, Jackson, and make sure your men do the same. I'm in charge here, okay? Lovejoy deployed me to set up this operation and you're going to have to fit in.'

'That's not how I understand it.'

He looked at me with bitter coldness; for a moment I wondered if I should be more frightened of him than of the Taliban. That was our first night in Vod Am. And that was our best night there.

Despite the heater and a bit of insulation in the ten-man arctic tent, it was so damned cold in the morning that it took all my willpower to crawl out of my sleeping bag and tell the other men to do the same.

The snow had come down steadily overnight, so our vehicles were covered with a few inches. Everything was white. Somebody had made a snowman and put fangs on it, adding something red to look like blood. A sign read, 'Taliban bloodsuckers will die.'

After we'd arrived the previous afternoon, I had the men connect up our mess tent with Alpha Company's. Back at Bagram, we'd practiced putting it up in just over an hour, but here they kept complaining their fingers were freezing and it took them twice as long. This all under the blank stares of some of Ditka's men. When I entered the mess in the morning, all of Alpha Company was on one side and we were on the other. There were no tables or chairs, but their side had some crudely made benches. My guys were standing or sitting cross-legged on the ground. There wasn't any talk. In all my years in the army, I'd seldom seen anything like it: a silent mess hall. Four electric heaters were chugging away.

Ditka didn't show up at the morning briefing. His first lieutenant, Harper, led it and told us almost nothing about what they'd been up to. He showed us a map of the area, showed us satellite photos, showed us where we were to patrol and where they would be. We'd be patrolling both north and south of the town, but on opposite sides of the narrow river.

'Stay on your side,' Harper said. And when he caught my look, he added, 'Captain says.' I kept my eyes locked on his. 'Sir,' he said.

The lieutenant was slightly chubby and acted like the type of person who was picked on as a kid and was now getting his revenge on the world. He was twitchy, and I suspected he had a mean streak not far underneath his smooth veneer. Perfect match for Ditka.

'We're on the same team, Lieutenant. Remember?'

'Captain wants you to stay on your side. Don't want friendly fire, right? If the snow continues, visibility will be shit. We're gonna shoot first and worry about who it is second. You stay in your area, we'll stay in ours. Those're Ditka's orders.'

'Let's make sure we talk to each other out there.'

'The briefing is over,' Harper said.

He talked just like Ditka, the second of his men in just over twelve hours who I wanted to pound. I took half a step toward him so he could feel my breath on his face.

'This briefing is over when I say it's over, Lieutenant.'

'Stay the fuck out of our way, Captain.'

I grabbed him by the collar but O'Keefe and Williams were on me, pulling me away.

'We're not at Bagram, *sir*,' Harper said. 'This is our show up here. Lovejoy sent us here first because he knows we can handle this shit. You guys are here to lend a hand. The captain says the best thing you can do is stay out of the way. Or use your hands to do something else.' At this, he made a jerking-off movement with his hand, turned, and strolled away.

And so began our first patrols at Vod Am. We strapped on our snowshoes only to take them off a few minutes later once we found stones where we could cross the river. Low mountains rose before us. We divided into our four platoons but, just to be cautious, I sent two platoons north along the river, the other two south, each with one translator. I didn't expect to find anything, especially with the snow covering the ground and cutting down visibility, but we'd start to know the terrain and my men could begin to get back into shape after six days stuck in the Strykers.

The snow started, stopped, and started again all morning. We regrouped for lunch. Heading south, the men had found nothing on this side of the river as far as they'd made it. North, where I went, there was a smaller village at a river junction—so small it didn't even seem to have a name. When we crossed the river into the village, we could see children playing in the snow. Men were cutting wood or talking; a group of women were beating clothes on the rocks just upstream, the icy water carrying faint traces of red and green dyes from the fabrics. As soon as they saw us, the children fled inside, the women stopped their work and watched warily, the men avoided our eyes. Our translator tried to talk to them. We learned nothing other than what I had also suspected from our reception back in Madud: Ditka had been here.

Four days, five days, passed this way. Venturing farther each day. Exploring the gullies and canyons cutting up from our side of the river and from the river that runs into the other village—neither had a name on our maps. We kept trying to talk to people in that village; we offered our medic to see people, but we got no takers.

Snow came and went, but the low clouds never left. The

cold got worse, plunging down to minus fifteen, minus twenty Celsius. We ate in our side of the tent—we too bought some rough planks from locals and made some crude benches. That much wood was a luxury around here. At 1,900 meters, trees are scarce and small.

At the end of each day, I was cold and tired from trudging through the snow. Sometimes we used snowshoes when the ground was flat, even though this often meant pushing knee deep, through the snow, and then wrestling them off to scramble up a hill or small cliff to see if there were any caves.

Six of my men had mild frostbite and were spending the day in camp; four others were sick; everyone was getting jittery. Just about everyone among the nearly two hundred of us stank: most of our clothes hadn't been washed in a week and a half. We didn't have a shower and although we heated water in big pots for washing dishes, bathing was just a cold splash of water carried from holes cut in the river ice. The only good thing about the freezing cold is that smells don't travel far.

Each day we were back in camp by three or three-thirty since night came early in the valley. I spent the long evenings talking to my men, playing cards, and reading. We listened to music on the Strykers' sound systems. We had two computers with a satellite link hookup, and my men took turns sending emails home, getting late news about Christmas, or sending greetings for the new year, which we all hoped would end better than it was starting. I had told the men about the beheadings—they would have heard it from Ditka's men and anyway I figured my men had a right to know. Besides, after a couple of days, ISAF HQ finally released the news. There was no talk of heads on spikes, of course, only that the bodies of the nine men had been found. I was guessing that in

Bagram word might have leaked out that they were beheaded. HQ was refusing to talk about our response, that *we* were that response, but I knew we weren't the only ones fanning out across Badakhshan and neighboring provinces—I knew 2nd Mountain was out there, and there must have been Special Forces and others.

I sent an email each day to Katherine, hoping that, somehow, one would get through. I tried to reach her through the satellite phone five, ten times, a day, but didn't even get a ring. I reached Sally, who said they hadn't heard from Katherine. Sally assumed the satphone was dead. I kept trying anyway. I'm sure some of my men were wondering why I was so worried about these clinic workers. I was feeling increasingly swallowed up by a sense of dread. Heads on spikes. Ditka's lost men. Kat out there somewhere.

One night I was taking a short walk around camp with O'Keefe. We stopped away from the tents and spoke confidentially. O'Keefe said, 'He's the worst I've ever seen. I mean, I've had some asshole NCOs and commissioned officers, but this guy's psycho.'

O'Keefe lit a cigarette.

We walked some more. The snowman with fangs had been rebuilt several times. The sign was still there: 'Taliban Bloodsuckers Will Die.' Tonight a second sign had been added. 'Bravo Company Pussies Stay out of the Way.'

I pulled off the sign and kicked the snowman over.

I marched into the command tent. Ditka's twitchy little Lieutenant Harper was there.

'Where's Ditka?' I said.

'Captain doesn't want to be bothered.'

I checked the mess tent. I checked each of their ten tents.

I checked the supply tent. I checked their Strykers. Finally, I checked their latrine tents. We even had separate latrine tents. The first one had three guys crapping and two more lined up outside yelling at them to hurry up.

In the second, the light was dim. One bare bulb hung from the middle of the tent and you had to duck so you didn't hit it. The electric heater was turned off and it was as freezing inside as out. Ditka's back was to me; next to him sat one of his men and their interpreter. Someone was lying naked on the wooden platform over the shit holes.

'Cold?' Ditka sneered to the person lying in front of him. The interpreter did his job. 'Tell me one fucking thing that makes sense and you might get a blanket.'

It was a teenager. The boy answered, whimpering, shaking. His hands and feet were tied by plastic cords to hooks that had been bolted to the wooden platform. There were welts across his chest and his thighs, some trickling blood.

The interpreter said, 'He says they are black *djinns*. They come in the night. They haunt people, kill them. You don't hear them coming.'

'Tell him I'm going to drop him down the hole.'

The interpreter did, the boy's eyes bugged out, tears pouring out. The interpreter said, 'He swears they are *djinns*.'

'What the hell's a *djinn*?' Ditka said.

The interpreter spoke without asking the boy. 'A spirit,' he said. 'Around here they hold to the old beliefs. There are white *djinns* and black ones. The black ones are evil. They possess people and make them go insane. They haunt houses and move things. They make you ill and die.'

'You tell this yak-herder that the only one around here that's going to make him ill and die is me.' The interpreter spoke. The boy was shaking uncontrollably. Ditka put his face right next to the boy's like he was going to bite him. 'Now you tell him I want to know where these Taliban are and what they're planning.'

The interpreter spoke, the boy responded, his voice barely audible.

'He is very afraid. He says he needs to find a *malang*. How do you say that? A shaman. He has seen the black *djinns*. They will come after him, unless he sees a *malang*.'

And then without turning around or changing his tone of voice, Ditka spoke to me, as if he had known I'd been standing behind him this whole time. 'Captain Jackson, I told you to stay out of my way.'

Ditka looked back at the interpreter.

'Tell him we'll continue this tomorrow. If he hasn't died.' The interpreter spoke to the boy.

Ditka moved away from the latrine and punched a finger into the interpreter's chest. 'And if you give him a blanket, you'll find yourself on the shithole next to him. Do you understand me?'

Then the boy spoke.

Ditka responded, 'What did he say?'

'He says no one is as strong as the *djinn*. He says you should be afraid of the black *djinns*.'

Ditka stepped up to the boy and stretched his hands toward his face as if he was going to gouge out his eyes.

'Ditka!' I shouted.

Ditka grunted, turned from the boy and left the tent.

I was on his heels. 'He's a fucking kid, Ditka.'

'This boy, Captain, was lurking around the village. He wouldn't tell us where he lived. He tried to run away when we approached.' He pointed a finger at me. 'I've warned you, stay the fuck out of my way.'

Ditka shoved past me. I thought about tackling him from behind, and I was taking a step forward when I heard the boy talking to the interpreter.

Ditka had disappeared in the snow. I went back into the tent. The interpreter was sitting on a stool, the boy was crying, trembling, pleading.

I pulled out my pen knife and sliced the plastic cords. I put an arm under the boy and sat him up.

'Hand me his clothes,' I said to the interpreter.

'Captain Ditka ordered me not to.'

I snatched the clothes off the floor. The interpreter started to lurch to the tent flap but I grabbed him and pushed him to the ground. I hissed at him, 'You move and you'll wish it was Ditka beating you up.'

I plugged in the heater. I helped the trembling boy into his clothes.

I pointed to the plastic water bottle under the interpreter's stool. 'Give me that water.'

I helped the boy drink.

He looked fourteen or fifteen. Could be a Taliban sympathizer or whoever it is up here. His skin was Caucasian pale, his eyes a striking grayish blue, but their shape was Mongolian. Generations of conquerors flowing in his blood.

'Tell him I'm not going to hurt him.'

The interpreter nodded. The boy dared a glance at me but then looked away.

'What's the story with these *djinns*?' I asked the interpreter. 'Is this kid bullshitting?'

The interpreter didn't hesitate. 'Oh no, he tells the truth.'

I studied them both in the dim light.

The interpreter said, 'He's more scared of the black *djinns* than he is of Captain Ditka. They are very powerful. He says he has seen them, these black *djinns*.'

The interpreter began talking with the boy again.

'These *djinns* move only at night. They can see in the dark.'

'Well, I can see in the dark with my NVDs, but that doesn't make me an evil spirit.'

The boy spoke again. The interpreter said, 'He says they can run faster than bullets. They can speak every language.'

'Which ones?'

The interpreter asked the boy.

The boy of course didn't know the names of the languages other than Tajik and Pashto, but he claimed there were many.

The boy interrupted the interpreter.

'He says your language.'

'English?'

The interpreter nodded.

I raised my eyebrows. 'What else?'

'He says the bodies are found without blood.'

'They're probably frozen,' I responded.

'These bodies have absolutely no blood left in them.'

'Tell this to the boy.' I paused. 'You tell him I'm a big deal *malang* where I come from and my men and I will take care of these black *djinns*.'

The boy stared at me through his one eye that wasn't swollen over.

Then I said to the interpreter, 'If you want to save your ass from both of us, from Ditka, from me, and even your goddamn *djinns*, then I want you to get out of here. You don't breathe a word of this to anyone. You come back at dawn and find the boy gone. If Ditka pushes you, you say I was talking to him when you left and he was still tied up and scared as shit. You got that?'

The interpreter started moving away. Too quickly.

I grabbed his arm. 'You go to Ditka now and I'll find you and kill you.' I waited until he said he understood and then I let him go.

I sat there with the boy and waited nearly half an hour until the camp quieted down, the music was gone, and the only sounds were the generators and the wind.

I held my finger to my lips.

He nodded.

There'd be guards at the gate and others patrolling, but we'd have cover from snow, which was coming down heavily. I unplugged the heater. I tossed the plastic cords down the shit hole. We ducked under the back canvas wall of the latrine tent. We were behind a six-foot wall of sandbags. On the other side were the coils of wire. I gestured my plan to him, hoped he caught on, then climbed to the top of the sandbags. He scrambled up beside me. I swung one leg over and got him to squat on top. The sole light was forty feet away and pointing out to the perimeter, only a glow through the heavy snowfall. I gestured again. I grasped his clothes. And when he sprang, I propelled him over the wires and into the snow outside our camp. It was the first thing in weeks I had done as a soldier that I felt good about.

It was two in the morning when I made it back to my tent.

Rodriguez woke up when he heard the rustle of my sleeping bag.

'Captain,' he whispered. 'There was a call for you on the

satphone. We tried to find you. Where were you?'

'Who was it?'

'A woman. Katherine. She said she was okay. Then we lost her.'

It was my job to stay calm.

Here's one thing I learned in the army: you can get used to just about anything. You get used to not showering for days, even weeks, and feeling itchy and miserable everywhere and having to put up with the reek of the men around you. You get used to functioning on no sleep with only the help of the drugs they're happy to dispense to you. You get used to the fact you're with guys just a few years past puberty who've been handed the power of life and death and yet spend some of their spare time constructing snowmen effigies of the Taliban and then throwing rocks at them while they laugh like seven-year-olds. You get used to being surrounded by guys swallowing Vicodin and oxys by the handful. You get used to seeing some guy strolling around in minus ten weather wearing only his Kevlar vest and absolutely nothing else. You even start getting used to the fact that a fellow commanding officer and his men won't talk to you and that you need to think twice about turning your back to them.

What I never got used to was losing my men. And I never got used to killing.

A couple of days passed. Ditka hadn't even asked what happened to the kid, which confirmed for me that he'd probably realized the boy knew nothing; he was torturing him simply because he could. The snow stopped, the clouds were thick and low. Each day the wind increased and now there were times it screeched through camp like a banshee.

The day for the supply drop came and went—low clouds, frigid temperatures, snow, and high winds don't make the best combination for choppers in the middle of the mountains.

Ditka's Lieutenant Harper announced without consulting me that we'd have to start rationing fuel for the generators. Ditka hadn't been resupplied in almost three weeks and our company had now been out ten days. We'd long used up all the jerry cans and had been syphoning diesel from the Strykers—five of theirs and two of ours were now empty. Only the mess tent and comm tent had heat and electricity, plus there was power going to the perimeter lights, and our radio equipment and other electronic gear. We kept the batteries for our NVDs and helmet communications in a couple of knapsacks in the comm tent so they didn't die in the cold—although with each day, more batteries were petering out. Men started sleeping in the mess tent, although there wasn't room for all us to sleep in there. I stayed in my tent to give a spot for one of my men and we piled brush and then snow along the tent sides to give us more insulation. We were still okay with food and there was talk of buying animals from the villagers.

One late night, O'Keefe, Williams, and I were outside, breathing the crisp, cold night air, one of the day's only pleasures. O'Keefe was telling us about his three-year-old daughter who he hadn't seen in more than a year. His wife and kid were back in Anchorage, Alaska, and when those of us from the south whined about the cold, O'Keefe would talk about skiing and winter camping. He knew more about snow than the rest of us put together.

But on this night the snow had stopped, the wind had died

down. We were looking up at the stars. I couldn't see Orion, and Williams said it was because it was too low to see with all the mountains in the way. O'Keefe had been quiet for a long time.

'What's up, John?' I asked.

'Day before we left Bagram, I called home. Heather said that Chelsea asked who her daddy was.'

'Man, that sucks,' Williams said.

I said, 'As soon as you're back, she'll forget it all. She'll know who her father is.'

'You guys don't have kids,' he said, and I could hear his voice almost cracking. 'A while ago Heather said she wondered if when Chelsea's older we'll be able to tell her it was worth it. You know, me being away like this, missing her growing up like I have. And...'

He didn't have to say it, but I knew what he meant: whether this whole damn war was worth it.

Out of the blue Williams said, 'Is it the night sky or are we drunk?'

'What are you talking about?' O'Keefe said.

'That's when we tell the truth, isn't it?' Williams said.

'What?' O'Keefe said.

'Us. Men. It's either when we're outside at night looking up at the sky, or when we're drunk. That's when you get the truth out of a man.'

'You think that up just now?' I asked Williams.

'Yeah, I think I did.'

We were out again as usual. Predictably, the wind had picked up and the clouds seemed syrupy thick; it was going to be another day without supplies. We had been travelling farther up and down our river and two smaller ones that joined it a kilometer north, but we were always limited by the short days, the slow progress through the snow, and the need to be back before dark. That day, I led my men north to the river junction, broke the company in half, and headed northeast along both sides of one of the smaller rivers. We inspected hovels—many had animals living alongside the family; we followed tracks and searched gullies and caves.

We'd found no traces of the Nomadic Northerners. All anyone would say—the few who would talk to us—was that they'd seen the black *djinns*. I'd been sending a daily report to Lovejoy by email and yesterday I'd phoned. I told him we should fall back, either to Madud where Ditka had lost his men or farther back toward Feyzabad where we'd been attacked. Lovejoy said he was considering it, but for another few days he was going with Ditka's instincts. So we were stuck here until they could send in enough choppers to airlift us out.

The days were tiring, cold, and frustrating. Everyone was edgy, constantly on the verge of frostbite, and feeling hemmed in. Everyone sensed that things could blow up at any moment between us and Alpha Company. What energy that didn't go into worrying about my men, worrying about our elusive and mysterious enemy, and worrying about Ditka went into worrying about Katherine. I had no idea how she was traveling or if she was still traveling. Maybe they had hired some yaks. One of the few villagers who talked to us had offered a pair of yaks for $16 a day each and I was close to saying yes.

CHAPTER 9

It's a bit past noon. We're on patrol again. Along the tributary to the north. Snow's still the same. Cold's still the same. No tracks. No sign of anything moving all morning. I'm out with nearly all my men. It's a two-and-a-half hour walk back to base and it's going to be dark if we don't get a move on.

'Vince, take your platoon and check out that farmhouse. Make it fast. We're running out of time.'

As the 4th Platoon heads off, O'Keefe comes onto the comm, his breathing sharp, excitement in his voice. 'I got something.'

O'Keefe and his eighteen men are on the other side of the river. Our side has scattered homes and trees; his has mountains that look as if huge chunks have crashed into the water over the years.

O'Keefe gives us coordinates and a description even though it means almost nothing since everything looks the same. He reports that his platoon is with him, more or less.

'What's that mean?' I ask.

'We're separated. I'm trying to get all of us back together.'

This is not a good sign. I order my platoon to head in O'Keefe's direction as quickly as possible. We cross at a shallow part of the river. We're the first to arrive where O'Keefe is supposed to be waiting for us.

He's not there. I call back to O'Keefe, asking him to report. Silence.

I yell: 'O'Keefe, report!'

Silence.

Rodriguez says he's getting a signal.

'Williams and Hoops, follow me,' I yell.

The snow has drifted and is deep, but the piles of rocks are huge. The rest of O'Keefe's platoon are just beyond a large rock some thirty meters from the river. I shout to O'Keefe's sergeant to make sure their fire teams stay close together, but to start searching.

I've still got my snowshoes on and I'm working awkwardly around the boulders.

I've skirted a boulder the size of a house when I hear O'Keefe's comm. His helmet, with its built-in comm, is lying on top of the snow. No O'Keefe in sight.

I yell into my comm, 'They've taken O'Keefe. Keep your men in their fire teams but spread out. Move quick. Ready to fire. But careful. O'Keefe's out there too.'

I direct the 3rd and 4th to space themselves along the river.

We radio Ditka. His men say they'll head up the river on both sides in case the enemy is escaping that way.

The snow has stopped and, for the moment, so has the wind. I can see half a kilometer in each direction. There are no tracks showing that the enemy has crossed the river and I can't see any tracks heading south. If they have O'Keefe, they've gone north deeper into the mountains. We're going to have to move that way. As I assemble the men, the wind starts whipping up along the valley and down through the gullies, stirring up the snow and making it impossible to see much beyond the next man.

Since O'Keefe disappeared about a hundred meters into a gulley north of us, it's our best bet. I take two platoons farther in, leaving the rest deployed in groups along both sides of the river.

We're not more than five minutes in when we see the snow stained red with blood. A lot of blood. A bloody trail for five meters. Then it disappears.

We follow the enemy tracks but the wind is covering them and creating impressions that may be leading us astray. Men crawl up the rocks trying to find trails, or caves, or blood, or tracks. Nothing.

An hour, two hours, pass. It's now 1430 hours. Even at a fast pace, we'll need more than two hours to get back to camp. With no moon or stars, I know I'll be risking injuries, frostbite, or further captures if I keep the men out.

I get Rodriguez to call everyone together, all eighty-five of us, at the entrance to the gulley.

I tell them I'm staying out with my HQ platoon. I order my lieutenants to take everyone else to the camp and be prepared to march out again at dawn.

They protest. They say we won't see a thing. They say we'll break our legs, get captured, fall between rocks, tumble off a ledge, freeze to death. When I don't budge, they say they want to help. But I order them to head back. The nine of us will be able to move quickly. I say I can't leave, not when O'Keefe is out here.

We search until dark. Then we sit in silence by the river, still on the side where O'Keefe disappeared. We aren't carrying NVDs because we aren't supposed to be out at night and didn't want the batteries to run down out here in the cold. I decide that if I hear voices we'll open fire. I don't think O'Keefe is alive, but if he is, I know he'll want to take our bullets rather than whatever death awaits him and, just maybe, kill some of these bastards.

We stay by the river for two hours, waving arms and shaking our legs to keep our circulation going. We try not to make a sound. But there is no movement other than from the relentless wind. Finally, we cross back to our side of the river and start the treacherous walk back to camp.

It's 2300 when we stumble back in, freezing, bruised, soaking wet with sweat, one man with a badly twisted ankle.

All my men are awake and as soon as word gets out that we're back, they congregate not far from the mess tent. I've lost O'Keefe, and all our weapons and satellites and billions haven't done shit. I tell them we're going to keep looking, we won't lose hope. I don't say that I think he's probably dead, but they all know it. I don't say we're probably searching for his body. I tell them we've got to sleep because we have to be up early.

I'm dead tired. But my mind tumbles into sleep only to awake with feverish dreams and half-formed images.

I'm tossing in and out of sleep. Seeing the spot where he went missing. Seeing the bloody snow nearby. Maybe his blood, maybe theirs. No one heard a shot, but the wind had been screeching—and it could have been the work of a knife or a rock. But why wasn't there a trail? It's not like they would have stopped to patch up a wound. Where was the trail of blood?

We use this all the time to track down enemy who are hit. What the hell did they do with O'Keefe? Half-awake, half-asleep, I imagine them wrapping up his body to take it away. I imagine them desecrating it. Then, in my half-formed nightmare, I see Ditka slitting O'Keefe's throat. I see the night stars and feel my whole body shudder. And then I see Katherine holding a crying baby but Kat is blindfolded and her hands are bound. She is calling to me, her lips are moving, but the wind is howling and I cannot hear a word she is saying. Then I wake up.

The next day our search is two companies strong. We leave the minimal number of men to guard the camp. Not an act of solidarity on Ditka's part, rather the smell of blood.

We find no trace of O'Keefe. Even the huge patch of blood is covered with fresh snow.

The following days are as dark as it gets. Foggy and overcast. I'm trying desperately to reach Katherine on the satphone. One day starts with clear skies and almost no wind. I'm through to Feyzabad and they promise to dispatch choppers immediately but they're delayed by some emergency, and by the time that's over, the thick low clouds have been pushed in by a ferocious wind.

Once a day—it's all I can justify because now the men only get three minutes of computer time every other day—I send an email to Katherine. All I want is a response that she's okay. Then I go to mush and say I can't wait to meet her in Bhutan when all this is over.

Alpha Company loses two more men: helmets left behind, blood but no bodies. They've now lost five. A day later, I lose three more—Whitby, Pencilhead, and Malcolm. I can hear Katherine's voice in my head. *They have names. They have—they had—lives.* One minute, I'm yelling at my men that I think they're fucking incompetent. I think it's their fault. I think they're dumbfucks who have never read a book in their lives. I need to blame somebody and the Taliban are nowhere to be found. Even Williams can't console me and he's trying his damnedest with his sheepdog face. Then the next minute, I'm like the father they may have never had: concerned, helping, patient, looking after them. I know I can't blame them for our losses. In the chain of command, the one to blame is me.

One of my guys has flipped, refuses to leave the Stryker, and has taken to pissing in an empty jerry can.

Arguments are breaking out over nothing. The packed mess hall is turning into a viper's nest.

One day when Ditka's company is going south on his side of the river, we say fuck 'em and go north on his side to see for ourselves what's up there. This side has the track, and the wind has cleared it of snow for long stretches. We make great time and come upon a deserted collection of houses. Not old deserted—people obviously live here—but deserted like everyone has suddenly vanished or fled. We break into squads to search in all directions. When I pass back through the village, I come upon Hoops and Delong. Delong is pointing his gun at a young man who's kneeling in the snow and trembling.

I ask Delong what's happening.

'*Hajji* here was walking around in the village,' Delong says.

Delong is one of the most respectful of my guys. I've never seen him mistreat a prisoner or a local nor use a word like that.

'So?' I ask.

Delong says, 'What's a *hajji* doing in a deserted village walking around in this cold?'

'I don't know,' I say.

'Maybe we should take him back to Ditka to get him to talk.'

'Delong, you don't report to Captain Ditka.'

Then I take a good look at this young Afghani. Seventeen at most. I think about O'Keefe and the other men we've lost.

I think about Katherine wherever she is. I think about the heads stuck with spikes. Suddenly I hate this boy as much as I ever hated anyone.

'Carry on,' I say. 'See what you can find out. Do whatever you need to do.'

I walk away and pretend not to hear the thud of a fist, and the moans of a boy fearing for his life—sounds that should have pierced my soul.

That night, or maybe the next one, I go into the mess tent. More and more I don't want to talk to anyone and I don't want to deal with Ditka's men. I'm long past telling myself some of them mean well. I hate them all. Whenever I see Ditka, my brain is a neuron away from telling my hands to lunge at his throat. It's easier to stay away from them all.

When I enter that night, everyone is dead silent, just like at our first breakfast. But this feels different, and what I feel in the air is anger, sadness, and fear.

I grab food and sit next to Williams, who tells me that one of Ditka's men killed himself. They just found his body. His buddies thought he was sleeping, but he'd taken a bottle of sleeping pills along with his psych meds. I'd guess that half the men in this tent are on these meds. I feel I could drown in the heaviness of that room.

The sadness: they lost a friend and comrade.

The anger: it happened up here at the end of the world. Why?

The fear: we all might end up like him.

Food stocks are running down. To supplement our MREs, we've bought rice, onions, lentils, and some half-frozen, limp carrots in the nearby hamlets, which aren't even on the map. Other than Vod Am, which is the only one approaching a small village, the two closest hamlets are a few klicks away. We've had some animals slaughtered. But even this food is hard to come by; these places don't have any more to sell. In Vod Am, there are two hovels that pass as stores: they have— *had*—a few bags of grains and a few dirty jars and bottles of stuff. We've found some farmers who will sell to us, although I wonder what they'll be eating.

Lovejoy tells me to hang in there. They've decided to pull us back to Feyzabad. The weather is supposed to shift in a few days.

Rumors swirl with the wind. Some of our men hear from villagers that Taliban are massing in the mountains and will attack any day. Villagers are saying that maybe these aren't Taliban but foul men who drink the blood of their victims. The *djinns*. Our men start believing all of it. Would this be laughed at if we were back at Bagram, if our men weren't being picked off one by one?

Again, just about the whole company is going up the river on Ditka's side. Again we don't tell Ditka. We pass the deserted village where I had let my men beat the shit out of that boy. We reach the next village. Like the one before, it's newly deserted. It's even smaller than the one before, maybe ten huts. Belongings have been tossed out onto the snow and it looks like animals have gotten into the meager food supplies. We call out. Nothing.

Third Platoon calls me from a grove of trees behind the houses.

Four local men and a boy are hanging by their necks. Their

faces are gray, stiff—they're dead. Their eyelids are open, but there are no eyes in the sockets.

'Captain,' one of my men says. He's pointing down to the boy's hands. In them he is holding what we guess are his own eyes.

We check through the trees. We look again in each house. We find an old woman, hiding under a dirty blanket. When she sees us she shrieks in terror, cowering, pleading with her hands.

That night, I find Ditka. He's outside smoking, staring up at the dark sky as if he could read the weather.

'We found some villagers lynched on your side of the river. Eyes ripped out of their heads.'

He blows smoke through his nose.

He says, 'And we should give a fuck?' He drags on his cigarette then speaks again. 'Sounds to me like you want to get your men killed. Taking them on our side of the river—that ain't a safe place to be.'

'Who the hell killed them?' I ask.

He drops his cigarette into the snow and mushes it with his boot.

'Who do you think, Jackson?' he barks. Then a glow comes onto his face with the barest hint of a smile, and he says, 'An eye for an eye.'

We're back in the area where O'Keefe went missing, now more than a week ago. The clouds seem lower and thicker than ever and the mountains rise only fifty or a hundred meters before disappearing in the clouds. It's a claustrophobic sight. The mountains are the walls and the clouds the ceiling of this tomb we're in, the tomb where my men are getting buried alive. Except for the sound of our walking, it's silent.

One of the platoons on the other side of the river calls for me. The river is now covered with ice, but we're still careful crossing. I find my men staring toward a small tree, afraid to go near. Something is resting in a tangle of thin branches. I go to the tree. I see a dog-eared photo of O'Keefe, holding his daughter with one arm, the other circling his wife. The photo is propped up on a branch as if on display. Hanging from a twig are his tags.

I take them down. I slip off my glove and hold the objects in my hand. I've heard people describe an inanimate object burning in their hands. I thought it was just bad poetry. But O'Keefe's small photograph and his tags burn my palm.

I look away in silence and then I yell at my men. I call them fuckin' idiots, going up to this tree, standing here, when this could be a booby trap or ambush. Even as I say this, I know it's ridiculous. Up here, there hasn't been a booby trap. Up here, no IEDs so far. Up here, the danger comes from something else; what, we do not know.

We radiate out looking for a trail, blood, scraps of cloth, anything. But there is nothing.

Another day without fresh supplies. We're further rationing diesel for the generators. Only randomly during the night do we turn on the perimeter lights. Fifteen minutes per hour for the heaters in the mess tent. Enough to charge batteries—not the Strykers', which are long dead—to keep our communications running. It's cold as hell and the wind feels like a hatchet thwacking into you.

Today we're sticking to camp or nearby. The plan is to burn fewer calories and get by with less food. It's a good idea and a stupid idea because now everyone is on top of each other day and night. Fights break out over a hand of cards or a comment about a girlfriend. I saw four of my men having a fistfight, I mean, really bashing each other's brains out. I broke it up, asked what was wrong, and they said, 'Nothing.' They said, 'We were just having some fun.'

The wind is so loud that sometimes it's hard to think.

The air is so cold that even the T-shirt guys from Alpha revert to winter jackets today.

In the late afternoon, Rodriguez is trying to pry a decent forecast out of Bagram about when the low clouds and the terrible wind are going to end. Instead, he gets this news: staff from a humanitarian organization working in Badakhshan province have been kidnapped. Which organization? No information yet. What district? Nobody knows. No word about who or how many or exactly where. My chest tightens so hard I'm scarcely able to breathe.

Another hour passes and then we find out. It's Kat's organization. District still not known.

With the satphone, I try to reach Kat. I try to phone Sally at her office, but the landline is out of order and her cell goes into voicemail. I send an email. Since I don't know where our information is coming from, whether it's accurate, I'm vague. I ask if she's gotten any news from Kat. I get a message back within minutes. Sally's heard nothing from Kat for two weeks but has gotten some third party messages that she and her colleagues are fine. No mention of any kidnappings.

Either they don't know, or it's actually a different organization, or the report is bogus—all of which are possible. When another few hours have passed and we get word it was a rumor, I'm relieved. I want to yell with joy and at the same time I want to scream at someone, anyone, for making me go through this. I am struck by the full force of what Katherine told me in Cambodia. She wants a life together. She is the home I will go to when this is all over.

It's barely been three weeks since Cambodia, but nowhere on the planet seems farther away. I force myself to visualize her smile. My mind slams me back to a picture of her chained in captivity. I force myself to imagine being together in Bhutan. I see her cold, wounded, scared. I try to think about what our life together will be. I hear her defying her captors, but soon she is crying for help. I find strength in Katherine's belief that I can be a good soldier. I try to forget I let Delong beat the hell out of that villager.

Later, I'm writing one of my emails to Katherine—actually imagining that they will reach her—when one arrives from Sally. She is short and to the point: they don't know where Katherine and her team are. Their satphone has died. Last they heard, the same heavy snow we've been facing was making their work treacherous; their supplies were running out. All Sally knows is that Katherine and her colleagues had been in Darwaz, and their plan was to make it on foot with local guides to Feyzabad. She guesses that could take as long as ten days.

What Sally doesn't say, and what I know, is that their likely path will take them along the other side of the great spine of mountains that flanks us and, perhaps, perilously close to where the Taliban are supposedly camping. The same Taliban who are picking off our men.

Sally ended her message with 'I hope this information helps.'

I want to blurt out the brutal truth, but I write with care: 'Please keep me informed. If you make contact with them, urge them to move quickly and with extreme caution. Get to Feyzabad.'

I want to say it differently. I want to say: *Get them the fuck out of there!*

I try to reassure myself that Sally and Katherine and their team know what they are doing. That they have worked in conditions like this for years, including with enemy combatants around them. I remind myself that the snow makes it almost as treacherous for the Taliban as it does for us.

In my head I tell Katherine what I feel for her, what I want for us. I tell her everything will be okay.

Just then Williams runs in.

'Captain!' It's Williams. Of course it would be Williams.

When I start telling him to leave me alone, he cuts me off.

'Captain, in the mess tent. Real bad.'

I race behind him and we're not even there when I can hear the shouts. Other men are also rushing to the tent. It's our company against theirs. There must be seventy men inside. Some have blood on their faces. Some are on the ground. Dazed, one man stumbles past me. Benches are turned over. Some of the punches are landing hard. Others, it's like the slugger just needs an excuse to hit something.

Above all the racket, one man bellows, 'You son of a bitch, what the hell are you—' It's an angry voice but it's also a cry of fear and is quickly drowned out. I turn to see who it is but there are too many men in front of me. I push through the crowd, throwing men out of the way, getting hit along the way but nothing hard.

The man yelling is Shortwave, one of our RTOs and a tech nerd. But this nerd's got a knife in his hand, its blade nasty and black, and he's repeatedly stabbing at one of Ditka's guys. At first I think he's just threatening, pretending. But then I see blood coming from the guy's mouth; each stab seems to be pushing deeper and deeper. My men are slow in stopping him.

I dive at Shortwave and take him down. I take out my pistol and fire it in the air through the tent roof. Stupid, but it gets their attention fast.

I scream for a medic. Three of my men grab Shortwave and pull him back.

Some of Ditka's men are stunned, some are screaming in fury, but for now all are holding back. One man, howling with rage, pushes through the crowd and drops to the ground next to his wounded friend, grabs him, cradles him, tells him to hold on.

Two medics, who were also in the fight, are now at his side. One gives CPR, the other rips open his uniform. There's blood everywhere. There is no Medevac here, no surgery.

'What the fuck was this about?' I begin yelling to my men, to anyone.

My men won't meet my eyes. Ditka's men look like they're gonna kill me. I know it'd take only one man to make the first move.

I grab Hoops, who's nearby. 'What the fuck happened?'

At this, there is noise, the crowd parts, and Ditka is on me, not physically, although he is an inch away.

'What the hell!' He looks at me. He looks at the men re-straining Shortwave right behind me.

'We'll bring charges against him, Ditka. This won't—'

'There'll be no charges, Jackson.' I feel his spit on my face. 'We settle this ourselves. Here.'

'We're US Army and we have rules.'

'Jackson, I make those rules now.'

I'm not going to budge. I'm not going to let him get to Shortwave.

Ditka must have felt my resolve. 'Jackson, you pussies will pay for this.'

None of my men dare sleep in the mess tent, so we add yet more branches and snow to insulate our tents and cram fifteen men into each one. The next morning I decide, using up energy or not, I've got to get my men out of there for the day. I leave behind two men to guard Shortwave, who I've put under arrest.

We make a feeble attempt at going out on patrol, not far from our camp, but at least we feel like we're doing something. It's another day of cold, blistering wind, and frustration.

We arrive back in the early afternoon and there's an email for me from Sally. *Captain Jackson - Katherine was in a group of our aid workers kidnapped on their way from Darwaz. No contact from them. Will keep you informed.*

It takes me two hours to reach Sally. She gives me the coordinates where Katherine and her group were last seen. It's only fifty kilometers away, but it's over a mountain and impossible to reach.

All this is confirmed when I call Bagram. I get through to Lovejoy. He already knows about Shortwave and of course the missing aid workers. I tell him we've gotta get out of here.

He barks at me over the radio. 'For fuck's sake, Jackson, act like a soldier. We'll get you out when we fucking well can get you out. Do your job.'

Next morning, as soon as light seeps through the low clouds, we resume our short patrols. An hour and a half, two hours max. We come back in, rest, and head out again. Ditka and his men are doing the same. Everyone is exhausted.

Mid-afternoon, my men and I are all back in camp. Finally, the sky seems to be clearing—there are gaps between the clouds. But the sun has already fallen behind the mountains and we have an hour and a half before it is night. I know our rescue will be delayed yet again.

All but one of Ditka's patrols have arrived back.

I go into the mess tent to get warm. I sit down and drift in and out of sleep. All day, all I have thought about is Katherine. I feel I'm stumbling. I don't think I can lead my men any longer. It feels like the camp could explode over nothing. That it could get even worse than what already happened in the mess tent.

There is yelling and we all rush outside.

One man has staggered back into the camp, babbling. Fucking deranged. We can't even figure out what he's saying. He's jumping around, yelling, clawing at his own face and pulling out his hair like he's trying to get at some torment tearing into his brain.

He was with Ditka's last patrol and it finally becomes clear: the rest of them were attacked. The rest of the men aren't coming back.

It will be dark in an hour, but Ditka says he's going out.

I say we're going too.

Ditka's out in front, faster, stronger, more relentless than anyone. It only takes him thirty minutes to find what's left of his men: blood and seven helmets. No bodies and no clear trail.

I know we can just make it back to camp before it's totally dark. Loudly, so Alpha Company can hear we're on their side, I tell my men we're coming back out as soon as it's light.

As if in response, Ditka bellows that his whole company is staying out until they find these bastards.

One of his men, I don't even know his name, says, 'Can't do that, Captain.' There is sheer terror in his voice. I've seen it before, when a man just can't take any more and cracks.

Everyone goes still.

'What's that you say, Private?'

'It's almost night, sir.' He shouts out the 'sir' like he's talking to a drill sergeant. 'They're gonna kill us out here. Sir.'

Ditka steps closer. I can see the private trembling.

Ditka says, his voice quiet, menacing, 'You go where I tell you to go. Private.'

'I can't, sir.'

Ditka doesn't answer. He cocks his head in the direction away from our camp and his men all start to follow. All except this one private. Twenty feet away, Ditka stops. Turns around. Sees this man standing there alone. Turns to all his men, and yells to no one in particular, 'You know what we call this in a war? We call this desertion.'

And with that, as if he covers those twenty feet in three strides, he's back in front of this private who is standing at attention, trying to keep his dignity. Ditka reaches down into the snow, and before I can even register what's happening, he grabs a rock, straightens back up, and smashes the private's face so hard that the front of his head caves in.

It seems like the private is still standing at attention, disobeying Ditka's will, maintaining what scrap of dignity he has left. Only the front of his brain has now been turned to pulp and there is no longer a 'he' to be left with anything.

The body falls to the ground.

Ditka turns to his men, holds the bloodied rock high above him and says, 'In my war, the penalty for disobedience is death.'

His men cheer and wave their weapons in the air.

My men and I are frozen, speechless.

I know we should leave, quickly get back to camp, and get away from him. Get away from all these men gone mad. But I can't.

'Ditka!' I yell.

He has turned and started off.

'Ditka!' I yell again.

He stops. They all stop and turn as if a single machine.

I look at him. I think about what I should say, and then I realize. What the fuck can I say?

He slowly, silently, walks toward me, his men not far behind.

Snow has started to fall. My men are behind me. The light is too dim to see Ditka's expression until he is right in my face.

We are staring each other down.

And that's the moment *they* hit us.

Shots from the darkness and then shouts from my men. Men falling around me. Men firing back into the night.

We scatter in all directions. I tumble behind some rocks. Our shouts, orders, screams, but other voices, too: muffled instructions in what might be Dari or Tajik. Our men are running, guns firing, bullets cracking through the air.

One moment I'm overwhelmed by the noise and fucking chaos, the next all seems silent, as if my brain can no longer process it all and desperately retreats into itself. I'm running, trying to find better cover, trying to get in with a group of my men, trying to find my platoon, yelling to my men to get down, to fire from the ground.

The chaos continues, falls off, then rises again. It is dark. I have lost my sense of time although it couldn't be more than minutes. Adrenaline and fatigue battle each other.

And then I finally start catching glimpses of them. The Taliban soldiers are moving at speeds that seem super-human, shots are fired and bodies whisked away before I can make sense of it. There are moments when I could swear they are flying. They leap into the air as if possessed. At times I look and think I see seventy-five or more of them, and other times I think there are no more than fifteen or twenty moving all around us.

I yell in my comm to whoever can hear. 'Stay down. They're all the fuck over the place.' But I think, *How the fuck did they have this many men right here in front of us?*

Some of the Taliban are hit and fall. Others come. More come. More than we can hold off.

I fall farther back, hoping to find a vantage point to regroup or find others still alive. Through the darkness I peer back and can just make out a Taliban stabbing one of our men. I shoot, hit him and he falls. I run low to our soldier and find him bathed in his own blood.

Fewer voices are now coming to me over the comm and although I can't always make out what they're saying, I hear pleading and calls for help.

I take shelter behind a low stone wall that must have been part of a farmhouse. I am freezing, drenched with sweat, panting loudly. I try to get my breathing under control and then wiggle forward and peer out around the corner. I can barely see through the snow and the darkness. The shots have become more infrequent and my first thought is that the fighting is dying down; my second thought is that's only because so many men have died.

For a moment, all is quiet. Then two short bursts of gunfire, and quiet again. I hear voices, whispers, strange laughter, in front of me, behind, I can't tell. I fall back to the ground behind the wall. I can't feel the ends of my fingertips and my lips are bleeding from being so dry. I lick the blood from them.

I whisper into my comm, trying again to reach my men, any of my men. There are only a few replies, disoriented, disjointed, desperate.

A scream, silence. A shot, silence. A burst of gunfire from one of us. Silence. Weakened shouts from all directions, then silence.

I come out through some trees and can just make out a man, forty, fifty feet away, crouching against a stunted tree. I think it's Williams, no sign of his gun.

I'm halfway to him when Williams spots me and yells, 'Captain, don't!'

Maybe I felt the sting. Maybe I heard the shot. Maybe I felt my leg burning.

The next thing I remember is waking up in a cave.

Maybe it was a house. I don't know.

For five days I am lost in fever. I think someone is caring for me. Somehow I was rescued. It would be days before I found out that everyone else had died except Williams and me. Every single soldier. Of the 193 who had gone north to Vod Am, only Williams and I had survived.

The Journal of
John Murakami Fox

October 22, London

'Not much reason to be there other than let the world know we can't be pushed around.' Alistair paused before completing his thought. 'Even if it is economically ruinous.'

I said, 'Not to mention the rather staggering loss of life.'

He waved his hand in the air, his cigarette creating swirls of smoke, the gesture saying, *When did that ever matter to us*?

It was my first visit back to London since late July. I had missed my nighttime talks with Alistair.

I said, 'And not a clue what was going on. Who are your friends. Who are your enemies. Not a clue about the culture. Not really.'

Alistair agreed and said, 'I have a theory about the Afghanis. Ever tell you this one?'

He had, but only once and it was so quirky, I was pleased to hear it again.

'You see, hospitality is one of the cornerstones of Afghani cultures. Note the plural, John. Always note the plural.'

I tipped my head to acknowledge his point.

'All of them, the Pashtuns, Tajiks, Uzbeks—'

'Hazaris, Balochis—'

'Nuristanis, Aimaqs, the whole lot. They may be violent, nasty buggers at times, but they are wonderful hosts.'

I will always remember a time I was travelling in Nuristan province with a driver and translator. Our car broke down and while the driver went to work, a family invited us into their house. Dirt poor. Literally: the floor of the house, like most in the countryside, was hard-packed dirt. They asked if we liked lamb. We said we did. And before we knew it they had slaughtered their only lamb, their treasure and their pride, simply to feed these guests in their home whom they owed nothing to, whom they expected nothing from, and whom they'd never see again.

At any rate, Alistair laid out his theory. He said, 'John, we send our soldiers into their country. There we are, in our red coats in one era or camouflage and helmets in another. They see this and say, "My goodness, our guests want us to provide them with a fight. What else can we do but give them what they want?"' With this, Alistair chuckled. 'It's all about hospitality.' He laughed again, amused by his own cleverness.

When he had wiped away his tears he continued. 'You know, there was almost no resistance when we went in. The Afghanis were clearly no match for our superior force.' He slowly mashed his cigarette into the ashtray.

'It's always been true that Afghanistan is much easier to enter than it is to leave,' I said.

'I believe it was I who first said that.' He looked up at me, his eyes lighting up.

'Yes, it was certainly true of the 1842 Anglo-Afghanistan War,' I said.

'That's precisely what I've been talking about, my friend. You didn't think I meant this infernal one, did you?'

I smiled.

'Oh,' he said, 'different excuses, different uniforms, and different types of idiocy. But, please, John, let us stay in the nineteenth century. This current century and this endless war really are too painful to discuss.'

When I assented, he smiled, but instead of continuing his nineteenth century diatribe, his face grew serious and I sensed what he'd been putting off saying since I arrived at his door. He said, 'Tanner's book. Your book. It's...'

He didn't complete his sentence, but I could hear his disappointment.

'The last chapter,' I said, 'it surprised you, too?'

'Is it the last?'

'I'm working on a concluding chapter to send to Tanner for approval. Williams dying; Tanner wounded, delusional, then rescued; and the army's cover-up.'

'So this was it? These were the revelations you got death threats over?'

I knew what he meant, and yet his words annoyed me. 'Alistair, there *is* a lot there, you know. A massacre of innocent women. The homicidal Captain Ditka. Army incompetence and cover-up. The inside story of perhaps the largest loss of US soldiers in a single battle since Vietnam.'

He waved a hand in dismissal. 'I was expecting more,' he said, his voice tired and sad.

I didn't say so, but so had I.

All those months ago in Charleston, Tanner had indeed recited a long, fairly coherent and convincing story to me. But like any verbal narrative, it rambled, repeated, backtracked, jumped ahead, and lapsed. Chapter by chapter, I'd worked hard and fast to turn our long interview into a book. When his rewrites and corrections came for each chapter, it took me days to work through all the things I had misunderstood or he'd forgotten to tell me or that I hadn't accurately depicted.

I had expected that by the time we got to the last chapter, he would have felt confident enough to open up, to truly account for this huge loss of life. Instead, he gave me two pages that barely explained how the Taliban rout of US forces could have been so complete.

'Well, at any rate,' said Alistair, calling me back to this story as if my book didn't deserve another word, 'our wars in Afghanistan made no sense. No strategic sense, no economic sense.'

'Alistair, I…'

'Come on, old boy, you tried. You came close.'

Half an hour later, just before he closed the door behind me, he said, 'Sad though. I thought we really had them this time.'

October 26, London

At first, a relief to be back in London. Already two dinners with Sandra and a play, *As You Like It*. I listen in a half daydream as she tells me about her classes, the book she is reading, the films she has recently seen. For the first time since she was a baby, I feel like a normal father. This could be a way to spend my days, I think, far from the adrenalin rush of the wars.

Today, a few perfunctory meetings with my longtime newspaper editor who said, in so many words, my days are numbered. Professionally speaking, that is. My kind just isn't needed any longer; even the august paper I do most of my UK work for has started printing the stories the army writes for the media.

And then tonight, I came home to find my apartment had been broken into. Laptop gone. Papers and various files taken. Drawers rifled. Luckily, I have everything backed up, including this journal, but I can't contain my fury and the intense feeling I've been violated.

I immediately phoned Alistair, telling him to make sure his windows were locked and his alarm turned on.

'What will they steal?' he said defiantly. 'My cognac? My pipe? My Mont Blanc? The photograph of my son?'

And there we had it. The thing most important to Alistair. Not simply a photograph, but the only photograph he had of his son as an adult.

The one who served in George Bush Sr.'s Gulf war in 1991 and was never the same afterwards. Sleeplessness, nightmares, long bouts of depression, unpredictable explosions of anger. Crying fits. Alcohol binges and drugs. The downward spiral finally coming to an end when he wandered in front of a passing truck in broad daylight.

October 27, London

'As I was starting to say the other night'—here Alistair tapped his pipe—'our succession of Afghan wars over the past hundred-and-eighty years has never made sense.'

'Did it ever make sense?' I asked, more to uphold my end of the conversation than to score a debating point. He knew this and ignored me.

'Much different from our conquest of India,' he continued. He examined his pipe. Scraped at the bowl. Thwacked it into the ashtray. 'Not that that excused us down there. But at least the India business followed some sort of perverted logic.'

And so, in his small living room that smelled of the leather of two grand old chairs, tobacco, brandy, and all those books, we put aside worries about the present. I momentarily forgot about the break-in and listened with pleasure to a history I had read about but whose intricacies I had never fully committed to memory. From the easy invasion of Afghanistan in

1838 to the massacre of 1842. The strange excesses of colonial warfare, in which the lowest officer was supposedly limited to ten servants but often had many times more. One general needed sixty camels to carry his personal effects, another two hundred and sixty. They filled their packs and chests with their best china, teas, cigars, port, furniture, uniforms, and tinned goods only to see it all disappear, along with their lives, three years later.

It was a mockery of a retreat, Alistair said. 'It was winter and we had to make it over the Khoord Kabul Pass, the Huft Kotul and the Jugdulluk Passes back to India. We had forty-five hundred soldiers and with them were twelve thousand others—wives and children, servants and whores. Akbar Khan played us like a master, delaying each stage with promises of protection. Our generals were divided, each with more hopeless ideas than the last. And wave upon wave of Ghilzais descended on us until no one was left.'

I ventured to say there was one survivor. At least I remembered some of my British military history.

'Ah yes, you're thinking of Brydon. William Brydon.'

'He was an army surgeon, if I recall.'

Alistair packed fragrant cherry tobacco into his pipe. Eventually he said, 'Not exactly. At the time, he was but an assistant surgeon with the East India Company. Remember, this was basically their show. Mercenaries of the empire.'

'A tradition the US has taken to new levels with all their contractors,' I said.

'Brydon is often depicted as the only one who made it out. There were a handful of others, of course.' Finally, he lit his pipe. 'And don't forget, some children and women were taken captive. Never recovered.'

'The blond-haired, blue-eyed people in the northern provinces?'

He said, 'Perhaps. But most of those likely trace back to another invasion of Afghanistan.' He waggled his pipe at me like a stern headmaster. 'Don't forget, John. This was where Alexander the Great discovered he wasn't so great after all.'

Later when I was leaving, I hesitated at his doorstep, glancing carefully up and down the darkened street, trying to spot someone sitting in a parked car or standing behind a tree.

'Anything the matter?' asked Alistair.

I shook my head.

'You're welcome to stay here for the night, if you like, old boy. I imagine these last days have taken their toll.'

I smiled at the offer; he was not usually the nurturing kind. He didn't have much experience at it. But then again, neither did I.

October 30, London

More stories of US veterans on the rampage and, now, a story of a gang of our veterans, in Bristol of all places. As always, I uploaded them to the website from my new laptop, then took a few minutes to leaf through the archives. Some postings were the expected bits of post-traumatic cruelty: barroom brawls, wife beatings, rape, murder. Others were new and bizarre: ex-soldiers organizing into gangs of drug dealers or small-time robbers hitting corner shops and petrol stations.

November 2, London

Sandra's all talk of hits and buzz. Tanner's and my e-book, although disappointing to Alistair and me, has done well. Our site is now quite the sensation. Over the past week, articles about the Vod Am Massacre have appeared across the Web and in major papers around the world. All the networks, from Al Jazeera to the BBC to the US cable stations, have done stories, and half of them have interviewed me.

So far, the army has refused to comment on Tanner's claim that Captain Ditka had murdered one of his own men and that the army's inability to get their men out of there or those soldiers' own exhaustion, faulty decision-making, and near civil war had led to the massacre.

Sandra is excited for me; her past scorn towards me seems to be at an all-time low. And although she's too polite to say so, assuming readers continue to download the book, I'll have the money to help her with the costs of university which, two months ago, I did not. So I say that to her and she beams with appreciation and relief.

I feel a sense of lightness, a pleasant glow that I have done my fatherly duty. But also a pleasant sense that I've gotten this story out, that I've managed to lift my voice above the downsizing and the outsourcing and the freelancing and the endless drivel that makes up most of what I do as a journalist.

Judith has received no fewer than twenty calls from agents representing studios, directors, and actors wanting to buy movie rights to the manuscript—all of which I've forwarded to Tanner without response.

It's all happened so fast.

But then I remember the death threats and the break-ins and the strange, all-knowing messages and I know I've stepped into a mess.

Later

I found myself jumping out from a tube carriage the second before the doors shut. Just to make sure I wasn't being followed.

I felt idiotic and was late for my appointment because the Metropolitan Line then suffered one of its interminable stoppages.

Meeting with the publisher of my principle UK gig. He, all ruffled up, dragged my editor and me onto the carpet. He had been visited this morning by a military attaché from the US embassy who informed him that one of his most prominent freelancers, me, is behind an oddly named website and a ghostwritten book that is attracting tremendous attention for printing terrible lies (although I interjected, 'or terrible secrets') about Britain's staunchest ally.

Since the cat was out of the bag, I admitted it was true. Yes, it was my website. My own editor, whom I've known for two decades, looked at me with astonishment, as if I were running a kiddie porn site. To my surprise, though, the publisher suddenly looked very pleased, hearing, apparently for the first time, about the e-book as well as the website. He appeared close to giddy just thinking about the publicity the paper will get out of this, including the nice touch that one of his longest-standing freelancers was getting death threats.

I asked if it would be possible to keep it all quiet, the website and death threat story, and he looked at me as if I were mad.

Later

I noticed two bearded men wearing round white caps loitering in the park across the street. I kept checking through the window until I felt like a complete idiot when their families met them and the men smiled with delight as they tossed their children in the air and warmly greeted their wives, who produced a picnic.

I wasn't foolish, I told myself. I knew about the US whistle-blowers dying in exile, and the hundreds of jailed or murdered journalists around the world. I had good reason to look over my shoulder.

Later

After dinner, Alistair rang me up and invited me over for a drink.

Our conversation meandered here and there. He asked, in several different ways, about my sanity. My old friend really is worried about me.

But we aren't ones to dwell on feelings and, each time, we quickly returned to our discussions of history and politics, past and present. At one point he said, as if still in the middle of last week's conversation, 'There was one thing I missed.'

'What's that?'

'Our man, William Brydon, the surgeon.'

I nodded. Sipped my single malt. Waited whilst Alistair re-filled his pipe and drew on it until satisfied with the burn and satisfied he was keeping up his old-fashioned image.

'Seems he kept showing up.'

'After he survived the '42 massacre?'

'In 1852 he was on hand when the British took Rangoon.'

'The Second Anglo-Burmese War?'

Alistair nodded. 'And then again in 1857, the Indian Mutiny. He was right at the heart of things in Lucknow, this time with his wife and children. Tens of thousands died. Not our

194

Brydon, who came through with flying colours. He had panache, that man did. Wouldn't doubt if he nursed a bit of a grudge against the wogs.'

He could see from my look that I found this expression offensive.

He said, 'His words, old boy. His words.'

.

November 4, London
Woken at 4 a.m. by a phone call.

A man's voice. Muffled and speaking in falsetto, so it was hard to pick out an accent of any sort. He said, 'We warned you.'

Later
Emailed short concluding chapter to Tanner. Words largely mine, so not sure what he'll think.

More important though, was my cover email: 'Tanner, is there something you haven't told me? If so, now's the time before it's too late.'

November 6, London
Email from Tanner that I should buy a throwaway SIM card and call him at the next of the list of numbers he'd given me.

Expected some debate about the draft chapter. Instead:

'Listen, John, there's more.'

'What do you mean?'

'I mean I didn't tell you everything when we got together.'

Long pause.

Tanner said, 'You still there?'

'What's that supposed to mean? That there's more?'

'I didn't tell you the actual ending. Something important

happened to me after the battle. Before they picked me up.'

'What exactly?'

'I've been writing it up.'

'Can't you just tell me?'

'It's complicated.'

'Why the hell didn't you tell me before?' I took a breath, trying to contain my fury. 'We're writing this book together. It's getting read in huge numbers.'

'Sorry,' he said, although he didn't sound sorry at all.

I waited for more.

Nothing.

'Well?'

'You'll have it tomorrow.'

November 7, London

Nothing comes.

Judith writes, 'Going crazy to get the final chapter.'

Judith rings me up to discuss the offers for movie rights.

Later she phones to say she'll auction the rights for the print book and movie rights the day after the final chapter appears. 'This is getting more buzz than you can imagine.'

Then why, Judith, do I feel a sense of dread?

November 8, London

New chapters come from Tanner.

Goddamn it to hell.

CHAPTER 10

Terrible pain woke me up. I thought I heard voices but I couldn't tell if they were in my head or around me. Then I focused on the pain blistering in my calf, which helped me remember where I had been, even if I didn't know where I was now.

I sat halfway up and stared down at my leg. I was still wearing my combat uniform, but someone had cut away part of the trouser leg so they could bandage it. I could move my toes and my foot; that was a relief. It was a neat bandage, put on by somebody who knew what they were doing.

I looked around. The old stone walls were roughly hewn. If the place wasn't centuries old, then the darkness made it seem like it was. It was musty and smoky. There was the slightest rank smell, like an old fireplace saturated with meaty grease smells too old and too deep to ever go away.

Next to a wooden door studded with heavy nails hung a lantern. A thin trail of smoke vented through cracks in the ceiling.

My whole body ached, like I'd been dragged across the countryside and dropped here. My head hurt. I found a large lump on the back of my head and I wondered if I'd been clubbed. I collapsed back down against the crude straw mattress and shut my eyes. It was cold, not quite cold enough to see my breath, but cold enough to be uncomfortable. Then I realized I was sweating. I touched my forehead. It was hot. Fever.

Later I tried to stand up, but the pain was intense and I slumped back down.

'Shit,' I said out loud.

'Captain, you awake?'

I rolled on my side and saw Williams leaning against the far wall, rubbing his eyes as if I'd just woken him.

'Jesus. Williams. You're alive.'

He smiled weakly and said, 'Hi, Captain.'

I asked where we were. He said he didn't know, and then, 'They've got me tied up, otherwise I'd move over there.'

When I told him I wasn't tied up, he said, 'I guess they figure you ain't going nowhere.'

I eventually found the energy to crawl over to him. We told each other what we remembered. Sitting next to him, my bad leg stretched out, I studied the small room. Near each of our mattresses were two buckets. One had water with a small plastic cup floating on top. It was pink. The other had a wooden top.

'Captain, you okay?'

'I'm fine,' I said, although I felt myself drifting away. 'Little weak... Anybody else...'

I woke up a little while later, or at least I think it was just a little while. I was still hot and had that floating, disoriented feeling that comes with a fever. I was sitting on my mattress and leaning against the wall. The cold from the stone seeped through my uniform and it felt soothing. Only then did I realize we were in a cave.

I opened my eyes. There was an Afghani in front of me, crouching in that legs-open sitting thing they do. He didn't move. He seemed to be studying me. There was now a second lamp in the room. The door was open.

I looked over at Williams but only made out a heap of blankets.

The man didn't blink and didn't look away. His look wasn't threatening. He was wearing the usual man-jammies, winter version, a wool scarf around his neck that covered part of his mouth, and a turban-like hat. He had the clear blue eyes, fair skin and chiseled features common in this part of Afghanistan. Another man came up behind him and set a plate of food down next to me. The man kneeling before me let the scarf fall down from his mouth and I could see his whole face. He smiled, just a slight smile, and I couldn't tell if his smile was kind or cruel or maybe both at the same time, like he was obligated by his tradition to treat me as an honored guest even if he was about to slaughter me.

He jutted his chin toward the food.

Even as their prisoner, I was their guest. It looked like goat and there was a piece of simple Afghan bread. The meat was cold but it tasted fresh. With this man's blue eyes staring at me, I ate, chewing carefully. I drank water with the pink plastic cup. I felt the frayed edges of the cup on my cracked lips. He nodded, as if affirming that he'd done his job as host and I was doing mine as guest. I finished the food and rubbed my hand across my mouth.

My fever had subsided a little, at least enough so that I could think straight. My leg still ached. I was cold and stiff. He was still watching me as I leaned my head back against the wall and closed my eyes. The act of eating had stripped me of energy. I thought I'd just shut my eyes for a second, but when I opened them again, the man was gone and the iron door was shut.

I had no idea if it was day or night. Though my head was still aching, leg still throbbing, I felt slightly stronger. Food must have done something for me. I managed to pull myself onto my knees and pissed into the bucket. I used the cup to pour some water into a cupped palm and did my best to wash my hands and face. The water was cold and I drank the rest of it in large gulps. I slumped back down, exhausted.

'Williams?'

'Captain. How you doing?'

'Okay.' I did my best to sound convincing. 'You?'

'Freezing my ass off. Still a little sore but I'm okay.'

'How long have we been here?'

'A day. Maybe day and a half. I think. No word about no one else.'

The squatting man was in front of me again. I tried to focus on him. This time I could see his whole face but he still wore the turban. Another plate of food. Looked to be the same as the last time but this time it was warm. He was smiling again: the same host smile. He was watching again: the same intelligent look in those clear blue eyes.

Then he spoke. At first I thought I was losing it, losing my mind. In perfect, British English, he said, 'Might we, Mr. Jackson, speak for a moment as gentlemen?'

He said, 'I know you would not breach your duty by disclosing anything, sir. We are both men of military training and tradition... At any rate, I know your name.' He tapped the name on my uniform. 'I can see your rank, and one or two of your men were kind enough to tell me the name of your company and regiment and what a terrible time you seem to have had.' Then he smiled. 'Although, of that, might I say I already had an inkling.'

He stood up and strolled over to Williams, looked down at

him without comment, and walked back.

As he neared me, he took off his turban and squatted in front of me again. He had dirty-blond hair, longish but well kept. Had I not seen other blonds up here, I would have taken him for British: the hair, the thin lips, the eyes—more gray than blue—the narrow jaw.

'If I may introduce myself: Captain Roger Pennyfield at your service.'

He gave me a second to react to this. I could see by the hint of a grin that he knew this was making no sense to me.

'Since I know how you came to be a guest in my cave… that is, one of my caves, Captain, and since you do not appear to be going anywhere soon, perhaps I might tell you how *I* came to be here. How all this'—he stretched out his hands in an exaggerated gesture—'came to be my abode.'

He paused.

Suddenly I felt very tired and hot again.

As I was drifting away, I heard him say, 'Not much to do in caves with so much time on one's hands. Tell stories, read stories, and plan how one's enemies shall die.'

My fever seemed to have abated a little. He was squatting in front of me again, staring at me. He moved his face closer to me. It was almost like he was smelling me.

'You know, Captain Jackson, the Soviets thought they could bomb the *mujahedeen* out of existence. You Americans ensured they would not. And then you thought that the hand that giveth could also be the hand that taketh away and you, too, thought you could bomb the *mujahedeen* out of existence.

'Is it that this country, with its poverty, simplicity, and backwardness, breeds such arrogance in all those who invade? Or is it perhaps your arrogance that leads you to invade? Whichever, none of you ever understands. Each century has given the world this lesson anew: First, to the British. Then, to the Soviets. Then NATO, then the Russians again, and then here you are again. A stadium blown up and you think all the blame is found here. I wonder who will be next to invade this country a century from now? The Chinese, perhaps. Or maybe India. I suspect I will still be here when they come.'

He tried to keep my gaze but I turned away.

'Oh, humor me, Captain. Two military men in a cave. Surely we might find some conversation to while away the time. Do people still read Chaucer?'

I didn't answer.

'I should like to think they still do. Surely a captain such as yourself knows of Chaucer's tales. So, might we, in like manner, think of ourselves as two of his pilgrims, amusing ourselves on our journey? It is a long way to walk in the snow if one has no tales to share.'

He seemed oblivious as to whether I took him seriously or if I spoke.

'My village vicar was a reasonably smart man, although influenced by the rigid dogma of our day. He thought the earth was but six thousand years old. This was a ludicrous claim even back then. We were early in Queen Victoria's reign, Captain. Some things we couldn't know. But isn't that always true? Some things, one just can't know. Trapped as we are within the vision, the narrow vision, that our position and culture afford us.'

He stood up and moved around. I felt I was watching a carefully staged performance. I made myself concentrate for a moment. I tried to look closely at his expressions, tried to ascertain if he really expected me to believe that he's been alive since Victorian times.

Then I closed my eyes and I felt myself drifting in and out of his monologue, in and out of this room in the cave, in and out of who I was and what had brought me here. I heard his voice but for a spell I no longer heard the words. For a while I couldn't concentrate beyond the pain in my calf.

I drifted back into the cave just as he said, 'We kill to live, just like you, Captain Jackson. But tell me, sir, what kind of life is left after you get used to killing?'

As he said this, it suddenly occurred to me that I hadn't heard Williams stir and I looked at the lump of bedclothes on his mattress.

'Williams,' I called out. 'Williams!'

'Don't worry, Captain, he's having a discussion with some of my men.' He shrugged. Spread out his hands. 'Do you understand the scope of this, sir? You and I are mere actors. Perhaps not even that. Mere props. We may not have aspired to such. I certainly did not, not by a long shot. They produce soldiers to carry out their particular designs. But, in the end, their responsibility is not to us. Perhaps it wasn't always so. Did you know that even Alexander the Great let his older Macedonian fighters go home after the war to have families?' His voice suddenly rose in fury. 'But what did Her Majesty's Army do to us? Tell, me Captain, do they treat you any better today?'

'Bring Williams back.'

'Tell me, Captain, and then I shall bring him back. How old do you judge me? Please. Humor me. One gentleman to another. One soldier to another.'

I turned my face away. I felt myself burning up.

'I am thirty-three—the age of Alexander the Great when he died. The age of Christ when he met his fate. Only I have been thirty-three years old for one hundred and eighty-eight years.'

I don't know when they brought Williams back. The lamp was out, darkness was total. I could hear him restlessly breathing, almost snoring.

Fever and exhaustion overtook me. I couldn't have told you if it had been Christ or Alexander crouching in front of me. I may have spoken to him, spoken to one of them, I don't know. I was desperately thirsty. I tried to reach for the water but I don't think the impulse even made it to my arm. But then I was drinking, the water wetter than water could possibly be.

I think maybe he was the one who put that water to my lips. I remember a hand holding my head. I remember how soothing it was.

My leg hurt like nothing I'd ever experienced. I thought, I need antibiotics or I'll lose my leg. I kept trying to convince myself that I would be fine.

'Williams,' I called out. It took all my energy to make my voice loud enough.

He answered me, feebly.

I said, 'You okay?'

'Yeah, I think.'

'Did they...?'

'No... Not too bad... I don't really remember what happened. I... I don't seem to have no energy.'

I forced myself to ask more. Into the dark, I said, 'Did you hear anything?'

'They speak that British English—sounds like a movie. Then they go into Pashto or Dari or whatever to talk to this one guy… There are a few others. Hostages or prisoners, like. In cells like ours but with bars instead of doors. But they're not any of our men. It was real quiet… I heard a radio… with that shortwave sound. The announcer said, "This is the BBC World Report."'

I don't think I said anything. I could hear Williams sitting up, moving.

'Shit,' he said, 'I feel so out of it.'

'Williams,' I said, trying to get him to focus.

'Thank God they didn't put the chain back on.'

'I need to know.'

I heard him crawl over to me.

'Williams, how many?'

'Maybe, five, maybe six. They didn't really ask me nothing about me. Nothing about our unit, our plans. Nothing. Didn't call me an infidel or videotape me or none of that shit they're supposed to do.' He spent the next few minutes rambling on like this.

Finally, I found the strength to interrupt him. Even pretty much out of it, I knew he was hiding something and I said that to him.

'So the weird thing is, Captain, all they asked about was you. Who you are. You know, family, if you have a wife, that stuff.'

When I came to, the man was squatting in front of me again.

'Ah, good day, Captain,' he said, as if he had been waiting

there for hours. 'So as I was saying,' and he launched into a long ramble about Genghis Khan, Alexander, some leaders I'd never heard of and some I had. 'All the greatest societies of their time. Are we seeing a pattern?' Then more rambling about the British Empire at the height of its glory: the East India Company its cream, and the British Army its crop— riding crop, that is.

Then he paused and walked back and forth, throwing out his arms like an old-style actor.

He squatted in front of me, as if wanting to make sure I was paying attention. 'Captain,' Williams called out. 'It's when he starts all this that—'

Before Williams could finish, my captor had leapt across the room and grabbed Williams, one hand around his neck, the other dug into his groin. Williams was gasping, I yelled, and then Pennyfield, or whoever he was, dropped Williams to the ground and gave him a kick so fast I almost missed the movement.

He calmly said, 'I hate to be interrupted.' His voice was both serene and sinister. He stood in front of me. I passed out.

'Are you with me now, Captain Jackson?' he said.

Every time I woke up he was there.

'Fever,' I said to him. It was the first time I spoke to him. 'My leg is infected. I need antibiotics.'

He stopped for a moment, moved his face closer to mine. Again, it felt like he was smelling me. He put his hand to my forehead. I pulled backward. He touched me again, this time resting a palm on my cheek.

'Yes. Perhaps we will do something about that, won't we? Wouldn't want you to spoil on us, would we now? And your wound is smelling. Not a good sign. We'll get someone to look at it.'

I no longer noticed any smells. Not the greasy mustiness of the cave, not the straw mattress or the wool, not my own stinking body, not my wound, not the shit in the buckets before they cleaned them out.

'So Captain, do you know anything about the 1842 Anglo-Afghan War?'

He waited, paused, as if he really thought I'd respond.

I imagined that if I could stay alert, stay focused, I could survive this. He waited, I nodded to say I was listening.

'You should have seen our troops when they were escaping. Thousands of the Queen's men. Some of the officers had wives. Some children. Some slaves and whores.

'Before we could leave—' He stopped, started again. 'Or, perhaps, by then, it would be more accurate to say, before *they* could leave, the Viceroy's head was impaled on the front door of his residence in downtown Kabul. It was a sight to see back then, Kabul that is. A city, capital of an empire, orderly, grand. I expect you've seen what it has become.

'How did the Viceroy, the very representative of the Empire, meet his well-deserved demise? The story was that an Afghan was sent to help the Viceroy and his family escape the marauding crowds. Instead, he was a spy who killed one and all. A bit of a mystery, actually.'

His eyes grew wider, brighter.

'The story my countrymen would tell at the end of their adventure here was patently and obviously false. Are you listening, Captain? It is very important you pay attention, particularly to this point. Do not trust the story that explains it all. But take it as a clue. A clue that you must keep digging.'

I had no idea what he was talking about.

He stood and walked to where Williams lay. He knew that would get my attention.

'It was the easiest thing in the world, Captain. By then I had let my beard grow to pass as one of them—my commanding officer had instructed me to do so. I spoke some Pashto, something which none of the Queen's men learned. I entered as if I belonged. They never suspected a thing.'

He crouched back in front of me. I could feel his breath, cold, without a smell. He stared in my eyes.

'I told him, of course, who I was and why I was killing him. But the truth was that the man I truly wanted was a surgeon, a chap named Mr. Brydon. He was the one who deserved to die.' He stopped as though considering this. He shrugged modestly and said, 'Perhaps none of you, when one comes to think of it, deserves to die. But I expect it is too late to have qualms about that. Mr. Brydon was the one who made us into'—he held his hands out, like an actor accepting his due—'into this.'

Some time later, I don't know how long, I woke up again to Williams calling me.

'Captain, there was a woman in here. I mean, she was like right here, looking at your wound.'

I asked if he could tell who she was. He said, 'I was pretending to sleep so I didn't really see her. She didn't talk or nothing, but they spoke to her in English. Then I heard her in the hall, getting all angry at them.'

I looked down at the new bandage. But the pain had only increased.

'She told them you need antibiotics, or...'

'Or what?'

'Well…'

'What?'

'Just that it won't be good for you. The head guy said you won't be around that long so to stop worrying.'

Of course I wanted to believe that the woman was Katherine.

Hours later, he was back.

'So, Captain, a little better after your nursemaid came? She does a fine job, doesn't she? I am thinking of keeping her around. She reminds me of someone from long ago.'

He was squatting before me again.

'She seemed most concerned about you.'

'Who is she?' I asked.

'But I was telling you about how pleasurable it was to kill the Viceroy, the very head of the British endeavor that brought me here.'

He stood and paced back and forth, three long strides in one direction, three long strides back.

'You may think this is monstrous that I should boast about cold-blooded murder. But please ask yourself how this is any different from your snipers on a rooftop? Or the pilot who fires missiles at a village? Or the drones you love using so much. Isn't cold-blooded killing what they—you and I and all our fellow soldiers—are trained for?

'But I digress. We were what you would now call an elite force. Looking back all these years, I choose to think we were the first modern soldiers, a century before our time. At any rate, we were absolutely singular. We had traveled by military steamer to Bombay, then overland to Afghanistan, kept apart from all the others. Brydon told only a very close few who—what—we were, and they kept us in suitable traveling conditions. Besides, it was cooler and more comfortable for us to travel at night. Of course, we didn't have your night vision glasses but then, again, we didn't need them. Eventually, the sun stopped bothering us, but in that first year it was very bad.'

I felt that disorientation that comes with a rising fever. I thought I was watching him steadily, but it was as if frames from a film were snipped out and I caught him on one side of our small room and then in a blink at the other.

I caught him saying 'Mr. Brydon.' And then, but not right away, 'An amazing man... even I should be generous enough to admit.' And then, 'When he was still in England, he heard talk of unexplained fatalities among returning sailors from the Royal Navy's West Africa Squadron. These men suffered every miserable disease the tropics could throw at them, but Brydon's genius was to notice something special.'

'What do you want from me?' I asked him, my voice barely audible.

Before he could answer, if he was going to answer, I felt my head spinning and he was wearing sailor's garb and the room swayed as if we were on the high seas. I closed my eyes and heard the crashing of waves and the shouts of deckhands. I willed myself to leave, to fall asleep, so I might dream of her.

Maybe it was the next day.

The first thing she whispered was, 'Don't let on you know me.'

Katherine was holding up my head, looking at my eyes as if examining me. Her hands, for a second, cured everything.

Even in my fever, I prayed this wasn't a dream.

I knew this wasn't a dream.

'Really you...'

'Don't talk. I'm okay.'

I glanced toward the door. One of my captor's soldiers was just outside.

In a normal voice she said, 'You were shot. The bullet went through your calf.'

'Who are they? Are they—'

'The problem is that it's badly infected. That's why you have a fever.'

'Who—'

Now in a whisper, she said, 'I don't know. They're obviously not Taliban. I'm in another room, about thirty steps to the left. They have me cooking food. To the right, beyond that is the entrance to the cave, but a man's always there.'

She unwrapped the bandage from my leg. The original wound was only a small hole on each side of my leg, where the bullet had entered and exited, but it was oozing pus, and a large patch around it was scarlet and so swollen that the red was shiny. The slight pressure of cloth against it felt like my skin was ripping off. I tried to stifle a groan.

'I've told them you need antibiotics.'

I whispered, 'We have to get out.'

She held up a small chip of a razor blade. She said, 'I have to cut open the wound and hope it will drain.' She held up a metal cup. 'This is warm salt water I'm going to pour on it.' She said, 'When I cut you open it's going to hurt like nothing you've ever imagined.'

I reached out to stop her. 'First promise you'll bring me a knife.'

She whispered, 'There's no way.'

'Bring me a knife. Next time you come, bring a knife.'

'They'll kill you, Tanner. You're not in any condition to—'

She stopped when the guard stepped into the room.

She said, 'I'm sorry,' and the razor chip cut into my inflamed flesh.

When I woke, Williams was with me, holding my hand.

I felt completely lucid for the first time in days. I told Williams that when she brought a knife I would kill the guard. I would go out first to kill the others. He would follow right behind with Katherine.

'Go to the right. Get her out of here,' I said.

'How will you get out?'

'Just get her out of here.'

'Captain, I—'

'That would be an order.'

CHAPTER 11

'Where is he?' I said, partly in confusion, partly in anger.

This time I was awake before my captor came in. This time I was waiting for him.

'Hardly a way to greet your host now, is it, Captain?'

'What have you done with him?' Williams had been gone when I woke up.

'You're hardly in a situation to be demanding.'

He lifted his eyebrows, as if to see if I had anything else to say. Then he continued.

'I was telling you about the vessel that sailed into Portsmouth harbor, sailors one and all returning home from Africa. It was sometime in November of 1839, a cold morning, but clear and dead still when the ship was sighted. It was early light and the captain of the port sensed something was awry. The ship appeared rudderless. The mainsails were down. No ensigns flew, no signals fluttered. Not a soul was spied on deck, yet they say it coasted toward the naval yard as if pushed by an unseen hand.

'Other sailors boarded her and found eighty-three men, all dead, pale and terribly gray as if they'd been bled to death. Her manifest said she had left the Gold Coast with eighty-five men. A young surgeon was rowed out and examined the bodies before they were removed and buried at sea.

'They left two unlucky sailors to guard the ship. And when the surgeon came back the next morning, these two were also dead. Apparently bled to death.

'This time our young surgeon asked for boats to be posted

around the ship, day and night. He stayed around the clock, for he had a hunch this might be more than a strange disease.

'On the second night, they spotted movement, swift movement on the deck. I expect you can figure out the rest, can't you, Captain?

'And so our good man Brydon, yes, the very same man who would later bring us to Afghanistan, brought four men out with him, men he could trust. They searched until they found them hiding in a dark room, these two infected men. They appeared healthy and certainly well fed. The light from the open door seemed to cause them great agony and they shrank backward, making them quite easily subdued.'

I didn't speak. But as mad as it was, I was listening to every word.

As if reading my thoughts, he said, 'It is very simple, Mr. Jackson. I want my victims to understand I am a victim too.

'Mr. Brydon was a man of science. There was much talk in those days about evolution. When I was at Cambridge, I read philosophy, but many of my friends were studying the natural sciences. There was a sense we were near a breakthrough in understanding how man had evolved. Some were even beginning to say this would allow us to perfect man. Mr. Brydon was apparently one such scientist.

'He carefully studied his prisoners. Their strengths, their weaknesses, their feeding habits. Let me assure you there was nothing supernatural. The prisoners could not defy gravity. When fed properly, they were very strong with tremendous stamina, but not superhuman. They were powerfully strong compared to even the strongest of soldiers and they could move extraordinarily fast—like sprinters, but over long distances—and yet, their metabolism was amazingly slow. So slow, conjectured Mr. Brydon, that they would age at one one-hundredth of the rate of other humans. They could be killed but it certainly wasn't easy. And, most wonderfully for his purposes, they were most alert, acutely alert, at night. They could see at night.

'Mr. Brydon was not only smart. He was a true believer that Britain was destined to rule the globe for generations to come. And what better way to do so than with a super-breed of fighting men?

'As a hobby, he had long bred pigeons, selecting their best qualities to obtain the most elaborate plumage. He decided to breed future soldiers in the same way. But his breeding attempts quickly proved disastrous. Many poor women died in the attempt.

'And then he had his moment of inspiration. He was vaccinating soldiers against the pox and thought perhaps he could do the same—but, this time, infect soldiers with this disease.

'There were ample test subjects in the prisons and the poorhouses. He went to work. It took him more than a year to succeed, that is, to properly isolate the viral agent, to get the dosage right, or perhaps simply to find a man who could survive the ordeal.

'It so happened that one night, there was a captain in the brig. Well educated. Promising but, unfortunately, he had gone AWOL. You see, the previous year he had brought a bride back from Jamaica. She was the daughter of a plantation owner and a slave, as beautiful a mix as the Lord makes on this earth. Our captain saw her and was mesmerized. Mind you, it was virtually unheard of for an Englishman, an officer, to marry a mulatto. But this young officer met her, fell in love, and managed to bring her back home.'

Pennyfield stopped, seemed to take my measure, and in a deliberately neutral voice, said, 'I believe you know the sort of exotic beauty I'm speaking of, Captain?'

In spite of the fever and the burning throb in my leg, I'm sure my reaction was painted on my face.

'They were back in England. He was stationed at Portsmouth and she, his wife, was pregnant. She lived twenty miles away in Chichester with his family. Our captain, no longer young, but a man of thirty-three, wanted to be there when his first child was born. He had no leave. So he left anyway. Four days later Her Majesty's soldiers found him sitting in his parents' house, his beautiful wife at his side, holding his son who was but days old. They dragged him from his house, his wife screaming, his son wailing, his mother terrified, his father cowed into silence. Back in Portsmouth, it was a nearly instant court martial and the brig.

'And there, I was selected by Mr. Brydon, in his fourteenth month of experimentation. There was no pain, just a scratch on my shoulder like the vaccination I had received for pox years before. They dumped me back into my cell, leaving me unaware of what was transpiring. Within hours, I felt a transformation rising within me as if the *me* I had always known was turning liquid and flowing away. Light burned my eyes. To even hold a limb out against natural light was to feel a fire burning me from the inside out. Unbearable pain. As if bursting into flame. But not a mark. Not a scratch. Just the most terrible pain.'

As he said those last words, Pennyfield unexpectedly dug his fingers into my injured calf so hard that I involuntarily screamed.

I woke to Katherine holding my hand. I smiled, weak, pathetic. She smiled. She helped me sit up and she gave me water and some food.

Williams was back on his mattress sleeping soundly.

'Kat, you have to bring me a knife. Today, tonight, whatever time it is. We can't wait.'

I told her that Williams and I had it worked out. That she should lead him to the door, follow him while I took care of Pennyfield's men.

'How will you get out?'

I did my best to smile. 'That's what soldiers do.'

Pennyfield was back.

'They observed me for a day. Shrinking away from the light, trying desperately to find absolute dark, even though my cell had no window to the outside and only a tiny slit in the door. And then night came. I felt my body come to life. As if I had woken from a thirty-three-year-long sleep. I felt strength and energy surging through me more intensely than when making love or charging against the enemy in battle.'

Pennyfield stood, walked across to Williams, who shrank backward, and then returned to his crouch in front of me.

'Mr. Brydon was there. My eyes were adjusting to the half dark. He explained what was happening. He explained what this disease was and what he was trying to achieve. He told me I would have fearsome strength, that I would see at night and live in terror of the day. That I would feed on blood.

'I was an intelligent and educated man. As you might imagine, I did not believe a single word he told me. I ridiculed him. I said, "There is nothing diseased about me. I've never been so healthy in all my life."

'Mr. Brydon placed a plate of food in front of me. I tried it. It was singularly disgusting. I spat it out. I accused him of bringing me rancid food. Brydon picked up a chicken leg and ate with gusto. Still I did not believe him.

'Brydon said, "Then if you will not be of service to your country, you may return home. I give you this opportunity. Now go. Be gone." I didn't move. Why should I believe I was being let out of prison? But the door was open, the guards were standing aside.

'Warily at first, I stood. I moved to the door and left my cell. I froze, waiting to be clubbed or shot. Nothing. Mr. Brydon led me past guards, through doors, down cold stone passageways to a gate at the side of the prison.

'"You may go," he said. "Take two days with your family." Brydon laughed. "Three or four if you would like."

'I started walking away. He reached out and stopped me, his voice sober, almost sad. "But heed my warning. You will be back very soon. Once you see what you've become."

'I was given a horse. I started at a walk, soon I was trotting, and by the time I reached the edge of Portsmouth on that cold, terrible night, I was flying in a canter. In less than two hours I was home. The house where I had grown up. The garden I had loved. It was January. I arrived at five in the morning and it was still very dark. But my beautiful woman was awake, wearing a white nightgown so pure I thought she was dressed in a cloud. She sat in the kitchen, the fire crackling, her nightgown pushed off her shoulders and our baby at her breast.

'She put our son down onto a fleece spread on the table. We fell into each other's arms and I knew I would never let her go, never let her out of my sight again. I had no time, and no desire, to explain the incredible story the surgeon had told me. We whispered sweet words and I told her I would never leave her again.

'I did not understand, you see. I did not know. I held her, I gazed at her, her shoulders, her soft neck, her uncovered breasts, her skin the color of cinnamon. She held me, moved to me, and I kissed her lips and her breasts and her neck and felt such fierce love and desire that I could not understand why her blood was on my lips and why her body was becoming lifeless in my shaking arms.

'And when I let her lifeless body fall to the ground, it was all I could do not to bring the young baby to my mouth.' Pennyfield cried out in anguish. 'My own flesh and blood!'

In his rage, he charged at the door, tore it from its hinges, and wrestled it into the hallway where I heard it slamming against the stone wall.

He returned, panting and breathless. He stood still and his whole body went calm.

He continued standing as he resumed his story, his voice raw. 'I didn't even remember I had a horse. Instead, I ran into the night, my body pumping with life in a way I'd never felt before. My life surging with the blood I had taken. I wandered, hid in a cellar for the day, disgusted, horrified by the blood that stained my clothes and, even more profoundly, stained my soul as no man's soul had ever been stained.

'The next night, when I could venture out again, I returned to Mr. Brydon. I planned to tear him to pieces. But as ill luck would have it, I arrived as the sun was rising. I should have hidden, biding my time, but they had been watching, waiting, and as I crumbled to the ground, they seized me.

'Brydon said, "I am sorry, I truly am. I did warn you but you didn't believe me." He shrugged. "Now you may serve your country. We will start with you and four others. You will serve your country as no men have ever served their country before.'"

Pennyfield stopped. He didn't speak for five minutes, maybe ten. At some point, I dozed off for a few moments. When I awoke, he was studying me.

I didn't mean to, but I laughed. Maybe it was the fever. Maybe I was going as mad as he was. Whatever it was, I laughed.

'It's a compelling story,' I said, 'but I know you don't expect me to believe it.'

Without saying anything, he lifted me up and threw me against the wall. I was holding my leg and struggling to breathe when he leaped over to Williams and snatched him up off the ground. Before Williams could raise his hands to defend himself, Pennyfield was tearing into his throat with his long fingernails and teeth.

I woke as one of Pennyfield's guards was half-carrying me, half-dragging me out of the cell. I didn't know that pain could ever be so bad. I did all that I could not to scream.

He dropped me onto another mattress. I didn't know what this move meant, but I was glad to be out of that tomb. I remembered Pennyfield's words. That he wanted his victims, at least some, to know the truth before they died.

Another one of Pennyfield's men brought me food. I ate the bread but was disgusted at the thought of eating.

I forced myself to sit up. For a moment, my head felt the clearest that it had in days.

Pennyfield entered. He was wearing a different shirt. He had washed. I wondered if I had imagined the entire story he told me.

His face solemn, he said, 'It is no longer revenge. It is our life.'

I said, 'Let her go. You have me. Do what you have to do. But let her go.'

'I believe she is fond of you.'

I didn't speak.

Pennyfield said, 'It is nothing to be ashamed of.'

'I'm not ashamed.' I took a deep breath and said, 'If any of what you told me is based on truth… If—'

'There is no *if*.'

'Then you know what it is to suffer. Leave her out of this.'

I was now sitting up, nearly standing, leaning toward him. I felt my brain clouding over, the pain returning in full force. I was shivering with cold.

Pennyfield said, 'So, you propose I let her live?' He gave the tiniest of smiles and left the room without another word.

Less than a minute later he was back. He had Katherine by the arm. He pushed her into the room toward me.

This time, she wrapped her arms around me, held me, kissed my face, told me she loved me, that she would always love me. For me to remember that she would always love me. And then Pennyfield snatched her away, just like that.

In the half-light, in the half-life, half-death state I was in, I feasted on her with my eyes. She was ragged and dirty but she was the most beautiful creature I had ever seen.

And then the fever rose again like a massive wave. I tried to focus, to think, but I could not. They were standing, staring at me. Pennyfield, observing me with his cold, silent eyes, Katherine… what was it she was trying to tell me? The noise of the crashing wave I imagined in my head was deafening. In my fever, in my delirium, I felt I was on a beach and I saw a knife washed onto the sand and I thought, how could I be so stupid? All her sudden hugs and kisses: she had been slipping me the knife. I slowly reached behind me, sure that I would feel the blade at my fingers. But there was nothing. I reached around again. Nothing. There was no knife. I twisted and turned like a mad man looking for a knife that wasn't there.

And then my moment of confusion was over.

I stopped and looked up at Pennyfield. Katherine was now avoiding my eyes.

'Tell him,' he said to her.

She mumbled something I could not hear.

Pennyfield shouted, 'Tell him.'

She couldn't look at me when she said, 'They're letting you go.'

My head was swirling again. Burning up.

I spoke, or I think I spoke. I think I said, 'They're letting *us* go? Don't you mean *us*?'

Now she looked at me, tears streaming down her face. 'They're letting *you* go, Tanner.'

She broke free of Pennyfield and ran to me. 'Tanner,' she cried in my ear. 'Go where we planned. In a year. I'll find you. I'll do whatever I can to find you.'

Pennyfield pulled her away.

'No. No. No,' I shouted at them until I couldn't call out any more.

She said, 'It was the only way.'

The next memories are vague. The *thump-thump-thump* of helicopter blades. Medics hovering. My eyes opening, closing, opening. The long flight, uncomfortable, a hospital, the pain, being moved, the longer flight, sleep, my leg on fire, more sleep. Finally waking up in a hospital. Ramstein. Then unsettling sleep.

I slowly emerged from the fog. A large room. Pale green walls, four beds, all empty but mine. End of a hall, no one passes by. They kept coming into my room. Surgeons deciding whether to amputate my leg. Starting physical therapy once they decide they can save it. A woman shrink trying to get me to talk about the trauma. I start telling her what happened, then intel arrives and I realize I need to forget. I know what will happen if I don't.

And then the medical discharge. They push me out into this world. Where we all get forgotten. The ones who manage to fit back in. The ones cast off like Cody, never to be seen. The ones the rest of you choose not to see. And the ones even worse off. The ones waiting to explode.

For a few months, I pretend to remember nothing. But I remember everything. I remember it all. I remember all my men killed in battle and many of Ditka's too. I remember Williams in the cave. And Pennyfield. And Katherine.

The Journal of
John Murakami Fox

November 8 (cont'd), London

'John,' said Alistair, 'I doubt I will read this any more quickly with you staring at me.'

I continued to stare.

I could swear he was reading slowly on purpose. Finally, he said, 'What is he after, do you suppose?'

'What's he after?' I responded, anger and sarcasm in my voice. 'He's either lost it completely or he somehow thinks we'll publish this shit and sales will go wild.'

'That is not a bad idea, by the way. But I am not sure that is it.'

I stared at Alistair for a moment. His look was calm and serious—his professorial, hypothesis-creating look. I was ready to throw my laptop across the room.

'You said you did not think he was crazy,' Alistair said. 'Up until now, all the rest has been clear, logical, the story of a good soldier told by a good soldier.'

'No, he didn't seem crazy. Quite the contrary, he's articulate and thoughtful,' I said.

Alistair fumbled with his pipe, then cleaned it and filled it.

'And he has done his homework,' he said. 'He has got the history right. Quite fascinating really.'

He lit his pipe, puffed at it, then gazed at the glowing bowl of tobacco.

I stared at him, angry at him for taking this so lightly, angry at myself for trusting Tanner. Angry for getting so absolutely taken. Or better yet, downright snookered.

'What is he after?' Alistair repeated.

I couldn't control my frustration. 'What's he after? How should I know? Fame? Money?'

'Again, perhaps not a bad idea in his position. No doubt sales could go quite wild with this vampire rubbish.'

I glared at him.

'But what is he hiding?' Alistair continued, as if prompting a group of graduate students rather than asking me directly. 'You see, on the one hand I want to say that he has had you, my boy. That he has gotten the hang of our book club. But that does not ring true.'

He took another puff of his pipe and continued.

'Could the whole story be rubbish?' Alistair asked, again in his pondering voice. 'Is Tanner not who he says he is? Did he make the whole thing up? We have to consider that possibility.'

'Why all the efforts by the spooks to scare me then? Why try to suppress a story that's absolute bollocks?'

'Maybe he knows more than he's told you so far. I have to say, I don't believe he's just playing with you in the spirit of our book club. There has to be something more to the story, John. Perhaps Tanner is not who he says he is.'

His curious smile faded. It seemed the longest time before he spoke again. His look turned serious, even dour.

'You know, John, I had such hopes for this book. I have been disappointed so many times. I truly do not believe these people will ever be held accountable for the things they do, whether it's what happened to my son thirty-seven years ago or last year at Vod Am. The victors not only tell their own story as the truth, they can crush anything and anyone that doesn't fit their lies. More often they simply ignore those of us who try to tell anything resembling the truth. And that's the worst, is it not? They watch us fade into an oblivion they have forced upon us.'

November 8-10, London & Hanoi

'What the fuck is this?' Judith screamed so loudly that I had to hold the phone away from my ear.

'We've been had.'

'You didn't write this?'

'Obviously not.'

'Does your *co-author*'—this was the first time she had referred to him as anything but your *captain* or *Tanner*—'actually believe that he met a vampire? A goddam army of them?'

'He never actually says Pennyfield was a vampire.'

'Fine, he only *pretends* he's a vampire.' She sighed theatrically. 'John, we're marketing this as a non-fiction memoir. Which, last time I checked, is supposed to be based on fact.'

'It all *is* true... Up until now.' I try to sound calm, but I knew if this were to be published, my reputation would be scorched.

'He told this to you in an interview and you patiently listened?'

'He told me the story up to the cave.'

'And you believe this?'

'Of course I don't believe this.'

'And now what does he say?'

'He doesn't answer my emails.'

'Now isn't that convenient. You need to find him.'

'I've been trying.'

'Try harder.'

'I'm leaving for the airport in ten minutes.'

I was on my way to Hanoi. 'I'll call when I get in.'

'I'll be asleep.'

'Then tomorrow.'

'This was going so well, John.'

'Except for the death threats.'

'That's precisely why we know it was going so well.'

Later

Flight delayed three hours leaving Heathrow. I can't sit still. I send emails to various friends. I try to find a book in the pathetic duty-free cubicle trying to pass as a bookstore. I phone Sandra and ask her if there is anything unusual on the website, but she says, 'Like what?'

I attempt to read. I wander around, feeling trapped in the crowds. A woman stares at me for the longest time. It's plain she recognizes me but then apparently loses the nerve to ask me if I am who she thinks I am. I loathe that I would have vehemently denied it if she had asked.

Finally we board the plane. I'm about to turn off my phone when a text arrives from Judith: 'I've showed it to a few people. Everyone loves it.'

I fired a text back: 'I couldn't care less. Do not share it with anyone else! I'll find Tanner and get it sorted out.'

In Dubai, it's a mad dash to my connecting flight.

On the plane, sweating from the run and the stress of almost missing my flight, I quickly check messages before yet another flight attendant pounces on me.

From Judith—apparently working late in her Brooklyn of-

227

fice: 'They're going crazy! Editors at Penguin Random House, Time/HarperCollins, and KFC-Fox. Will start taking offers tomorrow for the print edition.'

To Judith: 'I'll send you the real final chapter in the next four days. Do NOT show that chapter to anyone else.'

Interminable flight to Hanoi. Sadly, no longer have Wi-Fi access on the plane since Flight 6428.

Power outage at airport. No mobile reception.

Wait forever for luggage being carried into the terminal by hand. Stop waiting for luggage when I'm the only one left and it becomes clear my suitcase is lost.

Finally reach my hotel twenty-eight hours after leaving flat in London.

Hotel on generator power. Internet not working. A hotel staff member tells me, looking to the ground, 'That's what happens when we try to stand up to the big brothers in China.' Still no mobile reception.

Nothing to do but sleep.

When I woke the next morning, the power had returned.

Thirty-eight hours out of contact. Thirty emails from colleagues and friends; endless emails from the rest of the world.

Judith: 'Have you been kidnapped? Need to talk.'

My editor at the UK paper that buys a lot of my stuff: 'Are you mad?'

My daughter: 'Daddy. So cool!'

Cool? I thought. And calling me Daddy? But my stomach was sinking.

Another email from Judith: 'Changed my mind about last chapter. It's fantastic!'

Trying not to panic, I clicked onto Judith's e-book site. She had gone live with the new ending—the story of Pennyfield, Katherine, and the cave.

When I reached her, the first thing she said was, 'I knew you'd change your mind.'

'Of course I didn't.'

'You should. It's spectacular.'

'It's shit.'

She laughed. 'We usually only dream of these moments of success, John.'

'You had no right to put it up without my permission. You know that it's utter—'

'Read your contract.'

'It says I provide *content*.' I said this with derision. 'But I have copyright and I decide what I'm submitting for publication.'

'You submitted it.'

'I sent it so you would know what was happening.'

'My lawyer would call that a submission.'

'Take it down.'

'It says that once you send content to me, I will have full discretion over whether and when it goes live.'

'Take it down.'

'You signed it.'

'Judith, you have to take it down.'

'Have you seen the *Times*? Hang on.'

A few seconds later an email popped up in my inbox with a link to the *New York Times*. Judith said, 'The review will be in their print edition in the morning. Call me back when you've read it.'

I waited for the page to load, with the seconds seeming like minutes as I imagined the worst.

I skimmed the text: '…instantly being hailed… daring integration of fiction into non-fiction… suggests that a bizarre vampire story is no less absurd than our never-ending wars around the globe… clearly a metaphor for…'

I phoned Judith back, but didn't speak.

'Listen, John. I've been on the phone all afternoon. Everyone wants to interview you. The e-networks want you. People love this. Our system almost crashed from the e-book downloads. It's a madhouse here. Publishers are badgering me, the movie people are banging down my door. It's been years since we had an instant hit like this.'

I hung up.

I had work to do. I was in Hanoi for two interviews: one was paid work, and one for my own sake. The paid interview was with Shuk Fan Wong, the sole surviving leader of '2020 Democracy Now'. I'd met her three times before, once at her home in Guangzhou back in the teens, once in Beijing, and again after she was in exile. Her novels carry layers of political meaning—she had told me during an earlier interview that the only thing that had saved her whilst the trade union and student leaders, the journalists and academics, the lawyers, teachers and doctors, and other writers and artists were being rounded up was that she wrote very popular fiction. I was asked the week before by *The Guardian* to interview her in Hanoi, where she had lived in exile for nearly four years.

There were signs that the younger generation in China was bringing the Democracy Now movement back to life. Everyone wanted to hear Wong's take on it. Two other journalists waited ahead of me in the lobby of her apartment building in a fashionable corner of Hai Ba Trung in Hanoi. Book sales or Western governments, or both, apparently, kept her comfortable, and the Vietnamese government provided protection; there were two sentries outside her building and one in the lobby who eyed the three of us with suspicion. True to form, she was thoughtful and well informed of the trends and mood inside China. Her apartment smelled of jasmine and sandalwood and had a spectacular view of the city that kept distracting me.

Then there was my second interview. Amber Hayes. Amber was a Canadian journalist, a few years my senior, someone I had looked up to when I started my war corresponding. She had pursued the Drone Files case some six years back, got access to classified documents, and been forced into exile by the US under the Permanent Security Act, with the connivance of the Canadian government.

Her apartment was a shock after Wong's. It was above a fried noodle shop and looked onto a busy road. I had trouble hearing Amber's soft voice with the noise of trucks roaring by just yards away. I tried to look sympathetic but I kept thinking that the smell of frying oil would never come off me.

I asked her about the sequence of events leading up to her decision to go into exile. She must have thought me absolutely naïve as she watched my reaction. Phone calls late at night. Would-be bombs left in her apartment. Being tailed.

She had gotten used to writing copy for *Timeout Hanoi* and taking tourists on walking tours. What she hadn't gotten used to, she told me, was watching both her parents age and pass away while following it all from afar by Skype.

When I got back to my hotel, I quickly wrote up the interview with Wong and sent it to the *Guardian*. I didn't write up my interview with Amber. I had no place to send it, after all, and I didn't want to think about it. Instead I went down to the hotel pool, where all I wanted to do was float on my back and stare at the hazy sky.

I would soon be financially secure for the first time in my life. I could return to London for good, write whatever I want; Sandra would not be in debt because of her university costs. I could be the father I'd never been able to be. Only thing, rather important really, was that a story that implicated vampires in the Vod Am massacre had just gone viral with my name on it. And more important: with every chapter I wrote, I was getting the exact same threats that had led to Amber's pitiful life in exile.

November 13-17, Los Angeles and New York

At Judith's insistence I flew from Hanoi to Los Angeles for an appearance on a talk show. I didn't claim the part in the cave was true, only that this was the story told to me by a veteran calling himself Tanner Jackson. Next, I met with one of the producers who is gunning for movie rights and who wanted to shake my hand or something. He was a character straight out of his own movies, Cohiba and all. 'You've got to meet—' he said and reeled off a few A-list actors.

Then off to NYC for more media—by which time I had perfected my lines about the chapter in the cave being a metaphor to deconstruct the modern experience of endless warfare and the turning of men into killing machines. Then meetings with Judith to look at the draft contract for the book's print version.

I had acquired the fame I once thought I wanted more than anything. But what I really felt was that everyone was missing the real point of the book. It was an exposé, not a metaphor. Heads were supposed to roll, not explode with delight at how clever we were.

In all this, not a word from Tanner.

But no more threatening emails. Not a single one since the day after the vampire story appeared. My luggage no longer disappeared. My hotel rooms weren't searched. I don't think I was being followed. Then at last I received an anonymous email. *Hello Mr. Fox. We are very pleased you decided to cooperate. A wise move.*

And then there was the statement given by a US military spokesperson at one of her daily briefings. She laughed off a question about the veracity of the book: 'The US government has a firm policy neither to confirm nor deny vampire tales.' But when pressed about the account of the Vod Am Massacre, she would say nothing other than it had been the nation's greatest military tragedy in many decades and the US military wasn't amused, nor were the families of those killed, when anyone made light of it.

November 21, London

Alistair held up his cognac snifter in a toast. 'And now you may live the life of a gentleman.'

'Alistair, I'm fifty-four. I have no desire to...' My voice trailed off.

'Live like me?'

I shrugged and took another sip of his cognac.

'No sign of Tanner?'

I shook my head.

'Any fresh ideas?'

I told him about the anonymous email. I told him how

strangely unsettling it was *not* to feel watched.

Alistair said, 'It's somehow like that old joke about not wanting to be a member of any club that would have you.'

'They won, didn't they?' I said.

'Perhaps for now. But there has to be more. Whoever he is, Tanner knows more.'

November 22, London

It was four in the afternoon and I had two hours before I was to meet Sandra for dinner. It was almost dark. It was cold and wet.

I had been thinking again about Tanner's story of the cave. About Roger Pennyfield. I remembered Alistair's words the previous night. I remembered earlier in the month when he said that Tanner had done his homework, that he had got his history right.

Perhaps it was time for me to do more homework.

I looked up the hours of the Royal Victorian Military Museum and Archives. In its day, the Empire had a bureaucracy second to none; anything worth doing was worth recording on paper. Lists and orders and cables and reports abounded, everything saved for the files.

I arrived at 4:40. The commissionaire told me the building would close in twenty minutes. He pointed toward a hallway and said I was looking for the third door on the left.

The worn wooden floor creaked under my shoes. The air smelled of leather and dust. I heard the murmur of voices and the commissionaire cough. I went through the third door.

The woman behind the counter appeared old enough to have known Queen Victoria. Her sparse hair was pulled back into such a tight bun it strained her face. She tilted her head like a bird when I approached, as if a visitor were an odd thing.

'We are closing,' she said.

I gave her my best smile and my very best look of contrition. But what I said was, 'I'm sorry I'm so late. I'm writing a book, you see, on the Anglo-Afghan War of 1842.' She nodded. I said, 'My editor asked me to confirm the name of a young captain. I've tried searching online all day and couldn't find anything. And then I remembered this wonderful museum and archives.'

She said, 'Couldn't this wait until tomorrow?'

I said, 'You know how the Americans are. Everything done by yesterday. Everything must be online by first thing tomorrow and all that. Please,' I said.

She huffed, but was now listening. I gave her the name, explaining that Captain Roger Pennyfield had served in Jamaica and then was stationed in Portsmouth. I believed he had been in the Anglo-Afghan War in 1842, although I wasn't certain.

'This is no simple matter, young man.' She looked again at her watch. 'Especially at this late hour.' I smiled, patiently, hopefully, beseechingly. And then, like a conspirator, she winked. 'But I do love a good search.'

I followed her as she bustled from one room to another. I offered to help as she pulled massive volumes from shelves, but she shooed me away. She opened file boxes. I sneezed. She told me to step away.

'So far, out of luck,' she said. 'No such man served in the 1842 Afghan War.'

Strangely, perhaps, this was a relief. Not that I would have believed Tanner's story.

She glanced at her watch. 'We *do* close in five minutes…

But there is one more source I would like to examine.'

She ducked around another stack of shelves. I let my eyes drift along a row of leather-bound volumes, the old leather and cardboard starting to disintegrate.

She called to me, and when I rounded the corner she had a small volume braced against a shelf. A bony finger pointed at a page. 'And here is your Captain Pennyfield. Third Field Regiment Royal Artillery based in Portsmouth. Before that, the First West India Regiment.'

I started to read over her shoulder but she bristled at my proximity. She cleared her throat. Carried the volume to a table and let me read.

There it was: Roger Pennyfield was born 1808, attended Cambridge, wed one Rowena Crawford (daughter of Colonel Raymond Crawford; no mother listed). Rowena Crawford died in January 1841, the same year that Pennyfield is listed as dead. They were survived by a son.

'You see,' the woman said in triumph, 'he wasn't in the war after all.'

I walked in a daze down the hallway. Why would Tanner go to this much trouble to uncover such an obscure bit of history for a fabricated story? But for a second I let myself imagine Pennyfield's voice and I let myself wonder if any of it were true. My thoughts were interrupted inside the front entrance, where the elderly commissionaire asked if I were Mr. Fox. Before I could react properly, he continued. 'Sir, a gentleman was inquiring, and I told him exactly where he might find you. But he asked me to tell you he'll be catching up with you very soon.'

I had told no one I was coming here.

December 10, London

Had my first phone meeting with the acquiring editor in New York for the print edition. I explained that this book was not like my previous works, in which I'd interviewed sources and searched through contemporary and historical records. This was a memoir—Tanner's story. Some of the editor's questions were about the factuality of the text. Yes, I said, all the events checked out as best as I could uncover. No, there were no comments from the Pentagon because they had refused interviews as soon as I told them I was writing about Vod Am. Yes, names had been changed.

Why did Tanner write that ending? she asked. I said there were different ways to interpret it. She asked how I interpreted it. I said, truthfully, that I did not know.

And then she asked, 'What happened to Katherine? In real life, that is.'

I told her I had tracked down the story of a woman named Katherine Drewery—apparently nothing Sri Lankan about her. Nurse practitioner. Graduate of UNC. Lost in the field in northern Afghanistan almost a year ago. Presumed kidnapped, although could have died in an accident. Presumed dead.

I had even phoned her parents. When I said who I was and what I was writing about, her mother said, 'We do not want to talk about this. We have nothing to say. Please do not phone us again.'

January 15, London

I was being interviewed by a young writer from the *London Review of Books*, who was asking the familiar questions about the e-book and our decision to have a fictional last chapter. I had become very good at dissembling, if not outright lying.

Would we be changing anything for the print edition? I said he'd have to wait to see—although, I thought, it was actually I doing the waiting, that is, to hear from Tanner.

But then he shifted. He said, 'But what really interests me is not that, although it was ballsy, because it isn't the most important part of the book, is it?'

Startled to hear someone finally articulate what I'd been feeling, I said it was refreshing to hear that. No, the book was not meant to entertain, it was meant to expose the monstrosity of our wars in general and uncover one particularly horrendous incident.

And then he asked a question that sent me scrambling.

'The massacre. It hardly seems possible. Not as you described it.'

'Why?'

'It would soon be dark,' he said. 'They were exhausted, lacking food and rest. Far more dangerous to be out on patrol than at their camp. Why not just sleep the night and go out the next morning?'

'They were going out for only an hour. Jackson was trying to cool out Ditka. And he pretty much admits his own judgment was flawed by this point.'

'Point taken, but they were attacked right away.'

'No. It was half an hour, forty minutes later. Tanner was about to turn back.'

'Night or day, snow or no snow, how is it possible for a small Taliban force to defeat and kill two hundred of some of the best trained, best armed soldiers in the world? And leave only one or two survivors?'

'They knew the terrain. It was a large scale ambush. And it was lethal.'

'But—'

'And when Ditka killed his own man, their attention was turned against each other. The Taliban got the jump on them.'

'But—'

'With respect, how many battles have you observed? Have you ever been to Afghanistan?'

And yet, despite all my glib answers, I was disturbed by his questions for the rest of the day.

If there had been so much friction between Tanner and Ditka, what were they all doing together on the other side of the village? Tanner had made it clear they no longer patrolled together and, besides, a patrol wouldn't consist of over two hundred men. Tanner hadn't mentioned anything that would bring the two companies together. Yes, their men were getting picked off, but there was no suggestion of a major gathering of Taliban forces of the size that would have been able to carry out a massacre of that magnitude, nothing that would have lured them together to the far side of the village.

That evening, I reread our account of the Vod Am massacre. A few unanswered questions, but nothing impossible.

I started rereading Tanner's vampire tale. This time one paragraph struck me: Pennyfield says to him, 'The story they told at the end of their adventure was patently and obviously false. Are you listening, Captain? It is very important you pay attention, particularly to this point. Do not trust the story that explains it all. But take it as a clue. A clue that you must keep digging to find.'

These words seemed so familiar, plagiarized even, like I'd heard them or read them elsewhere. I put various word strings into my search engine, but it brought up nothing at all.

January 16, London

I wandered along the Embankment. It's way too warm for January.

Are you listening? Pay attention.

In Charleston, walking with Tanner on that long afternoon. 'Are you listening, Mr. Fox?' he had asked at one point. 'Pay attention,' he had said.

The same words that Tanner had put into Roger Penny-field's mouth.

I rushed to the Westminster tube stop. Slammed my Oyster card onto the turnstile. Ran through the heavily armoured station and impatiently waited. Jammed into a crowded car. Half ran all the way home from the station.

I booted my computer and accessed my recorded interviews with Tanner. Fast forwarded, stopped, listened, fast forwarded, stopped, listened. Two hours later, I'd made it to the end. Nothing.

I rewound to the walk in Charleston. Started again.

This time found it within twenty minutes, just as I remembered. Tanner's words to me were almost exactly the same as ones he'd given Pennyfield.

'The story the Pentagon told was obviously false. Fox, are you listening?… It's real important you pay attention. Particularly to this point. Okay?'

I said okay.

'There's not going to be a story that explains it all. Anyone tries, just take it as a clue.'

'For what?' I said. 'A clue for what exactly?'

'To keep digging.'

January 19, Washington, D.C. and Baltimore

In the queue in the arrivals line in Washington I worried I would be yanked from the line, locked in a small room for—what were Homeland Security now allowed? Two days? Four? How long did they hold the Wikifreedom 5 before they were charged?

The clean-faced Homeland Security official ran my biometrics. He seemed to hesitate a few seconds too long. I forced myself to remain calm. When he finally said, 'Welcome to the United States,' I smiled.

Now that I was in I wondered if I would get out.

There was a fluttering of snow on Interstate 95 to Baltimore. It seemed a tease because this winter, unlike last year's, was far warmer than it should have been.

The bar hadn't changed: the same smell, the same dirt, the same competing fogs of depression and desperation.

Two of the guys I'd met before were there. The white guy with the angry tattoos running up his arms and the quiet black guy. They were drinking and staring like zombies at the television.

I stood in front of the table.

They looked up, maybe recognition dawning, maybe not. They turned back to the TV.

I sat down.

'Sorry to hear about Cody,' I said.

They didn't speak. They didn't look at me.

'I'm the journalist who was in here back in April.'

'We know.' It was the white guy.

'I wrote a book.'

'We know that too.'

'Listen, I need to get in touch with Tanner again.'

'I thought you wrote a book with him.'

'I did. But he's gone now.'

White man shrugged.

'Something else happened in Vod Am. Worse than what we wrote, I think.'

The black man spoke. 'Definitely worse than what you wrote. But they won't let you tell it, will they?'

I started to speak, then shut my mouth. In another place or time, his voice would have seemed like that of someone mentally ill, either schizophrenic or paranoid or both.

The white man said, 'If Tanner's gone, means he don't want to be found. They don't take kindly to soldiers who talk too much, know what I mean?'

January 20, Charleston

I rented a car at the Charleston airport, an oversized monster SUV that used a tank of petrol just getting out of the parking lot. It was disturbing and comforting to be in the South again. Even after The Storms and The Spill, it was still its old self, stuck in its own time and proud of it. Trucks with Confederate flags painted on the side or draped in a window. Kudzu swallowing up trees, telephone poles, and dilapidated houses. Oversized people. Friendliest convenience store worker on the planet when I stopped to ask for directions. In the city, there was an overripe smell in the air coming from the Charleston Bay.

I checked into the same hotel and found an Internet café to see if there were any emails to the new account I set up last night in Baltimore.

Whilst still up there, I had logged into the usual vet-blogs, then left messages asking about the Captain. I asked new questions about Vod Am, not saying who I was. Sent texts to all the numbers the Captain had ever given me. Phoned an Air Force colonel, whom I'd once helped get out of a minor jam when he was stationed in Bagram. Said I was still researching the Vod Am massacre. Asked if he could set me up with someone to interview.

'Can't help you.' He didn't use my name and hung up without saying goodbye.

The only email was from some poor veteran who asked if I could help him find his family.

I walked the same streets I had walked with Tanner, feeling foolish that I'd even come here. When I'd met him here back in April, it was clear he'd ridden his motorcycle a long way. It makes sense that he wouldn't have invited me to meet him near where he was living. And I didn't think I would find him hanging out here: his final email to me said he was out of the country and there was no reason to think he was lying. But maybe he had known someone here; maybe that's why he met me here.

I wandered through parks, hoping to find some men who might be veterans. I didn't imagine there'd be women among them, but when I finally found a group, there was one, looking as pissed off and blanked out as the men she was with.

I was tired and had turned into an old graveyard in hopes of finding a bench and the quiet company of the long dead. Wind-worn gravestones, their inscriptions lost to time, and Spanish moss hanging from trees with tangles of crepe myrtle and wild rose now brown for the winter. Even The Storms couldn't wipe these out.

Three men and a woman had taken over a small patch of mossy grass. Two were talking quietly. One wore a battered

US Air Force flight jacket. Another was sleeping, his head on the woman's lap; she was stroking his head and staring at the sky.

The two talkers clammed up when I approached. The woman ignored me.

I asked if they'd been in Afghanistan.

They asked why I wanted to know.

I said I was a journalist.

'You're a Brit,' one of them said.

'I wrote a book about the Vod Am massacre.'

The woman turned her eyes to me.

'My name is Fox.'

The woman spoke, her voice almost childlike. 'I heard of ya.'

'I wrote it with a captain, Tanner Jackson. He's disappeared. I'm trying to find him again.'

They spoke to each other quietly.

The woman said to me, 'We don't think he's from 'round here.'

I asked if there was anyone I could talk to who might know him.

She gave me the name of a bar.

I ate lunch and then returned to the Internet café. Finally, I forced myself to go to the bar.

With Wild West perfection, heads at one of the tables popped up and eyes glared at me and, seeing nothing interesting, turned away. The floor was sticky. The air smelled of fried food and bodies that had consumed too much alcohol and taken too few showers. Two televisions pounded out competing sporting events. The bartender, who looked as if he snacked on steroids, was wearing a DeathTorrent T-shirt, although he looked more country than heavy metal.

I slid onto a stool at the bar. It took the bartender a while, but he finally made it to me. He didn't ask me what I wanted, just stood there and waited for me to speak.

I ordered a beer from the tap.

I swiveled halfway and examined the room. White, African-American, Hispanic men, worn out T-shirts, jeans, cowboy boots, half-shredded work boots, and the one hostile group of white men wearing combat boots all shined up as if to show they meant business. Their hair was military short and they had an aggressive look.

The bartender filled a plastic pitcher with beer and carried it to their table. They talked softly for a few minutes before he returned.

He polished glasses with a grimy dishtowel and finally returned to face me. He said, 'Some of my customers are wondering who the hell you are.'

I started to speak, but he interrupted me. 'Let me put that different. Some of my customers are wondering if you're some kind of cop. Maybe NSA.'

'Do I look like a cop?'

'How about you should answer my question.'

'I'm a journalist. From England. I co-wrote a book about the Vod Am massacre.'

The bartender returned to his cleaning. He eventually made it back to the nasty-boy table. He spoke to them and they all turned and looked at me. One of them called out, 'Seen any vampires lately?'

I didn't think it was the time to talk about deconstructing the modern experience of endless warfare; they had a point.

The bartender filled a half-pint glass and put it in front of me although I hadn't asked for a refill.

'You probably shouldn't hang around here too long.'

'I'm trying to find Tanner. The captain in the book. My co-writer.'

'You lost your partner?' he said, his voice mocking me.

'He's disappeared. I need to find him. There was more to the story he told me. I'm worried about him.'

'Vampire story just don't make sense, does it?' he said.

'You read it?'

He shook his head. 'But folks been talking about it so much it doesn't seem I really need to.'

'You a veteran?'

He looked me hard in the eyes. He nodded.

Only when I acknowledged this by nodding back did he speak. 'Word was he was through here. Staying low. Never talked to no one, or if he did, they stayed quiet.'

'Anyone here who—'

'You didn't pay for the drink.'

I put a twenty down on the bar. He put my change onto the bar then continued his chores. He replaced a couple of the beer coasters along the bar. The one nearest me was upside down. He'd written a phone number on it.

On his next pass near me, he said, 'This guy might know. Text him, don't call, right? Say the bartender told you. Be vague, you know what I mean? If he comes in, I'll tell him you were here.'

I slid from the stool, thanked him, and started walking away.

'Hey,' he said harshly. I stopped and turned slowly around. He jutted his head toward the bar. 'Take your change.'

Later

I sent a text to the number.

Then I returned to the hotel and asked the young woman at reception if there was a bookstore in town. She gawked at me as if I'd asked if there was a zoo with dinosaurs. 'Books?' she said. 'I think they sell them at Walmart.'

She returned towing the manager, who told me he thought there might be a used bookstore on Broad Street. I went there and bought a ragged old copy of *Heart of Darkness*, which I hadn't read since school, and returned to my room to read.

Text came through: 'Can't help.'

Later

Judith sent me the final sales numbers for her online edition. Said the final payments to Tanner and me should have gone through by now. The book was now offline until the print edition appeared.

I called Sandra. She asked when I'd be coming home. I said I hoped it would be soon, and that when I came back, it was going to be for good.

I said, rather brusquely, 'Listen, I have to run, but let's talk very soon.' It was her suggested code.

Normally my cold tone would have been expected between us. But for the first time in many years, I think she really wanted to talk to me and I to her.

Thirty minutes later I was at an Internet café, a different one than before, and I presumed she was too. I followed the instructions she'd given me before I left London and found myself on an obscure chat site, the two of us using fake names to speak to each other. I knew she was good at all this, but I still worried that I could be endangering her, not to mention helping any government agency that might want to find Tanner.

I chose words carefully and explained my problem: no way to find the captain.

I typed: 'I phoned his banks. They hung up on me.'

'No idea where he went?'

'One or two wild guesses. Doesn't really help.'

'No contacts where u r?'

'Apparently not.'

'So all u know r the banks?'

'And account numbers.' He'd given me those to give to Judith back when I first met him, although I was sure by now those accounts were only pass-through accounts.

She said she'd talk to a few people.

I wrote back: 'Careful.'

'Tomorrow. 9 a.m. your time.'

January 21, Charleston

I awoke early feeling an alcohol- and jet-lag-induced dread. Had that sensation of not recognizing the room I woke up in and not remembering for a few seconds where I was. Knew that just about anyone could figure that one out from credit cards, rental car, airline manifests. Started feeling a reality-induced dread.

The story was still swirling on the Net, now being stoked by a steady dribble of news. The studio that bought movie rights had just signed some young director whose first movie had appeared as fifteen-second Twitter feeds. The print edition was being rushed for the mid-summer. Our own website was being followed in the mainstream and social media.

Lots happening, but luckily no threatening messages. Or,

perhaps, strange that there were no threatening messages.

No one breaking into my hotel room. No one following me.

Perhaps that only meant they were being careful not to spook me. Perhaps they wanted me to lead them to Tanner. Or perhaps no one really cared anymore.

Or perhaps it meant I was just getting paranoid all over again.

Later
Sandra: U have his account numbers, right?
Me: Yes.
Sandra: When u do a transfer into his account, u can include a 99- character message.
Me: You sure?
Sandra: Daddy!
Me: Listen—if you ever don't hear from me for 3 days, take down the site.
Sandra: Drama queen.
Me: I'm serious. Take it down. Dump the domain. Wipe out your hard drive if it has anything about the site.
Sandra: I told u it doesn't.

A pause before my response.
Me: I love you.
Sandra: Drama queen… Love u 2.

I love you. Words I hadn't heard in a very long time. Words I hadn't said since she was a child when I was still reading her bedtime stories and we both lived in the same house.

Later
Finally found a combination that was less than 99 characters: 'Paid attention. Didn't trust story that explained all. Need the

real ending. I'm here where we met.'

I found another Internet café. Logged into a small, anonymous offshore bank account that a respectable lawyer I had dated for a few months had once set up for me in the Jersey Islands. 'Just in case,' she had said. 'In case what?' 'Who knows,' she had answered.

I transferred ten pounds from that account to Tanner's with my 99-character message.

January 22-27, Charleston

I try to kill time. I read books. I get disgusted with the news feeds. I try to see how long I can go without reading them. My record was four waking hours. I make it to four and a half.

I visit the old slave market. I take a drive to a nearby beach. Dolphins used to swim here. Sign says, 'Toxic: No swimming.' I can't recall if it's residual nuclear from the Tupelo incident or if it's chemical. I remember those old *Simpsons* episodes when the villain would throw the victim in the toxic mix, but now the villains seem everywhere and we've all been tossed into the stew.

I imagine there will come a time in my life when I want the days to drag on in slow, syrupy seconds that never seem to pass. But now I'm just bored out of my skull. And afraid that I'll never find Tanner again. That the true story will never come out. And that my illustrious career will end with the story of Roger Pennyfield.

January 28, Charleston

I drank too much again last night and my sluggish head took forever to register the knocking at my door. I fumbled for the bedside light. More knocking. My knees were sore as I stumbled to the door, rubbing my eyes.

I was barely thinking when I opened the door, and my heart skipped a beat when I saw a man standing there. Central or South Asian. Afghan. Involuntarily I lurched backwards and started shutting the door when I realized he was wearing the hotel uniform.

I forced a smile. I noticed a large manila envelope in his hand.

'This came for you, sir.'

I tipped him and closed the door.

I slipped on my clothes and ran down the stairs to the front desk.

'This envelope was just delivered to me.'

'Yes sir,' said the clean-cut young man behind the counter.

'Did you see who brought it here?'

'Yes sir.'

'And?'

'I don't know. A guy. Jus' kinda average.'

'Medium height, you mean?'

He nodded.

'What colour was his hair?'

'Black, curly-ish.'

Not Tanner.

'Tattoos?'

'Bunches.'

Definitely not Tanner.

'When did he drop it off?'

'Oh, 'bout five this morning. But he told me to wait until later to give it to you.'

I returned to my room.

I remembered the package left in my apartment in Islamabad. Rooms had been blown apart with smaller envelopes.

I weighed it in my hand. I ran my hand over it to see if I felt any wires or bulges. I tore a small opening along one edge and I saw a sheaf of paper, perhaps twenty sheets in all.

I ripped it open and read.

THE VOD AM MASSACRE

Time is frozen. It seems like the private is still standing at attention, disobeying Ditka's order, maintaining what smidgeon of dignity he has left. Only the front of his brain has now been turned to pulp and there is no longer a 'he' to be left with anything.

The body falls to the ground.

Ditka turns to his men, holds the bloodied rock high in the air, and says, 'In my war, the penalty for disobedience is death.'

His men cheer and wave their weapons in the air.

My men and I are frozen, stunned.

I know I should say something, challenge Ditka, arrest him, threaten him.

But I turn and lead my men away.

If I hadn't turned away, perhaps I could have stopped him. But it isn't only Ditka. It is all his men. Every moment we are near them is another moment closer to a battle between us.

It's pitch black when we make it back to base. Maybe because we're all exhausted or maybe because we're still stunned from having seen Ditka kill one of his men, it takes a moment to make sense of what's hanging from the makeshift flagpole at the main 'gate.' It's Shortwave's head. After the fight in which he killed one of Ditka's men, we had left two men to guard him. Today, though, we had left him unguarded when we went out for this final patrol. I had thought since we were helping find Ditka's men that Shortwave would be safe.

I'm tired and confused and my first thought is that Shortwave left camp and was killed and the Taliban left his head here.

As I think this, one of Ditka's sentries greets us with a friendly, 'Evening, soldiers. Welcome home.' And then he looks at the swinging head as if we could have missed it. He says, 'Seem to have a bit of a situation here. A real shame.'

His voice is rattlesnake junior to Ditka's senior.

He says, 'You're late, Captain. This is Bravo's night on sentry.' He grins at his two buddies, who have Afghan scarves tied around their heads.

'What the fuck happened to Shortwave?' I shout.

'Can't say I know, Captain,' Ditka's man responds calmly. I can't tell if he sounds slightly drugged or just sounds like Ditka. 'Our guess is, he went out after you on patrol and enemy got him. It's a scary place up here.'

My men look at me to gauge how to react. Anger and sadness cloud their faces. My finger is on the trigger of my weapon. I take down Shortwave's head and, trying not to think what I have in my hands, I put it down on the snow and cover it.

I gather my men. I tell them to keep their weapons ready and keep a watch on the perimeter of our base but to wait for my command. I tell them not to talk to the few Alpha sentries or to anyone from Alpha if they come back. I tell them there will be no reprisals.

I go to the comm tent to call Bagram, to tell them that Ditka and his men have gone totally feral, that we're all going crazy, that they'd better get us the hell out of here whatever it takes. But Rodriguez arrived before me and he is standing, back to me, shoulders slumped, looking down.

He moves aside to let me see.

All the equipment in the comm tent has been destroyed.

I dig into a bag where I left my computer; it too has been smashed. Rodriguez races back to his tent, where he dropped his gear. The satphone has been destroyed.

I send men to the Strykers. There too, the antennae have been torn off and the equipment inside has been savaged.

I don't even bother to ask if any of them have satphones with battery power left. I know those are long gone. Everyone has their weapons drawn like they're going to be attacked any second.

I gather my remaining officers and NCOs. I can feel the ripples of fear and anger, madness and desperation, traveling back and forth among them. All of them look exhausted.

'We're leaving before first light of morning. Pack all the rations that are ours, dry clothing, ammo, first aid, and leave behind anything you don't absolutely need. Post two sentries at each tent while the others pack.'

Williams has been with me the whole time and when the others leave, he gives me a look that shows he knows what I'm thinking.

Keeping his weapon at the ready, he moves closer.

I stare at the camp for movement. I stare trying to understand that this once was a base, that we once had a common mission, that even with all the tension with Ditka, we were the same army.

Now, in the dark night sky, no stars showing, nothing but a few lights from our tents, I feel desperate and desolate.

Finally I speak. 'I wish there was another way.'

We were going to walk to Madud in the morning.

On the way here it took us a day to drive from Madud, but we were walking for half of that and a lot of time was spent trying to find places for the vehicles to cross. We'll walk back in a day and a half, maybe even one long day. We'll be away from Ditka and his men. By then the weather will clear and they will get us out. And if not, we'll get what food we can in Madud and keep walking to Feyzabad.

We're packing up to leave before the sun comes up. Rodriguez is trying to pull out parts to make a radio, but Ditka's men have done a thorough job. My men look like zombies, no sleep, cold as shit, sleeping and patrolling in the same clothes for weeks, no showers, no shaving. When I so much as dip into a tent, they almost jump—except half are too tired to jump. I tell them they need to sleep. For those who still have working batteries for their helmet comm and NVD, I tell them we're not going to collect them but for them to take their batteries from their helmets and sleep with them inside their sleeping bags so they'll stay as warm as possible. Williams organizes a sentry outside of each tent and they do short, sixty-minute shifts. We'll be up at 0500. We will leave at 0515. I tell them we don't want a sound. They can eat, cough, piss, and shit when we get the fuck away from here.

I can't sleep. I listen for the return of Ditka and his men. I pray they'll return so tired they won't take notice of us. I pray they won't return. I keep seeing Ditka smashing the head of his own man as the rest of his men cheer. They don't train us for this shit; this is not what we came here to do.

Then my mind goes from rehearsing the morning departure to sheer torment about Katherine. I send her messages in my head that all will be fine, that I will find her, that she will survive. The kidnappers only want ransom. That they won't hurt her... I try to find comfort in words that even I don't believe.

At 0430, I go outside to clear my head. Williams is instantly beside me, his weapon in hand. He whispers, 'I heard you get up.'

I nod.

'Any sign of Ditka?' I ask him.

He shakes his head.

We go to our sentries closer to the gate. They tell us Ditka's sentries left and they haven't seen a sign of them and that none of Ditka's men have returned. This may not be a good thing, for they were south of here and might still be along the route we'll be taking to Madud. The last thing I want to do is run into them.

I remember Ditka torturing that boy in their latrine. I whisper to Williams that there's something I need to check. Our guns ready, our flashlights pointing, we go into their latrine tent. It's a gruesome, horrific sight and our flashlights madly flick back and forth. There are bodies. Four of them. Three on the ground and one on top of the shitbox. That one is headless.

The bodies on the ground have frost all over—as if the moisture from piss and breath has condensed on them. From his boots—which is all the clothes he is wearing—I can see that one of them is an Afghani soldier, and I can make out enough of his face to know it's the translator. The one I forced into silence as I helped that boy escape. The one I had promised I'd protect.

Another is an Afghan man. Old and naked except for the scarf stuffed into his mouth. He's missing all his fingers and the frozen stumps are raw and black.

The last is a woman. Young, naked, black hair, frosted. For a second I think it's Katherine, but of course it's not. This woman is not much more than a girl.

There is no time to bury them, no time to cover them. Not even time for Williams and me to bow our heads, but I'm so tired and my brain is so fried that, even in the midst of this horror and even with my heart pounding like mad, I fight an urge to close my eyes and sleep.

We're just out of the tent when I whisper, 'Wake 'em. We're getting the hell out of here now.'

Packs on, weapons ready, the men line up in silence at the gate. They know what's at stake. Whispering, Williams and I count off the men. We started with a hundred and eight: Our eighty-eight from Bravo, eighteen Stryker commanders and gunners, two translators. We've lost O'Keefe; we've lost Whitby, Pencilhead, and Malcolm, we lost Shortwave. It takes two tries, but we miraculously account for everyone.

Two men, both with bad frostbite, are being carried. Three others are supported by comrades.

My original plan had been simple. Madud is south along the river. It's the same track that we drove up on and that we walked along the evening before looking for Ditka's lost men. At least for the first hour, it won't be a problem to find since the snow is packed down. After that, depending on how far and how often Alpha Company has traveled the trail, it might be harder to find, but we have our snowshoes and it doesn't really matter if we are over a field or a trail. We'll make it just fine.

Fine, except that Alpha Company hasn't yet returned. They

probably stayed south of the camp since that's where their men were when they were picked off. And it stands to reason that if we head along the river we'll run into them, either coming back or still out there searching up all the gullies. We leave the camp.

We walk as quietly as possible until we're well away from the camp. I pull my four platoon leaders plus Williams aside. They should know what I'm thinking.

'We're about to make the walk to Madud longer, much more difficult, and much more dangerous. Williams and I found three villagers lynched in the latrine tent. We all saw what Ditka did to his own man. They destroyed the comm gear. I don't know what's in his head, but we're not staying around to find out. And we have Taliban nearby.'

I tell them that going north is not an option—we have no idea how far the trail goes or if eventually we'll be able to make it across the mountains to Tajikistan. There is only one way. We will go through the village and take the trail that heads west, up higher into the mountains, and then, eventually, circle back to the river several hours south of here. It is possible we'll still run into Ditka.

The snow will be deeper, the track more dangerous. It will add at least a day to our journey. None of them asks about the one thing we don't know: is this path going to take us closer to these elusive Taliban we've been chasing?

We set off through the village, then we pass the small farms and scattered huts. It's deadly quiet, and this unusual quiet is made eerie because I'm seeing it all in the green glow of the night vision device.

We stop at the last of the sparse trees beyond the last of the huts. My men finally get their breakfast, the last of our MREs eaten standing or sitting on their packs. Their platoon leaders brief them about what we think lies ahead.

As we eat, the sky begins to grow light. It will be some time before the sun rises and even longer before it reaches us in the valley. But the wind has stopped; we've gone from bone-chilling cold to bearable cold. It is still too dark to see whether the sky is clearing, but there are no stars so I don't have much hope.

We set off again, now able to shed our NVDs, at least those of the men who still have working batteries. The land here, on the powerful flanks of towering mountains, is desolate. There is a great weight under us, all around us. As it grows lighter, features begin to emerge—strange rock formations, frozen waterfalls, snow blown into dunes.

Some of the men are now talking softly. Williams comes up beside me. 'You got something else on your mind?' he says.

I ask him if he remembers Katherine from the NGO meetings.

He says, 'She the one you went to Cambodia with?'

I don't bother asking how he knows.

'Yeah, her.'

'She the one who phoned you?… Rodriguez told me.'

Without saying much, I tell him I knew her back home, that we were together and that she was part of the humanitarian group that was likely kidnapped.

He nods; he knows I don't want to talk about it.

After dawn, we hit the first patches of fog. We push forward. There are stretches where the wind has blown the snow away and it's almost bare rock and dirt. Other stretches where the snow is deep and we need our snowshoes. Most of the time

I don't have a clue if we're on the actual path. But we fan out, and occasionally, where the snow has cleared, someone will see what looks like frozen animal tracks or human footprints made when the road was muddy.

We've been steadily climbing. The valley has narrowed appreciably and is starting to feel like one of the gullies we've been searching up and down for the past few weeks. With every step, it feels like we're walking into the innards of the mountain. The patches of fog get thicker as we climb.

We no longer see the trail—maybe it's there under the snow, but who knows if we've lost it and are just randomly wandering up the mountainside.

In mid-morning, we reach a landslide. Sometime after our maps were drawn and the latest satellite images shot for this remote, non-militarized part of Afghanistan, a portion of this mountain crashed down on itself. It's a broad field of jagged boulders. It would be difficult to cross in the summer; with the snow, ice, and heavy packs to throw off our balance, it will be almost impossible.

I ask Lieutenant Quinn of 1st Platoon to send a team across. Somewhere in the midst of the anxiety and numbness, I register our smooth-functioning chain of command as a fire team goes out. It gives me a momentary sense of comfort. After all these men have been through, they're functioning like professionals and I'm proud of them.

When they return an hour later, they report they made it to the far side of the mountain slide, but there, the mountain rose steeply and there was no sign of any way through. We might pick up the track we're on, but we might also get lost high in the mountains.

There's no option. We turn back.

I feel the spirits of my men sink. We'll have spent the better part of the day getting colder and more tired. Unless we spot a trail that we somehow missed, we're going to be right back where we started, right back with Ditka and his men.

I pull all the men together. I say it sucks. I tell them we'll get through this.

We make good time returning. A hundred and three men beat a pretty good trail in the snow and we don't have to search for the path. Even as the fog grows heavier, you just have to watch the man in front of you, he watches the man in front of him. The one at the front watches for the boot prints and compressed snow.

By the time we reach the first of the trees outside the village it is mid-afternoon. The sun has been covered by clouds all day, but I'm certain it has already slipped behind the mountains and it won't be long before it starts getting dark. The fog has become a thick wall around us. Trees have ghostly limbs, clumps of soldiers appear and disappear.

We hear voices, at first indistinct, tenuous.

I don't think it's the villagers. We're not near enough and there are too many voices. The villages we've just gone through have several dozen residents at most. And they don't sound right. I can't make out a word they're saying, or even what language they're speaking. The fog seems to distort everything.

We hear shouts and murmurs, strange laughter and moans, and the fog tosses the sound all around us so there's no way to tell whether it's coming from off to the left or right or from someone who's about to tap me on the shoulder. Or stick a knife in my back.

Only a third of us still have communications through our helmets. I give the hand signal to halt—and it takes longer than it should to register because visibility is poor and the signal must be relayed back. Our column has become ragged so I tell the platoon leaders to get their men back into their squads.

'Quiet,' I whisper. 'Everybody silent.' The sounds of their movement and whispers are muffled by the snow and fog.

I whisper and the message gets passed along: 'Fourth Platoon, flank left, a hundred meters. Third Platoon, flank right, a hundred meters. Second, you guys hold position until I say move. First, you're with me. Take it real slow. Careful.'

The voices continue. I think we're moving in their direction, but they seem to pop up and disappear, like they're swirling around us. Voices without words; words without bodies.

Slowly we move forward, weapons ready, alert: blind men in the fog.

I hear a cry, off to my right, I think.

'Fourth Platoon, report,' I say into my comm.

No response.

'Fourth Platoon, do you copy?'

Vince's voice comes on, desperate, confused, baffled. 'I don't know where they came from.'

Nothing more. I try to reach him. Nothing.

Then I hear JoJo from 4th. 'I can't see but—' and his voice cuts out.

'Jenner! Fourth Platoon!' I yell. 'What happened to Vince and JoJo? Find them.'

Now I think I see the first of the tiny stone houses of Vod Am, but they're indistinct shapes in the fog, squares amid the tangle of the trees.

I pull my HQ platoon and 1st into a huddle. 'Williams. Salsa.' I stop and look around for a third and spot Salsa's best friend out here. 'You too, V-Man. With me. The rest, stay right here. Together. We're checking out those trees.'

As we take the first steps, I hear movement, maybe footsteps crunching in the snow. I reach over, touch both of them to get their attention, and motion for them to follow me.

There's someone there, I'm certain. I know it can't be any of my men.

'Stop,' I yell in Tajik. 'Come out, hands up.'

Nothing.

'Who's that?' I yell in English.

The snow begins, wet snow, heavy clumps in the middle of this fog and it's like a wall of white in front of me. I can barely see beyond the men at my sides and the trees are shape-shifting under each gust. Suddenly I hear not just one person in the snow but dozens.

The four of us hit the ground and maneuver our way behind a tree. Over the comm, I whisper to the other platoons that we have possible contact with *hajjis*. Today that's what they are to me.

We see the ends of their rifles first. Williams and Salsa are looking at me like they want to know if they should open fire. My heart is pounding so hard I could swear anyone within a mile can hear me. Before another second passes, there's a mini swirl of the fog and I see it's Alpha Company.

'Ditka! Alpha! It's Bravo, hold your fire,' I yell.

Ditka's men continue moving. Finally, they drop to the ground and two of them fire at us.

Over the comm I yell at my men, 'Bravo, hold your fire.'

'Ditka,' I scream, holding my head down. 'Hold your fire!'

Ditka's voice booms through the fog. Now it is clear. 'Where do you think you can run, Jackson? Didn't I tell you what we do to deserters?'

Before I can respond, Salsa calls from behind.

'Captain.' It sounds like he's hurt.

'What?'

'It's...' his voice sounds like a little boy's.

I look behind me. V-Man is splayed on his back, his heavy pack underneath him. His face, what's left of it, is a mess of blood. He's not moving.

'What the fuck?' I yell as I stand up.

I'm very aware of my gun as I walk toward Ditka and his men.

'Who fired?' I yell, now looking at Ditka. 'Get your fucking gun off me.'

All of Ditka's men are now standing, rifles ready.

'Who the hell fired?' I say again, now just fifty feet away from Ditka and his men.

I hear Salsa crying in agony. I glance back, he's on his knees, slamming his hands into the snow next to V-Man, crying out, 'No. No. No. No.'

Ditka and his men remain motionless, their rifles still at the ready. I can barely see him through the fog.

A bank of fog is moving in again and Ditka's men are getting swallowed up.

From behind, Salsa's rhythmic cries have quickly changed from agony to fury, the *no*'s are getting louder, turning into a strange, visceral growl. My eyes are locked on Ditka, although he is disappearing into the fog. Behind me I hear sounds and sense movement, but before I can react, Salsa has charged past me and is running at Ditka, screaming, 'You motherfuckers!'

'Salsa, stop!'

But it's too late.

Ditka opens up on him and instinctively I dive behind the tree and to the ground.

'Take cover,' I yell to my men, but the fog is now thick again, providing its own cover and confusion and leaving us all disoriented. Shots are coming from both sides, bullets are whizzing overhead.

'Bravo, this is friendly fire!' I scream out loud. 'Hold your fire. Stay down. Repeat: Hold your fire.'

The firing intensifies.

The next seconds seem like hours.

I hear shots and screams, some coming over my comm, some echoing through the fog. I hear men running in the snow or across patches of hard ground. I hear a rooster and a dog. The fog appears and disappears and I catch sight of men down, blood on the snow, and I'm yelling into my comm and yelling for both sides to hold their fire.

I'm running, trying to get in with a group of my men, trying to find my platoon, yelling to my men to get down, stay low, and hold their fire, but men are lost in the fog and the snow. And I now realize it's growing darker and soon it will be even harder to make out who is who and what is what.

The firing jolts me every time it stops and starts again. I don't know if my men are to the left or right of me, in front or behind, and I don't know where Ditka's men are either, or maybe all of them are mixed together.

I'm moving from tree to tree, trying to find my men. Out of one hut burst two soldiers from Alpha Company. They're firing as they fly from the door and I throw myself behind a wall. I don't want to shoot at them.

I see two more of my men fall and I slump back down in anger and disgust and sorrow but mostly confusion. I haven't been trained to order my men to fire on our own troops. There has to be a way to stop this.

'Ditka, can you read me?'

Nothing but static.

'Ditka! Can you read me? Tell your men to cease fire!'

I hear more shots and I hear shouting. Fewer voices are now coming to me over the comm.

The snow stops, the fog is patchy again, and I spot a few soldiers but can't tell from which company. I think they're moving toward the center of the village. I move to circle around them. Staying as low as possible, I run through a small, ragged farm and its ghostly orchard. I think I see more faces looking out from a solitary window. I reach the village and head toward the center, moving slowly, cautiously, running low from one house to another, finding walls to duck behind.

It's getting darker by the minute.

Then there's shooting again, calls, screams in all directions, but now the voices seem farther apart, scarcer.

I come out through some trees and spot Rodriguez.

I call out but he doesn't answer.

I'm halfway to him when he yells, 'Captain, don't!' and Ditka steps out from behind the corner of the shed, his rifle pointed at Rodriguez's neck.

Ditka's voice is calm, almost friendly. 'Throw away your weapon, Jackson. Far.'

At first I don't move. I haven't dropped my gun but neither have I aimed at Ditka.

'Come on, Jackson, be a good boy or your kid here gets a bullet through his neck.'

I'm only thirty feet from them.

Ditka barks, 'Now, Jackson. You have four seconds to throw it away from you.'

I toss my rifle.

'And now your SIG.'

I reach for my service revolver.

'Carefully,' Ditka says slowly.

I throw it away and as I do, Ditka fires, killing Rodriguez at point blank rage.

I recoil from the shot. Rage explodes in my head. I don't even think as I lunge at him, and I see him smile as he turns his gun on me and I swear in this split second in the half dark I can even see his finger starting to tense to squeeze the trigger and I hear a single shot and I am still lunging, and in this millisecond I'm trying to register what has happened and where I've been shot and I reach Ditka right as blood is spreading across one side of his face and neck and I tackle him, bringing him down.

As I reach him, I look around to see where the shot came from and spot a small man. He's wearing a ragged wool coat and a scarf wrapped around his head and across his face. I hit the snow with Ditka under me and I'm thinking I should reach for Ditka's weapon when the man steps forward, pointing an old rifle at me. I raise my hands to show I'm not armed.

He steps closer, the rifle still pointed down at me, and he pulls the scarf away from his face. It's the young man whom Ditka had been torturing that night when we first arrived in Vod Am—the boy I saved.

He shakes his head. I hear the word *djinn* several times. He points to Ditka and says, '*Djinn.*'

Before I can say anything or even react, the boy has run off into the approaching night as quickly as he came.

Ditka's weapon is on the ground near us. I kick it away. Only then do I turn to him. He is alive. In the dim light, it appears that the bullet passed through his cheek and jaw. He's bleeding badly but he's breathing. His eyes are open and he moves a hand to his wound as if to assess the damage.

Gently, I remove his helmet. I help him steady his hand over the wound. He moves his mouth slightly but makes no sound. His breathing is shallow but steady.

I stand up, leaving Ditka lying on the ground. I look around in search of others—anyone, Alpha, Bravo, or enemy. I listen for voices or shots. In the increasing darkness, I see no one and hear nothing but the wind.

I snatch up Ditka's rifle and sling it on my back.

Ditka mumbles something that I can't make out.

I walk a few steps away and pick up a large rock. I hold it with both hands and walk back to Ditka. I kneel beside him. I raise the rock high above my head. I give Ditka a moment to focus on me. His eyes find mine and widen in panic as he sees the rock. With all my remaining strength, I bring the rock down on his face.

I speak again into my comm, telling my men to report. No replies. I yell out, telling them to make it back to the camp. That we're under attack from both the enemy and Ditka's men. That Ditka is dead. I pick up Ditka's helmet and call to Alpha, 'Ditka is dead.' I say it again.

No response.

I'm now running at full speed, tripping over a body in the near dark. It's one of Ditka's men and I snatch up his rifle and ammo and keep running. There are more bodies, most shot, a few with their throats slit, surrounded by snow that's streaked with blood.

I think I see shapes, but it's now almost completely dark.

I'm still running. I stop only when I spot one of my men and check him for movement, sometimes shaking him to see if he responds.

Then I hear a groan and I see a man sitting on the ground, slumped against a tree. I get to him. It's Williams. I don't see any wound, there's no blood.

'Williams,' I whisper loudly, shaking him.

Again he groans.

'Captain,' he says, and I see his mouth forming a smile. And then it is forever gone.

Maybe I heard the shot. Maybe I felt the sting. Maybe I felt my leg burning. Yes, that part I remember.

After that, only images, scrambled memories, pain. Half carried, half dragged into a cave. Voices. Dark, cold. Light. Someone washing the wound on my leg. Piercing blue eyes; perhaps the young boy again.

A long darkness. Light and dark. Agonizing pain in leg. Burning up. Freezing cold.

This happened. Or I dreamed this happened: Katherine comes to me. She places a cool, wet cloth on my head.

'Katherine,' I say.

'Shh. You're going to be okay,' Katherine says to me in my dream. 'You're a good soldier, Tanner.'

The Journal of
John Murakami Fox

January 28, New York
Judith put down the pages and sighed. She popped out her contact lenses and rubbed her eyes and then grabbed her glasses from the drawer. Finally, she tapped the small stack of pages. 'You sure this is from Tanner?'

'Of course.'

I had received the final chapter only seven hours earlier. I had packed, then raced to the airport and caught the first flight into La Guardia.

'Well that certainly changes things,' she said.

'It doesn't change anything. It's the real story of the massacre.'

'And the one we sold for $2.4 million for book and movie rights?'

'I told you not to publish it.'

'John, they love the vampire. But they're not going to like this.'

'I don't care. This version is the truth.'

'But the vampire ending is so much better.'

'Please, you can't be serious.'

'John,' she said, looking straight into my eyes. 'We've got no choice on this.'

'Of course we have a choice.'

'Those threats you were getting?'

'What about them?'

'And then they stopped?'

I just stared at her.

'Now, it's my turn.'

She opened her desk drawer, took out a folder, and from it removed two sheets of paper. She handed them to me to read.

It was a letter on crisp government stationery. 'Under the Permanent Security Act, you are required to immediately and without delay surrender any materials, documents, affidavits, testimonies, or written accounts that you have in your possession or have access to related to the Vod Am Incident.' And then it recounted, at length, the penalties, including imprisonment, for disobeying this order.

I reread it, twice. Judith said, 'I'm not planning on going to prison for this, John. And I don't think you are either.'

'So the rest of the book, as it stands, they're fine with? It's...' I began to half shout, half grumble.

'Evidently.'

'This is nonsense. We can appeal,' I said.

'We could, or could have, back in the first Afghan War, back before the Permanent Security Act.'

My fury was matched only by an overwhelming sense of powerlessness. My shoulders slumped and I felt myself sag down into my chair.

For once, Judith spoke softly. 'I'll pretend I never saw this version,' she said. 'And unless you want me to be sending your royalty payments to an account in, say, North Korea, I'd suggest you do the same.'

January 31, London

I returned to a London that was colder than I can ever remember. The weather report blamed new wobbles in the Gulf

Stream, but all I knew was that most of England had been locked in below-freezing temperatures since I'd left for the States two weeks ago. Car batteries were dead, Tube service was erratic, homeless people had died by the dozens, and everyone was complaining that their houses and flats felt like walk-in refrigerators. Ice was appearing here and there on the Thames.

Alistair, though, seemed content with the 'spot of cold' and was a study in browns and oranges: Heavy wool sweater under a baggy tweed jacket. Fire blazing in the hearth. Pipe fired up in his hand. A snifter of cognac beside him.

His mood, though, was more unsettled than I'd ever seen in him. Not too different than mine.

He told me to go for a walk whilst he read Tanner's new ending. When I returned, he was terribly agitated. He was pacing the floor, manuscript in hand, flipping through the pages.

'John. It's all here.' He slapped the pages emphatically. 'It's damn well all right here.'

'Judith received a warning under the Permanent Security Act. Won't even consider fighting it. To her it's done. Over. The vampire story is the ending and this… this part never existed.'

'Damn that stupid woman! She's a coward.'

He turned and looked out the window into the sunless, cold park across from his flat.

'So what do we do now, John? Publish the true story on our website? It will go viral, you know. Heads will roll. It will be the scandal the world will talk about for a long time.'

His eyes lit up with this possibility, this chance to expose the war machine.

He now stood up and walked over to the window with a vigour in his step that I hadn't seen for years. I wished my mood could match his.

He repeated, 'So what do we do?'

I mildly appreciated the 'we', but it was actually a question of 'me.'

'Do we, I, have a choice?' I said.

I really didn't think they'd harm Sandra or Alistair, but I know what has happened to those who have exposed the hard truths. From Snowden to Politkovskaya, Saro-Wiwa in Nigeria to my colleague Amber in Hanoi—men and women forced into lifelong exile, murdered, or executed. Yes, we can get information out; it's impossible for them to stop it all. But the big stories? We know what they do to those who tell.

But—yet another *but*—if I bury the story, my worry for Alistair would be different, for I knew, in the most profound way, that I'd be letting him down forever.

Alistair turned back from the window.

'I suppose our man Tanner has had to face this same dilemma,' he said.

'Where do you think he is now?'

'Hopefully somewhere far, far away,' I answered.

I bundled up and ducked my head into the freezing night air. This time, I knew for certain I was being followed. Two men, their faces in the shadows, followed me as far as the Tube station and stood and watched as I went through the turnstile. At my stop, a man and a woman were waiting when I left the station and followed me, openly, to my flat.

February 1, London

I need to decide.

I can't decide.

This is my profession, my duty.

I don't want to spend the rest of my life in hiding.

I would be betraying everything I believe in.

I don't want to be killed or rendered to one of their secret prisons. Or packed away to one of the official ones.

I need to say yes to publishing the true story of the massacre on our website. Whatever it takes, I told myself with resolve, I will make sure the real story sees the light of day.

I dressed carefully, as if going to, what?... I laughed. My funeral? A party? An awards dinner? No, perhaps simply a celebration of sorts, a grim celebration, for I was going over to Alistair's to tell him what I had decided.

When I arrived, Alistair was on the phone, his expression somber, which well fit my mood of resignation and determination. When he saw me, he waved me in with a silent gesture. I could tell he was trying to cut the conversation short, but when he did, he handed me the phone. 'It's really for you,' he said. 'Sandra.'

'Hello, my dear,' I said.

'Daddy, someone sent an email to the site just now.'

At first assuming it was a threat, my heart started to beat faster than it already was.

But then she said, 'Have you heard of a man named Doug Abernathy?'

Of course I had, because it was Tanner's real name. I had tracked it down soon after our first meeting when it was clear the army wanted to keep Tanner under wraps. Even though it would have been a feel-good story to have uncovered a survivor of the Vod Am Massacre, they obviously didn't trust that he remembered nothing or, if he genuinely did not, that his memories would not return. I had told Alistair, but no one else.

'Is it Tanner?'

'Why?'

'Just wondering. Anyway, you should see this. I just forwarded it to you.'

The email had a link to *The Tennessean* and an attachment.

The Tennessean article from January 29 was the sort we've been posting on the website for the past three years. In short: the FBI, with the assistance of US Army Intelligence, raided a house in Nashville, where a veteran of the Afghanistan War was apprehended. The FBI said that 'for security reasons' no details were released, but speaking off the record, one agent said that the individual was 'highly dangerous' and appeared to be plotting 'a major attack'. Citing the provisions of the 2021 Public Safety Act, and the subsequent Permanent Security Act, the man's name was not, and would not, be released.

The attachment was a blurry photograph of a computer screen. Glare, perhaps from a desk light, blotted out certain words, but it was clearly some sort of initial psychiatric note.

Doug Abernathy
31-year-old single unemployed man, wounded veteran with past memory loss but no psychiatric history, apprehended by police. Considered dangerous. Very agitated. Complained of being under surveillance and of an army 'cover-up.' Appears frightened for his life. No evidence of substance abuse.
On examination: agitated, seems to be responding to visual

hallucinations, paranoid. Anxious but not depressed. Possibly suicidal.

Impressions: Schizophrenia or delusional disorder

Plan: admit for further assessment; antipsychotic medication to reduce agitation and paranoia.

It was Alistair who finally broke our silence.

'John,' he said. 'John?'

I raised my head and felt I was seeing him for the first time in years. He was old. Not ancient, but somehow I had missed how much he had aged in recent years. I had always seen him as a perpetual middle-aged man, but those days were clearly behind him.

'John, you will never be able to come home again. Publish this and you will be in hiding, perhaps for the rest of your life.'

'Then they win.'

'Or locked up. In prison. An institution. A military base.'

I thought of never seeing Sandra again. Of dying alone. Of psychological torture. Of being forgotten. I thought of the sadness in Amber's eyes and her lonely apartment. And then back to Sandra, the daughter I had all but deserted to pursue my career, the daughter whom I was finally getting close to. But instead of saying any of this, I replied, 'Then what has been the whole point?'

'We tried,' said Alistair. 'Indeed we tried.'

'This is the cause I've chosen. Isn't this exactly the sacrifice I knew I might have to make?'

Alistair said, 'Yes, that is all true. Instead, you would be sacrificing the truth, but that is what men always do in war.'

'If I say "not me", you'd call me a pompous ass.'

'Oh come on, John.' I noticed he had dropped the *old boys*

277

and *old chaps*. 'Have you always told the whole truth? Did you never censor yourself knowing what would or would not get printed? Or how you would be judged? Did your editors never distort what you wrote and you acquiesced?'

Of course this was true. But all I could say was, 'But I always did my best to get the story out.'

'Of course you did, John. Of course you did. You would not be my friend if you had not always tried to at least come close to the truth.'

We were silent again, until Alistair spoke. 'I have long admired... no, more than that, I have long been in awe of those men and women who sacrificed their lives or their freedom to speak the truth.'

I nodded, but he was barely paying attention to my reaction.

'Perhaps,' he said and then, for a moment, appeared to think about what he would say next. 'Yes, perhaps my deep admiration is because, deep down, I could not do so myself. I do not mean I would not save a life—I believe most of us would run into the blazing house to save our child. Would we not?'

An image of Sandra pulsed into my brain. I said that, yes, I thought that I would.

'But,' he said, 'give me time to think about it? Face torture just for telling the truth? I would equivocate. Find excuses. Or,' he continued, 'perhaps I would simply realize I should save myself to continue the fight. Losing the battle and all that, but hopefully helping win the war.'

'Not good enough,' I said. 'If we always run from the battle, we will never win the war.'

'At any rate,' said Alistair, 'who would believe this new account? There is no one alive to confirm it, is there?… They are very good at what they do. Have to give them credit for that.'

I said, 'Yes, but someday the evidence will come out. If not a witness to the massacre, then autopsy reports. Investigators' reports. Something, someday.'

'Then it will,' he said.

I bristled. 'Does that give me an excuse to bury this? That perhaps, maybe, someday, somehow, the truth will be known? If I go along with that, am I any less a coward than Judith is, as you so aptly noted?'

'I don't know,' Alistair said, his voice weary and defeated. He stared, again, at the photograph of his son. 'But I do know this,' he said. 'Right now, I'd give up all of this for just one more day with my son.'

Clock Tower Square, Thimphu, Bhutan

It is a glorious summer day in the Himalayas. On all sides of the small city, the green mountains are free of snow. She watches clouds get snared by distant peaks and then contort to pull free, as if the ancient rock and the ephemeral vapor are playing a child's game. The air is thin and pristine—she feels closer to the sky. As the guidebook says, it's one of the few places in the world where the air is still air.

In the ten days since she arrived, she has come here each day. She sips tea and writes and stares up at the mountains. She imagines her father once passing through here those many years ago and seeing this clock, just as she sees it to-day, still the old analogue kind. She imagines him in the cof-fee shop with all the other foreigners checking email over the slow Internet connection.

She came because she has read stories of the man who vis-its the square now and then and tells stories of a massacre back in the second Afghanistan war. For the few tourists who come to the tiny capital of Bhutan, he is considered a source of good fun. Some days he tells of vampires, and other days he recounts a fratricidal battle between two companies in the US army. But even those two accounts have conflicting and convoluted versions. It is something of an obligatory memen-to of a trip to Bhutan to share the version you heard from the crazy American man who swears he was once a captain in the US army.

It has been ten days and she is due to leave tomorrow. She still has not seen him and wonders if he has died. She has visited monasteries and palaces, and gone for short hikes. But still, this is what matters. She has come in hopes of meeting him.

She is reading and does not see him approach. But when he is near, she looks up with a start. She knows he must be in his sixties but he still looks youthful, although it seems that an outdoor life has left his skin with a leathery tan.

'I'm the captain,' he says. 'Perhaps you have heard of me.'

She smiles and says, 'Of course I have.'

'Buy me a tea and I'll tell you a story.'

She looks at his clothes. He doesn't appear to be someone who needs to have his tea bought for him. His dress is simple but elegant: a light pullover sweater, emerald green, made of very fine wool or perhaps silk. Crisp, ironed blue jeans. Hiking boots she'd seen in business class lounges. His white hair is on the long side, but neatly cut.

'Yes, I'd like that,' she says.

She goes to the coffee house and buys two cups of tea. She returns and places one cup before him.

'I'd like a special version of the story,' she says, once they have both taken a sip of their tea.

'Yes, don't they all… But you needn't worry. Everyone gets a special version.'

'What I mean, Mr. Jackson,'—she catches his eye—'that is, I assume that's who you are, is that I actually want to hear the truth.'

He stares at her, squints suspiciously, then shifts his weight forward as if to stand up, his anger barely hidden. 'I really don't feel like talking today.'

Before he can rise, though, she pushes her phone toward him, slides a finger across the screen and a photo appears.

It is of her and an older man, smiling, side by side.

'John Fox,' she says, 'was my father.'

He holds the phone for a moment and as he studies her and then the photo again, his brow softens, he appears to drop his guard.

'Your father, is he…?'

She shakes her head. 'He died two years ago.'

'He was young.'

'Not so young. He was eighty-three. But in the end he was happy.'

'That's good.'

'He would never talk about it, though, his one great story. And his greatest disappointment.'

'I'm sorry to hear that. Him passing, I mean.'

'It was your story.'

He seems to consider this. 'There are, as you said, many versions of that story. Did he ever tell you how it all ended?'

'That's why I'm here. He had a final chapter, but he destroyed it.'

'Yes, of course.'

'He never told me why. And he never told me what really happened.'

The man holds up his hands, palms upward, in a theatrical shrug.

'Please,' she says. 'It's time to tell the real story.'

'The real story…' he says, speaking into the air.

She waits.

Slowly, he begins to talk. His story meanders from childhood memories to a long-lost love to military training and deployment to Afghanistan. At times he seems in a trance. Mostly he is coherent; occasionally he loses the thread—characters change names and dates are convoluted. Sometimes she hears a hint of a Southern US accent. Other times, though, his accent seems English and she could swear his sentences sound Victorian.

She interrupts him only once during his long monologue.

'Are you really Tanner? I mean the man my father called Tanner?'

He pauses and gives her a glare that denounces her impertinence.

'Does it really matter?' he asks, his voice weary. 'I was a soldier. That's all that matters.'

She stares at him, unsure what he means. For a moment she focuses on his eyes. She remembers her father saying that Tanner's were brown. This man has penetrating blue eyes. Then again, she never knew which details about the soldier he called Tanner were real. She realizes she has been staring and lets her eyes wander, unfocused, across the clock square.

The man waits until, again, she looks at his eyes.

'So, precisely which story might you have come for? One that begins in an army hospital? Perhaps one in a cave? A massacre, maybe, in which brothers kill brothers? Or one that commences in the year of our Lord 1840?'

She knows the look on her face gives away her confusion.

'Tell me,' he continues, his accent hovering somewhere between British and American. 'How many ways do you think they have invented over the centuries to take an honest man, turn him into a soldier, rob him of his humanity, and then conceal the truth? Just how many times must I tell this story again?'

ACKNOWLEDGMENTS

Co-writing a work of fiction is lunacy. But when the process works, the book emerges even stronger than had we been writing alone. As challenging as it was to merge ideas into a coherent whole, eventually it truly became *our* book. It's been a wonderful experience of patience and flexibility, literary comradeship, and, most of all, friendship.

Thank you to those friends, family members, colleagues, and total strangers who told us their stories of Afghanistan, shared their reactions to earlier drafts of the book, or took the time to answer our questions. These include Samara Andrade, Sean Baine, David Fenton, Nathan Kaufman, Victoria Lee, Dean Piedmont, Maureen Simpkins, Manav Sachdeva, John Scott, Brian Sparks. and Gillian Strudwick. Thanks to many others, including a very helpful doctor from Médicins Sans Frontières, who chose not to be named.

This is a work of speculative fiction. The country called Afghanistan that appears in this book both is and is not the real-life country that has suffered so much during centuries of foreign invasions and internal strife. The military strategies, characters and events in our story, though, are all completely fictitious.

Thank you to the team at World Editions who bring to publishing the craftsmanship and personal commitment to books that seems, sadly, a relic of a bygone era—in particular publishing director Eric Visser, publishing assistant Corien Ligtenberg, and interns Thaïsa de Leij and Rowan van Meurs. Thanks to our proofreader Anne O. Fisher. Thanks so much to our editors Ann Patty and Marie-Lynn Hammond.

As always, we'd like to thank our families for their forbearance and encouragement—Suy, Nina, Betty, Chloe and Liam. We forgive them their doubts for our writing a book with 'vampire' in the title.